VALA

VALA

Part 1—The Awakening

LUKE FITZPATRICK

Copyright © 2014 by Luke Fitzpatrick.

ISBN: Softcover   978-1-4990-8636-2
           eBook   978-1-4990-8637-9

All rights reserved. No part of this book may be reproduced or transmitted in any form or by any means, electronic or mechanical, including photocopying, recording, or by any information storage and retrieval system, without permission in writing from the copyright owner.

This is a work of fiction. Names, characters, places and incidents either are the product of the author's imagination or are used fictitiously, and any resemblance to any actual persons, living or dead, events, or locales is entirely coincidental.

Any people depicted in stock imagery provided by Thinkstock are models, and such images are being used for illustrative purposes only.
Certain stock imagery © Thinkstock.

This book was printed in the United States of America.

Rev. date: 05/21/2014

To order additional copies of this book, contact:
Xlibris LLC
0-800-056-3182
www.xlibrispublishing.co.uk
Orders@xlibrispublishing.co.uk
624240

CONTENTS

Author's notes 7

Chapter 1   Welcome to my mind 11

Chapter 2   It all starts with a bang 20

Chapter 3   Ripples 27

Chapter 4   Earth and Vala 37

Chapter 5   Endless Sleep 45

Chapter 6   Open Door Through A Closed Window 51

Chapter 7   First Born Steps into Reality 63

Chapter 8   Friend or Foe? 69

Chapter 9   Lesson 1 75

Chapter 10   Realisation 81

Chapter 11   Tired and Hungry 91

Chapter 12   Lesson 2 97

Chapter 13   Running Out of Time 103

Chapter 14   The Tunnel Boars Tunnel 110

Chapter 15   Descending, Ascending 120

Chapter 16   The Wall 129

Chapter 17	Vala	138
Chapter 18	Time To Get To Work	145
Chapter 19	Into The Lion's Den	154
Chapter 20	Where Do We Go Now?	164
Chapter 21	Fire Fight	177
Chapter 22	Run	187
Chapter 23	Safe At Last?	195
Chapter 24	Back Where We Started	202
Chapter 25	Nothing More To Lose	209
Chapter 26	Right In The Corner Of Your Eye	216
Chapter 27	Dig Deep	225
Chapter 28	It's All Over Now	234
Chapter 29	It Was All An Illusion	240
Chapter 30	Wake Up	248
Chapter 31	Hunted	255
Special Thanks		261

AUTHOR'S NOTES

Hi, I am the author of this book, Luke Fitzpatrick. For those of you that have read this book I really hope you enjoyed it, and for those of you that are about to embark of the adventure that is Vala I hope you like it. I first came up with the idea for Vala when I was walking home from college one day and I thought to myself how odd it was that I could easily predict the actions of people, how people seemed to live some sort of routine every day of their lives, and then it started happening to me, to a point where most people I knew I could predict what they were going to say and do because of this routine they live. Then one day I asked myself if the world was real, and thus Vala was born, I wanted a man to live a similar life to all of you and myself, working and paying bills, only I wanted him to find a new life and realise that there is so much more than we thought we knew about the world, so many more questions to be asked and situations that no one has ever lived.

For those of you that do not know, Vala is the first book of three that I hope to write, perhaps four if this one is popular to read, I have already planned and structured the other two books and their stories, I see this book as more of the introduction into Vala and the other two explore the more uncharted parts, the more extreme creatures and of course, space, for those of you that have not read the book yet I will say no more as I do not want to give anything away before you begin.

I want you all to know that you can easily write a book just as I have, it is not hard, and if you have a good idea then I am sure it is worth writing down and start by showing a friend your idea then go from there, I believe that there are thousands of fantastic stories that each and every one of you could write, and I would love nothing more to read them all, so if you think you have a good idea for a book then go ahead and try,

Just to give you more of an insight to the idea of Vala and the context behind the plot and the storyline, most of it was thought up as I wrote the book, I would think of a new idea and write a note at the bottom to insure that latter on I put that very idea into the book. Honestly the storyline was going to start off as just a normal man living his normal life and writing a journal of all the weird stuff and coincidences that happened within his life, then I decided that he should break free from that life, and then I wanted Vala to be more beautiful and more interesting then Earth, and so on and so on until I decided to put so much more into the story and the book, and I hope you enjoy reading it as much as I have enjoyed writing it.

So these have been my personal notes, everything you have read was something I personally typed for my readers and it has not been edited by anyone, I just wanted to let you know that I really appreciate you taking the time to read this, and I truly hope you love it, thank you.

PART 1
AWAKENING

CHAPTER 1

WELCOME TO MY MIND

HAVE YOU EVER wondered why it is that when you walk down a road the wind always seems to blow towards you? Never from behind, or the side, always towards your face. Or why you hear someone shout your name, but when you turn to see who called you there is no one there. Or when something odd happens and you mention it to someone they always seem to say it's happened to them as well, however you never see it happen, they just tell you that it did. How many times have you left a room, building, toilet or anywhere and bumped into someone or seen something and if you left that place even a second later or before you wouldn't of seen it, what are the odds of that happening? I bet it's always you stuck in traffic jams, waiting in queues and saying the words "what are the odds"? Over and over again. Have you ever wondered these things? Because it's all I have thought about for over a year now.

Even now, with the wind in my hair and the sound of nothing but the early morning birds filling up my ears with music, it is still all I can think about. One day I hoped it would change, that my routine would become random and I could no longer predict what my girlfriend would say or do, or my boss or anyone for that matter, it seems my life is a book that I've already read a thousand times and now I can't take it anymore, a year ago I swore today would be the day I change everything, I've been planning it for a year now, down to the smallest detail and it has engulfed my life with this constant feeling of numbness, mindlessly going along waiting for this one unique day to come along and now that it is here, I am afraid. So much effort has gone into this, so much feeling and if it messes up then that is all on me, whereas right now I could push my rested hands on the ledge and say goodbye to everything, the ground was far enough away to kill me, I wouldn't have to worry about today going wrong because it will end on my own terms, finish the book for the first time with a different ending, and different day. No matter what I think, no matter what I do, I know I do not have the courage to jump from this roof, my heart was in throat and sweat on my palms, and even though my body clearly thought it was possible that I would jump, I know I won't.

Saying this in my head I placed my hands on the side of my building and pushed, not to throw myself from the empty shell of a building to end the empty shell that is my life, it was to gently bring my body to a standing position to go back down stairs and write in my stupid journal about this situation and how it made me feel, it seems writing these days is the only thing that calms my mind, it makes me realise that I have control over my thoughts, my mind belongs to me, my body may be the worlds to play with and control but I can think what I want inside the walls on my skull.

My life has always been hard, going to college, working or losing jobs, it's the same thing just a different day, but I have always questioned how this world can remain so big and yet so un seen by my eyes. This last year is what changed my life, from the start of me believing that my life wasn't real, that there was something else going on, right to this day where I have been keeping a journal of every little phenomenon, every coincidence and detail in this book, there are hundreds, it's unreal . . . . No pun intended.

Anyway, my name is Leo, I am 22 years old, I live with my girlfriend in a broken down apartment building, working most days of my life to earn what small amount of money I can to buy essentials just so I can go on living in this fake world I have been placed in. I'm about 5'9 so not very tall, dark brown hair, blue eyes, a small stubble beard and medium length hair that I always try to style because its calming, but it never looks right, oh and a few scars from a car crash when I was younger, both my parents died in it, that's a story for another day.

"Leo are you writing in that bloody diary again"?

That's the love of my fake life, trust me to fall for a psychotic bitch, should have been gay, would have been easier. And to answer her question yes I am writing in my diary, because if I don't use this pen on some paper I'd use it to stab you to death, I think I'll keep that in my head, if I told her she'd kill me.

Would a sane person put up with a relationship like this? I hear about people doing it, and see it on the T.V, but as I said before I never see it in person, just hear about it, maybe it's just me. However people do more insane things in this world, I mean when I think about one thing in particular I just don't see how this can be real. People work every day of their lives, millions of people, billions, and they earn a small amount of money for a lot of work, spend it on essentials just so they can keep living, then they put on their TV to hear a man tell them that he runs their country and he has some new laws for them to follow. This man makes it harder for these people every day and takes their money in the form of taxes, the money they work hard for, he then puts police around to keep him safe. But these people go on everyday living this fake, lonely life, working to eat and giving their money to someone who gives them rules in return, tells them to obey and listen. They then turn over the channel to see more people doing little work for millions and love them? Why? Do actors, singers and footballers deserve all that money for doing nothing? One day of work a week and your job is what others do for fun? How do these people not see that it is all fake, it is a house of cards, we could all live happily without these idiots running our lives, no money, no jobs, they did it before us we can do it now. Live on the land instead of killing it, one day they'll wake up like me and see how insane this is, we could all live happy and free, enough of everything to share, it's not for some to have loads of and others to have none, but everyone to have some.

I could go on and on, and I used to, until I figured out that seriously no one can be that stupid, it's too insane when you think about it, which means these people will never wake up, never realise how crazy it is to live like this . . . . Because they are not real, maybe their actors, or computer programmes, but they are not like me, they are not real. After today I will know the truth, I have been waiting for this day for months now and it's finally here, I know there's something else going on, this can't be true, I want answers, today I go looking for them, for the truth to my life.

So welcome to my mind, my thoughts and my actions, I already know I'm crazy so I might as well talk to myself now, an inner monologue. I've stopped writing, time to start my last day, my apartment was one floor, our corridor was long and went straight from the front door to the main room, as you left the main room on the left you had the kitchen, a small, dull and rather pathetic kitchen. On the right there was a lounge, that was a bit bigger and I usually kept it pretty clean, we had an average size television in there and a sofa, like most normal people. Right now I'm hungry, so I think its breakfast time. Opening the door to the kitchen I could see my girlfriend placing her cup in the sink and turning around to look at me. I smiled, I hated her but seeing her always made me smile for some reason.

"Good morning angel" I said still smiling

"You were in there for ages; I'm going to be late now, well done"! She hissed pushing pass me.

I guess I should have known she'd be angry at me about something, she always is, like I said, it's a crazy relationship, not fun and filled with constant arguments, the best kind of insanity . . . Love.

Right . . . . It's time for Sugar puffs, god I love Sugar puffs, yum yum yu . . . Wait a second.

"Hun, where are the Sugar Puffs"? I said, with general sadness in my voice, I really like Sugar Puffs.

"I threw them out, there was only a few left" she yelled back from the bathroom.

I must admit, I did think about picking up my empty bowl, which should be full of Sugar Puffs and milk now, and throwing out the window, but I decided against it, we can't afford another new bowl. However I now have to find something else to indulge on this morning, let's see what else we have. Now as I said before, we can't afford a bowl, one bowl, so we didn't have much food in most days, our jobs were pretty average pay and only just got us food and a roof over our heads.

"Crap" I said out loud looking into my practically empty cupboard, we have one bag of prawn and cocktail crisps left and the rest of the stuff is her diet food, which even if I was lying face down in a desert and some hot, gorgeous and sexy redhead came riding over to me on a camel or something, and said

"I will sleep with you and carry you home to safety if you eat this diet food"

I'd rather die, well maybe that's not true, I'd tell her ok but I want her first, then after, I would refuse to eat the food and then die smiling.

"Screw it" I said picking up the squashed, last packet of crisps and started walking towards the front door, out of the kitchen, grabbing my jacket and bag, I pre-packed it the night before with everything I need today, the day I have been waiting for so long.

"Bye, I am off now" I yelled opening the door. But didn't hear a reply, I paused for a second, thinking, I suppose I'd better check up on her, just in case.

"Babe"? I yelled once more, this time louder.

"Yes I heard you, goodbye" She screeched still in the bathroom, Jesus what on earth is she doing in there? I feel so sorry for that toilet and mirror.

I walked out of my apartment and into the building corridor, it was a worn down corridor, as if someone had ran through it with a flamethrower, torching everything and then urinating all over the walls. It was a sluggish Brown colour, with doors on the sides and stairs in the middle, leading from the bottom straight to the roof. My landlord lived on the same floor as us . . . .

"Damn" I said remembering that today I had to give her the rent I owe her, she has ears like a hawk, if any part of my body touches the floor outside of her room she will know it is me straight away and come out. Any other day I would try to sneak past, but today I'm late, and I truly don't see the point as I will never be setting foot in this building again, not after today, my last day. So screw it.

I started running, down the corridor and straight past her room, the door opened almost instantly and my overweight and badly dressed landlord stepped out, the smell of cats and fatty food wafting out the door, she had yellow teeth, faded blonde hair and arms like cranes. Her husband, believe it or not, was way scarier.

"Oi, where are you going"? She shouted swinging one arm at my head; I ducked and slid on the ground right below her, kicking the floor to lift my body back to a running position so I wouldn't lose any speed.

"You look lovely today misses Hanover" I yelled as I launched myself down the stairs and around the corner at the bottom of our flight, swinging myself on to the next set and then the next. I didn't dare turn around in case her husband was there, I could hear her calling him, and stopping around above me. My bag was flying around on my back as I jumped over the bannisters to get down the stairs quicker.

Finally I reached the bottom floor and slung open the door, I was struck by the freezing weather outside, it was like walking through a thin sheet of ice cold glass, wow it was cold, flipping up my collar on my jacket and tucking my hands into my pockets hoping for some warmth, I was outside, and on my way to work, goodbye building, goodbye baby and goodbye landlord, If I had a third nut sack id tell you all to suck it as I wouldn't waste any of the two I have on you lot, time for the answers I want, it's time to start my last day in this fake world, one way or another this will be my last day here.

The road to work was long, not far, just long. We lived on a main road, you could see it from the windows in our apartment, it was always busy, even really late at night I could just lie in bed and hear the cars driving past constantly, one after another and then the occasion 'beep'. Outside the building we have a small path on the road next to the main road; it takes me through a nice, surprisingly quiet walkway, every morning id walk down this walkway and just stop at this small bridge half way down, just stop there surrounded by the dying trees, they were dying because of the fact this lovely little path was right next to a main road, stupid idea really. Anyway id just stop on this bridge and stare straight into the water bellow, just a small stream of water right below the bridge, it was calming but I found it so hard to believe it was actually there, every day id pick up a stone and just drop it into the water, and every day it would splash.

I had a dream one night, that one day I dropped a stone into the water, as I did hundreds of times before, it didn't splash, not even a twinkle, I stood there staring at the water, wondering, and as I stood there staring it just grew, and grew, and grew until it was as tall as the bridge, towered in front of me like an obelisk, then it lunged forward as if to drown me, that's all I remember of the dream, I think I woke up after that.

Something about the water, it was so beautiful and yet so sinister at the same time, I looked into and it just felt like someone was staring straight back at me. Anyway I am already late, so can't stare to long. I picked up the pace now, today has to go exactly to plan for it to work, the timing every detail and that includes going to work. I know it's crazy going into work on my last day, but I have to pick up my final pay check, that last brown envelope with cash inside, then I'm free to leave work. It's not that far now. At the end of this path you came straight back on to another main road, this one was the one that my work was on, take a right at the end and there it is.

The boring, dull, pathetic looking building, it might as well have been a prison. It looked like one of those containers you get at construction sites, the one that they do all their paper work in and have meetings about what trees to kill and what land to tear up in search of black treasure, liquid gold, otherwise known as oil, or coal, copper, hell anything completely irrelevant to life, just tear open the earth and reach in, take what you want, not what you need, that should be the motto of the companies that do it all. My work place however did not do that, we sold and manufactured vacuum cleaners, I was a sales rep, I'd sit my fat ass on one of those chairs, in my cubicle and pick up the phone, cold calling idiots to ask them if they would like to buy a product I'm sure they already have. It's not that bad though, sometimes I get calls as well, and I have to give advice on how to help them work their vacuum cleaners or any other queries they may have, I'm your guy, pick up the phone and call me!

As I stood there looking at this building I smiled, not a big smile because if someone walked past and just saw a man smiling at a building they'd think I was crazy, maybe I am, who knows. The reason I was smiling was because this is the last time I will set foot inside this dark grey, damp, old looking building. This is the last time I'd walk through those double doors and clock in, but also the first time for a few new things I've decided to do today. My hands were cold now, I could see my breath in front of me, I might as well of had an invisible cigarette in my mouth, it would have had the same effect. My hands were deep in my pockets now and yet still freezing, my ears felt like they were being stabbed by millions of tiny pins, god this weather is ridiculous, and yet I prefer it then the hot. With cold weather you can warm up, however with hot weather it is so much harder to cool down.

"Leo" A voice yelled from behind me as I stood there still smiling at the building.
I turned around to see a man crossing the road, waving at a car to say thank you for letting him cross in front of it. I started laughing as recognised the man now jogging towards me.
"Wayland" I chuckled back at him, opening my arms to give him a hug, taking my hands out of my pockets made me realise just how cold it really was.
"What are you doing outside man? You'll freeze out here" He said to me with a smile on his face, his nose red from the cold.
"Just, waiting for you mate" I didn't like lying to my friend, but I knew it was for the best.
"Come on then, in we go" His voice now quivering from the cold, he places one arm on my shoulder leading me into the building. I'd known Wayland for years now, he was my oldest and pretty much only friend now, I may not think the world is real, or know it, but I pray that he is, I've known him so long, he is like a brother to me.

We entered the building, still talking about the weather and laughing about it, until we got to the front desk and had to check in.
"Wayland Manning" He said to the lady at the front desk with a wink, she was not impressed by that, you could tell as she glared back him before entering him to the clock in system, we both just looked at each other and started laughing again.
"Ah hem"! She coughed at us, and then looked at me.
"Leo Cathrey" I said through the laughter, smiling away. That was one thing I liked, laughing, I watched comedy shows constantly on the TV at home, and read comedy books and even had a joke messaging service on my phone, but none of that made me laugh as much as hanging out with Wayland, he always did stupid things and messed around, it made my days at work so much more interesting.

We started walking off again, now that we were both clocked in. There was an elevator but it was broken, so we had to use the stairs, our work floor was on the third floor. We were hugging each other as we walked up the stairs, still laughing. We finally reached the door to our work, a big, strong looking door; blue with no windows and one long sliver handle to open it. Wayland placed his hand on the door handle and looked at me with a smile.

"Ready for work"? He said smiling still.

I just nodded, but quietly, under my breath I muttered something, just quiet enough so he wouldn't hear me.

"I have been ready for this day for too long my friend".

CHAPTER 2

IT ALL STARTS WITH A BANG

AN EMPTY CUBICLE, nothing in it, just an empty cubicle, then place a computer inside that empty cubicle, a keyboard, some pictures of a girlfriend on the sides, a cup on nothing, just floating in the air, a desk below the cup to fulfil the laws of gravity, places a pot on the desk with pens inside, a rubber at the bottom of it, hidden amongst the pens. Then finally a chair in front of the desk, but not an empty chair, this chair has a human shaped battery, placed there to fuel the world it lives within. This battery will go about its days fuelling the world, none the wiser that he is pawn, placed there for reasons even he doesn't know. This battery is running out of power, this battery is getting useless to the people who use it, this battery is me.

God this is boring, the clock couldn't tick any slower, I've only been here an hour! That can't be right. What's that? A noise? I looked at the desk and saw my phone placed there, just ringing, sitting there and looking at me as if to say.

"Pick me up, pick me up, pick me up" hell, after a while it actually sounds like that.

My hand reached forward and just hovered over the grey phone, just waiting above it. I placed my hand on top of it and pull it off the hook; now my face not only consisted of a stubble beard, but also a phone that might as well have been stuck to it.

"Denning and Son hoover services, Leo speaking how may I help you"? I said with a dead and relentless drone, bored of the sound of my own voice saying those words.

"Hi, my hoover doesn't work" a woman said down the phone to me, she sounded older, and quiet, but also tense.

"Right, urmmm is it plugged in"? I said with question in my voice

"OF COURSE IT'S PLUGGED IN YOU IDIOT"! She screeched down the phone at me, and carried on screeching in my ear, through my new head accessory.

"ARE YOU CALLING ME AND IDIOT? SAYING I DON'T KNOW HOW TO PLUG IN A HOOVER"? She carried on yelling.

Now I get this sort of call once a week, maybe less, with these stupid people who half the time have not plugged it in, however as it was my last day I felt this temptation fill my body, this warmth, this tranquillity, I developed a smile across my face and began to breathe in, as if to tell myself that I was about to shout back at this woman, my grip tightened around the phone and then suddenly.

"Please hold". I whispered down the phone in a tense, shaky voice, placing her on hold and leaning back in my chair, hands folded behind my head. Then after staring at the ceiling, a breath out, inhaled from my mouth. That was way too close, if I shouted, if I lost my head, there would have been no pay check waiting for me at the end of this day, and that check is so important, without it everything I have waiting for, this day would be just like every other, and these last few months would have been wasted, all because I couldn't keep my mouth shut. But I did, and now I am quiet and calm again.

After that close call I decided I needed a break, I think I'll go to the conference room, see if Wayland is there. I stood up from my desk and started walking to the conference room. This was a room that was used to hold meetings between our companies and other companies, or sometimes just staff meetings, but because it was very rare that a meeting was actually held there, Wayland and I would use it as a lunch room. On my way to the room I found myself stuck, I looked around at the cubicles beside me and couldn't see a reason why I would be stuck, then I sharply turned around and found my floor manager behind me, holding my shirt. The floor manager was basically the person in charge of all the people in their cubicles, while the boss was on the same floor, she preferred doing absolutely no work, and hiring this douche to do it for her instead.

"Where do you think you are going?" He said with a snare in his voice. He was a bit older than me, but with those few years he had on me, he also had a lot of attitude. Big nose, pointy ears, glasses and a short bowl of a haircut, he looked like those nerds you see in films, the ones that our also running around winding everyone up, this guy was kind of like that, except with power, which made him ten times worse.

"I am . . . ." Thinking on my feet here,

"Getting some water" phew, I thought to myself

"Well hurry up, we don't pay you to drink" He moaned back at me.

"You're flies are undone" I said quietly under my breath, funny thing is, he didn't hear me, nor did he notice until he went home.

The rest of the day went rather quickly to be honest, it was a nice change, maybe it was because regardless of how much I hated my job, I loved the idea of today, and everything in this day made me happy, made me smile. My work was done now, I was finished for the day, but at the end of every shift each staff member has to fill out an assessment form talking about their customers. The reason for this is that every conversation on the phones, held between us and the customer is recorded, and they want to hear our side to every conversation in black and white, I don't know why, nor do I ask why, but to me it sounds like a stupid idea.

I just sat there now, waiting, dreaming and wishing of something new, something different, maybe I will find it, maybe there is a light at the end of the tunnel . . . . My thoughts wondered away from my day dreams to something else. I forgot all about the flashing light on my phone, on my desk in front of me and instead was looking at something else. A man, tall, skinny, not really an attractive man, he had thin, worn hair and spots which was odd considering his old age. This man was not any ordinary man, but my bosses' assistant, a man of super powers, for you see this man, this old, ugly man was bringer of happiness and love and I found myself staring at him with a gleaming smile, just looking at him walk towards me. I was not looking at his eyes, or his face at all however, but his hands, they were not empty.

"Leo Cathrey" He said handing me a brown envelope. Now usually this would not make me that happy, id barely smile, but today this man found a different reaction from me.

"YES!!! YES YES YES YES!!!" I jumped up and screamed, hugging the man.

"You, you son of a bitch I love you" I said to him, picking him up of his feet and swinging him around. But it was over before it even began.

"What on earth is going on here?" My boss said, coming out of her office. Now my boss was a completely horrible woman and I hated her, but even I had to admit she was very attractive, which is probably what lead me to do something I'd wanted to for a while. Walking over towards her smiling I started shouting.

"You are the most arrogant, psychosocial woman I have ever known, you heart eating vulture, don't go out looking for love because with an attitude like yours you'll just find guys like me." I was right in front of her now, he mouth wide open with shock, I had always been quiet and taken her verbal abuse until now, always the good little worker for this fake world, well today is different, today is the end. I grabbed her round her waist and pulled her towards me, forcing her head close to mine and kissing her, she was fiercely striking my face and kicking me, but I held her head there for quite a while, I like to think I felt her kissing back, maybe it was just my imagination.

I finally pulled away and let out a big breath.

"You're Fi . . . ." Before she could finish her sentence, I decided I was a mind reader and knew what she was going to say, so I ended it for her.

"Amazing? I know, but that's not important right now, I quit" I said, god it felt good, this warm feeling all around my body . . . . And then it started to feel, not so good, painful, wait a second.

"Get him out of here" My boss yelled. Two big security guards had a Taser in my back, shocking me, I can honestly say I have never been in so much pain, this was like someone injecting you with millions of tiny needles, and them all filling your blood around your body, jabbing into your veins, trying to escape, and it was horrible.

I then found myself in the parking lot outside of the building, well not in it, I was being held at the door by these two guards. Now the effect of a Taser isn't pleasant, in many ways it is like being drunk. So in my head what I was thinking, what I am thinking is

"Let go of me you big apes, this is assault, who do you think you are?

But what came out was,

"Thank you kindly for the lift my good friends, now if you wouldn't mind taking me to the shop where I will buy my bike . . . . I love you, did you know that?" I then started crying for some reason.

"Why don't you love me?" Still crying I muttered too one of the guards.

"Weeee" Why was I yelling we? Then a loud "BANG!" As I flew into the side of a bin, ah that's why, I thought to myself.

"Totally worth it" I blurred out, my mouth half open on the ground below me. I just lay there for a bit, trying to recapture my spinning head, that all happened so fast, I don't even remember parts of it. I flipped over onto my back and stared at the sky. It was so calm, like water, but above us, weird how they are so similar and yet completely different in almost every way. A plane was overhead; I could see the trail of white smoke coming from behind it as it glided along through the blue ocean of sky.

"Get the hell out of the way" I heard a man yell suddenly, I looked to my left and to my shock, there was a car bumper inches from my head. Car horns filled the air, it turns out I was on the road, could they have really thrown me that far? I looked back at the door, it was not as far as I first thought, but still that must have been some throw. Stumbling to my feet I placed one hand on the car bonnet for support.

"Sorry" I mumbled, trying to walk to the side of the road, falling over multiple times before reaching the curb. I turned around sharply as I approached it and sat down, barely on the curb, but just enough so I could rest and not be in anyone's way.

Suddenly a thought crossed my mind, my eyes widened.

"Shit, oh no, no no no no." I said over and over again, looking around, panicking, but they were nowhere to be seen. My bag, my pay check, even my jacket, they were all gone, there is no way the security would let me back in after what I did, even to get my stuff. This day I had been waiting for, this day of all days, how could I be so stupid, everything is ruined now. Still sitting on the curb I placed my head in my hands, I felt like crying, letting it all out, screaming, I had planned this down to the letter, every detail, and yet without my bag I can't do anything except go home to my pathetic life, my fake, lonely life.

However a familiar sound arose, footsteps filled the air, along with a ringing from my ear drums I could only assume were from the Taser. I looked to see where they were coming from. As I looked on my right I saw Wayland walking over towards me, smiling and barely hiding his laughter, he was carrying my bag and what looked like a brown envelope.

"You are one crazy bastard" He said chucking my bag at me, and throwing my jacket on my head, he could no longer contain his laughter, sitting down next to me, placing his arm round my shoulder and wiping the blood from my check. I started laughing as well, just a little, more of laughter out of relief, I wouldn't have to go home now, this day could continue as planned.

"What in god's name possessed you to kiss our boss? Did you think she'd give you a raise or something?" He said laughing as he spoke.

"I figured I might as well go out with a bang" I said, no longer laughing, just staring back up at the sky.

"I thought you liked your job?" He said staring at me.

"Look Weyland, don't look too much into this, but I have to go now, I won't be coming back for a while" I said to him with nervousness in my voice, wondering what he would say, how he would react.

"Ok" He chuckled out with a smile. Ok? I thought to myself, that's it? After all these years, I started staring at him; he looked back at me and laughed.

"Leo I have known you for years now, I can see you're not happy, and I don't blame you, no offence but your girlfriend is a bitch" He could barely finish that word as we both broke out laughing.

"And if some time away from all this is what you need, then go luck man, I hope it helps." Hearing him say that made me smile, although I had my doubts he was even real, it was nice having some support, some confidence from someone.

We both stood up, and gazed up at the sky, I put on my jacket and bag, he handed me the brown envelope as I finished getting ready, I knew it was time for me to go, I can't be late.

"Where are you going? Why is this pay check so important? Surely you have money" He said to me, both of us still staring at the sky above, the blue of the sky; even though it was still bitter cold.

"A bike" I said

"I am buying a bike"

He looked at me confused, but then he smiled.

"Good luck Leo, I'll see you soon" He quivered out of his mouth, hugging me, I could tell he wanted to laugh and cry at the same time, we had been friends for so long now; it was sad saying goodbye to him. After we finished hugging, I just nodded at him and walked away, didn't look back once, just walked down the road with my bag on my back and the wind blowing in my face again, never from the side, always in my face. I wiped the rest of the blood from my head; I guess part of me was bleeding from when they launched me out the door. I knew Wayland was watching me as I turned the corner and carried on walking.

I couldn't help but think about what he said though "see you soon." I thought to myself many things at that time and felt many feelings, doubt, worry and I was scared, I hadn't be scared before, but what if I was wrong? Could I be wrong? However the wind still blowing in my face gave me the smallest glimmer of hope, it was a constant reminder of how much I wrote down in that book, how many examples I had of this world being fake, this can't be real I thought

"This can't be real" I quietly muttered as I repeated it in my head.

But the main thing that went through my mind when I thought about what he said, that he'd see me soon, was three simple words . . . .

No you won't.

Chapter 3

Ripples

"**£4000?**" I said

"You said it was £4000 and that's how much I could have it for?" Anger filled my voice, along with a strong frustration.

"That was then, this is now, its £5000 or nothing" the man replied, a smile across his face, god that made me angry, I wanted to grab him and take the bike, maybe it was the cold weather that was making me think so aggressively, maybe I have just had enough of waiting for this day to finally end, I honestly don't know, but this isn't me, I wasn't thinking like me, I was angry, tense, I had given up completely, on this life, on this world, on everything.

"Look I have exactly £4000 here cash, you said 4000, the price was 4000, you promised me 4000" I was now shaking, and he could see it, there was no way he was going to give me this bike for that price, he could sense I was desperate.

"Sorry, I don't know what to tell you" he said back to me, that smile still glued to his face, his ugly, oiled covered face, you could see hand prints on his cheeks where he had been wiping the fluids away, not exactly a nice man, he was overweight with no hair, stubble all over his face, hairy, basically a typical car junky. The shop itself was a small establishment, it was far from work, almost in the middle of nowhere, took me 3 hours to walk here, I didn't feel like taking a bus or a taxi, didn't really have the money, but mostly it was just because I liked walking. It was a dirty shop, has bits of car parts everywhere, a small, broken pump out of the front of it, broken signs and vehicles, and the inside of it was as black as this man's face.

However there was one good thing about it, and that was this bike, a black and red 2008 Honda CB1000R, beautiful and very cheap when compared to most other stores, but that wasn't because I was lucky, it was because it looked like it had been driven of a cliff and back up again, rust and damage everywhere, but they had been my favourite bikes for a while and I wanted this day to be perfect, I had to have this bike.

"Isn't there anything I can do to have this bike for £4000" I pleaded with the man.

He breathed in and raised his finger towards me, but suddenly a phone started ringing from the backroom, and the man's point turned into a wave of announce, and he just walked off into the backroom, grunting as he walked. I waited for a bit, he was talking very loudly, I could make out the whole conversation from where I was standing, something about a pub I think, wasn't really paying much attention to it to be honest, I was staring at the bike in front of me. The shop around it really made it look so much more worse than it actually was, I loved the bike for what it was and what it could be, everything I could do to it that I couldn't do to myself, let it fulfil its purpose in this fake world. The sun was shining through the broken glass that I guess used to be a window, reflecting of the bike, it looked like some sort of sign, the bike was glowing, the oil around the floor near it just made it look so much better, helping the reflection light the room, I looked over to the room where the man had gone into, I couldn't hear him on the phone anymore, but nor could I see him.

Leaning over the bike I could see the keys in it, oh I really wish I didn't just see that, perhaps just a feel of the bike, one sit upon it, that's all I need, just one sit, then I'll leave, find something else. I walked slowly to the side of the bike, all the while my eyes where half glued to the bike, watching my hand glide over the faded paint, and half glaring at the door, worried that any second now the man would walk back in. I lifted my leg, very slowly, my leg barely even touched the bike, it reached the other side of the bike and I grabbed the handles, then slow as ever, I moved down, placing myself on the seat, a smile grew across my face, I knew I had to have this bike, today is my last day, it is going to go how I planned it and not even slightly different, I picked up the helmet beside the bike and placed it on my head, sliding down the visor when it was tightened and fastened safely.

My hand reached for the ignition, turning the key in the slot, the engine sparked into life, roaring, filling the shop with this loud purr, funny how I sound can make something look more attractive, even the shop looked better. The man suddenly came rushing into the shop; a crowbar was tightly gripped in his hand, my thoughts dramatically changed.
"Get the hell off that, NOW!" He screamed at me, I dropped the brown envelope on the floor, I put the exact amount of money that the bike should have cost in there, I wasn't a thief, I wouldn't take this without paying, well technically. A year it took me to save up the amount for this bike, a year it had been sitting here, close to a year anyway, the day was finally here; time for this day to end I thought to myself, I had a destination to go to and this was how I was going to get there.

Footsteps were filling the room now, along with the sound of the engine screaming, the man was running towards me as fast as he could, the room wasn't far from the bike, but time seemed to slow down, this all lasted no longer than ten seconds, but it felt like an hour, a lifetime. Tightening up my bag on my back, gripping the handle bars and taking one last quick glance at the man, who was now extremely close, I could smell his fowl stench increasing, nesting in the back of my throat, time to go. I pulled back on the throttle, the back tire ripped into the floor, screeching and sliding all over the shop floor, I could feel the man grab my bag, but at that speed when he tried holding on, he just fell straight on his face and I was safe, or so I thought.

I didn't realise that the garage door was closed, there was no way of getting the bike out of the shop, that was that, I was going to have to stopped and try and run from this man, I looked around to think about where I could run off to when I ditched the bike, I saw the door towards the shop area open, through the aisles of the store, old snacks and dirty magazines will surely make some good cover as I run from him and his crowbar, actually, I wonder how wide that door is, all of this going through my head as the bike still moved toward the closes garage door. I looked forward and panicked, pulling the bike left as hard and sharp as I could, there was a loud bang as I flung the bike and myself straight into the closed door, banging against the metal, screaming out in pain, I was on the floor with the bike on top of me, I could see the man finding his feet over the other side of the shop, crowbar still in his hand.

"Shit" I muttered through my helmet.

No, no no, I grabbed the bike and started pushing, crying out in pain, my back and legs completely pain filled from the crash, trying to lift this bike off of me, pleading with it to just move.

"Come on you bastard" I yelled, my hands red with pain, it was so heavy, but I was full of adrenaline, and the fear of this big ape of a man coming over to me and beating me senseless with that bar was helping me a lot. The bike was moving back to its upright position, I looked over at the man and saw he was now on his feet and limping towards me again, cursing and screaming as he walked, his face blue with pain and anger, eyebrows touching the top of his nose, spit flying out of his dry lips every time he threw another curse at me. My heart dropped, he was very close.

The bike bounced back onto its wheels, I was already on it, and the engine still running, the man knew he wouldn't get to me in time, I was already pulling back the throttle and launching myself forward to the open door into the shop, this didn't slow him though, just made him change tactics, he raised the crowbar and threw it at my head, smashing the side of my visor and denting my helmet, I ignored it as best I could, still flying forward. The bike reached the door into the room, sparks flew from the handle bars as they brushed the sides, old chocolate and other random supplies flew through the air as the bike broke through aisle after aisle, I was struggling to keep it under control and almost fell off, but then there was a light as I blasted through the final aisle, it was the shop window. It was bright outside, and yet still insanely cold, but I wasn't worried about that, all I could think was the fact that any second now I was going to be driving through a shop window, I grabbed the brakes so hard I thought they might snap off, the back tired lifted off the ground, but it wasn't enough, the bike reached the window and went flying straight into it, shattering the glass and almost throwing me from the bike.

The speed I was going helped a lot, it meant I could keep going when I got out of the shop, I shook my head to get the glass off and pulled back on the throttle again, the bike chocked and jolted itself forward and onto the road, glass was all over me, I could feel a big piece on my back between my bag and jacket, there was nothing I could do about it now though, not while I was so close to the shop with that man still inside, no doubt he would have called the police as well, I had to go and fast. Reaching the road I moved into the higher gears on the bike, its speed suddenly started dramatically increasing, I decided to go up another gear, the bike was now flying forward, screeching as it went, leaving nothing behind me but dust and a crazy, probably very angry man, I was on my way to there, finally, after all these years it was going to happen, of course first I wanted to stop and check my bag, check that I wasn't injured and get rid of this bloody glass digging into me, but after I had done that, I was heading straight there, my last day had finally come, I was ready.

"Bag, check" I said to myself, feeling all over, trying to figure out if I had forgotten anything, there was no turning back now, so I was really hoping I hadn't. Smiling away I got back on my bike, no, I hadn't forgotten anything, and even if I had, so long as the bike still worked and I had my bag, it didn't really matter. I settled myself on the seat and check my bag again before turning the bike on, putting it into gear and driving off again, god I love that sound.

"Brrrrr brum brum" I blurred out of the cracks in my helmet, singing along with the bike and laughing at the same time. The road was long, a nice long straight road, I opened up the bike, putting it in its highest gear, swerving from one side of the road to the other, dodging and sliding between the occasional car, watching the trees on the side of the road becoming green and brown blurs in the wind. I could feel a fierce blow of air coming through my helmet, it felt like someone pushing my head into the back of my helmet, forcing my eyes to almost close, at the speed I was doing this was very dangerous, the broken visor offered no wind safety, and yet I didn't care, I pulled the throttle to its fullest, going faster and faster. I could not even turn my head to see the trees anymore, the sun had disappeared behind some clouds, darkening the sky, if it rained id have to slow down, I didn't really want too. One way or another world ends today; my world anyway, so might as well do what I want.

Why a bike? Why not a car? I asked myself this question a few months ago, a car is safer, and in general better than most bikes. The reason I chose a bike is because I have a theory that it is harder to fake, a car journey seems so easy to fake as you're basically in a box with TV screens around you, or as some call them, windows. But a bike, you are right in the television, much harder to fake, and I don't want to make this easy for them in anyway, so however I can make this harder for them to fake, I will, maybe cause a slip up, a glitch.

The journey went by rather quickly, the bike was very fast, I think I got flashed by a few speed cameras as well on my way, but honestly that really didn't make any difference, and anyway, I was here now, sitting on my bike, waiting in the queue of cars, one of the cattle of people smelling the sea air, looking across the ocean. The dock was at the end of that long winding road I took to get here, after my stop I didn't need to stop again until I reached it, so I just carried on going.

"Please stand away from the ferries doors, they are now opening, board with care" a voice came from the speaker phones, they were located pretty much everywhere, someone really liked hearing their own voice.

Vehicles started moving forward now; and before I knew it, it came to be my turn to move forward, but I didn't move, I just sat there. What is the point in moving my bike a couple of feet a minute, wasting all that fuel and energy, when I can just wait until all the cars in front of me are on the ferry and drive straight on. People started beeping me behind, I didn't want to cause any confrontation with anyone so I turned the bike on and moved forward slowly with the crowd of cars, the sheep with wheels. It was a nice, normal looking boat, big back door open, excepting the sheep, and it floats, I suppose if it didn't, I probably would be going on a different one. There was a loud clang as I drove onto the platform, or door, I don't know what it's called really, the big thing that comes down at the back of the boat to let cars on. And then it was straight into a small car park underneath the socialising and sleeping parts of the ferry. Turning of the engine, I left the bike next to an old car, well it looked old.

"Ah, you're here Leo, finally here" I said to myself with a smile. One year I have been waiting for this day, it feels like so much longer, a year is a long time, but a lifetime is longer, and for a whole lifetime I have been living this fake, boring life, following the pointless situations and never questioning the endless amount of coincidences that occurred, today, soon, that all ends forever. I couldn't stop smiling, didn't really know what to do now, had to pass the time until the boat started going, I am pretty hungry, maybe some food. I started walking towards the stairs, in hope of finding some sort of canteen or food court upstairs. People were pouring into the staircase, rushing and pushing up the stairs, rude arrogant people all in a rush to get nowhere, there are thousands of seats on this boat, and yet they would rather push, doesn't really make any sense.

The stairs were packed all the way up; dull orange walls surrounded them, with dull people to fill the space between them. When I finally reached the top I saw a long queue for what looked like the food area.

"Hmmm" I mumbled to myself looking around. So clearly I was supposed to queue up, the boat would leave, and I wouldn't get to do my trick, my plan.

"Screw that" I chuckled still looking around.

"Ah" I said with a sigh of relief, walking over to something sticking onto a wall, a vending machine, no queue for this. I pulled put my last bit of cash, the exact amount as a sandwich from the machine, I would say what are the odds, but I have had this day planned for a while now, I know the system, I learned the patterns, I knew how much to bring. I placed the money into the machine and received my sandwich.

"Better get to the side" I said looking at my watch, walking to the doors to get out to the side of the ferry, when suddenly I heard a voice.

"Excuse me" Oh shit, I bet it's the police. Turning around slowly I was pleasantly surprised.

"Hello" I replied with a smile, it was a beautiful woman, long blonde hair, dark brown eyes, a perfect hourglass body, and an adorable smile.

"I was wondering if you could help me, my bag is really heavy, and my room is so far away, would you mind helping me carry it." She said with that beautiful smile. I had no idea where this ferry was going, I didn't need to know, but I guess it's far if people have rooms.

"Stand clear, the ferry is departing" A voice came on the intercom, I smiled again, but not at the girl in front of me, more at the timing, I felt like something didn't want me doing my plan, queues, and what sane man would say no to this gorgeous girl?

"No, sorry" as it turns out, I am insane. I've often thought I must be to believe something as crazy as I do, but this decision was not one of an insane man, I had no time for their games and deception, if I was late then I could not be certain of my plan working.

Walking past the woman, her blonde hair brushing my shoulder, her mouth open from shock, I don't believe she has ever heard the word no until today, oh well. I could see the door to the balcony, it was a glass door, I grasped the handle and pulled it open, stepping out into the blistering cold, hitting me like the side of a steel sword, I could smell the ocean air, and see the port behind us, men were running around below throwing bits of rope around, unlatching and tying up different parts of the boat connecting to the dock, the engine rumbled, I leant forward and gripped the rail to lean over the edge and check that we were ready to embark. Everything looked ok, no rope left on the boat, no men running around, and the engine spitting out water as if to tell the helms man that the boat was ready. I smiled, taking off my rucksack and placing it on the floor, unzipping the top of it quickly to reach for the one thing inside, a small see through bag, very heavy, but small none the less. I pulled it out of my bag with both hands and left my bag open on the floor, returning to my spot leaning over the edge of the boat.

Opening the bag I removed one item from inside and placed the open bag in my pocket, so I could reach in and remove an item at will, it almost pulled down my trousers due to the heaviness of the contents inside. I leaned out further over the edge and held my hand out as far as I could, looking at the water below I released my grip and the item fell from my grasp, falling through the air and creating a small splash as it hit the water. There's something sinister about the water, I kept repeating this in my head, the water scared me, it looked fake, too unreal, too unexplored. The stone that I had dropped in disappeared quickly, and the ripples soon faded with them.

"Ok, so far so good" I said, the wind quietened my voice and made it impossible for anyone to hear. I reached in my pocket and pulled out another stone, and then another, dropping them one after another as the boat continued into the ocean, every time I would look at the water and wait for the ripples of the first one to fade before dropping in the next, nothing changed, and I was running out of stones.

"The waters real" I said in disbelief as I realised I was out of stones, feeling around my pocket I couldn't find anymore, I guess I was wrong.

My eyes widened, my mouth opened and a smile grew from check to check.

"What do we have here?" I whispered to my own ears as I reached down to the floor surface below grasping something and raising it to my chest, as if it was a baby bird that I just found, fallen from its nest, looking back at the shore I realised just how far out we were now, must have been a few miles from the dock, the shoreline almost completely faded under the mist of the sea. I leant over the edge, almost completely over the water now and held out was arm as far as I could, and just as I was going to drop it, I paused. Could that be it? Is it just this small area? I stepped down from the ledge and walked a few paces back, towards the door, but just as I reached the door to enter the boat again I suddenly turned, running towards the edge of the boat and throwing the stone I found as far as I could, launching it into the sky above, I had never thrown something as far as that before, the weight, the wind, everything was perfect, it all carried the stone into the grey of the sky above.

Barely making it out in the distance as it came crashing down into the water below, but something different happened this time, something even I couldn't have predicted. There were no ripples, not even a splash; it just appeared to disappear into the abyss. I looked in disbelief, did I just see that? No, it was too far; perhaps the fog hid the splash. The stone now gone faded, never to be seen again by my eyes.

This is what I came here for, I needed proof and I now have it, I have never been so scared in my life but I know what I saw, and today is my last day, it was always supposed to be my last day, and it will be, I climbed on the side on the rail and looked down into the water, splashing against the side of the boat.

"I am not your puppet anymore, today I die, so you can never use me again" I yelled as I jumped from the side of the ferry, plummeting down beside the hull, greeting the water below, this was my last day, I always knew it would end like this, I just didn't want to believe it, but now I have no choice, even if this world is real, even if I was wrong, I have nothing to go back to, no life to live, no happiness, only death to await, I wanted to leave this world on my own terms, and the fact that I now was drowning amongst the waves of the ocean and feeling the splitting cold of the current ripping through my flesh meant that I had, I was free from the relentlessness of my life, my last day had come, and I was finally at peace, finally happy, and yet so afraid of death at the same time, and insanely cold. Neither the less, here I was, in the empty abyss, dying.

This all seemed to happen so fast, looking back at this day, it was too quick, did I rush this, could it have ended differently? It doesn't matter anymore. For some reason I seem to be falling quicker, being dragged to the darkness below, maybe I over looked some stones in my pocket, the darkness was rapping its cold, dead hands around me, freezing my body, I tried to breath but found myself swallowing water, trying to cough it out and breath even more just meant I was filling up my lungs more and more with this salty liquid, this is the end, I could see a dark mist descending over my eyes, kicking and trying to swim, but nothing could change the outcome now. My eyes closed, that was that, I was dead, no more girlfriend, no more best friend, no more work, nothing, perhaps I was wrong, maybe this world is real, either way its ended for me now, my eternal sleep has begun, people say you see a light, all I can see is never ending darkness, which I will now call my home.

But then something happened, something magical and disturbing, something I never thought possible, I was alive, I felt my heart beat through my body as if nothing had happened, as if I was at home asleep, or eating my Sugar Puffs, I was living in this abyss, how is this possible?

"No, that's not possible, this cannot be real" I tried to say but could not talk without swallowing this black ocean water, I was in disbelief as I watched it come towards me, grabbing me and dragging me into this light, this blinding, pure white light, beneath all these waves, way beyond saving it found me, how is this possible, I couldn't see a body, all I could see was it floating on my jacket, dragging me up and into this light, a hand.

What was going on? This must be a dream.

Chapter 4

Earth and Vala

Was I blind? I can't see a damn thing other than some white light, perhaps I am dead?

"You're not dead" a voice said from beyond the light.

"I'm blind then" I replied back, who was this person speaking to me? By the sound and tone of the voice I could tell it was a female, not sure how old, the voice was somewhat familiar and calming, a nice feeling of tranquillity filled my body, I felt at piece simply by the sound of this woman telling me I wasn't dead.

"No, just very stupid" she said turning of the white light, a hospital light it seemed, one dentists use to check your teeth for damage and other things wrong with them. Looking around I realised that I was in a hospital, there were other patients on beds similar to mine and green curtains covering me from their view, computers were on desks, nurses walking around, the only thing that made it look less like a hospital and more like some mad scientists lab was the equipment, it was all different, I did not recognise any of it, it looked like something from the future, but then again if I had drowned maybe this was something they needed to help me?

The woman was looking at me, smiling, she then began to pace up and down beside my bed, looking at some sort of hand held laptop in her hand. I reached out and grabbed her arm to stop her walking; she looked down at me with utter fear pouring out of her eyes and facial expression.

"What happened?" I whispered to her.

"You drowned" she replied, her shoulders un-tensed and I let go, she began to walk off

"And then we had to pull you out" She loudly muttered as she walked down the corridor. Did she mean out of the water? How did I get here? How am I alive? I was so far under the water the only people that could have saved were inhabitants of the lost city of Atlantis. Just as she disappeared around the corner, two men came around the corner where she had gone, pacing towards where I was laying. Both of them had plan boring suits and sunglasses, the suits were pure white and completely clean, they looked like some sort of authority, but no police officers I have ever seen wore a uniform like that.

"The director will see you now" one of them said, nodding to the other as he finished his sentence.

Suddenly the other man grabbed me, holding me down; I was too weak to push him away.

"Get off, what are you doing?" I yelled, wriggling and shouting at them as the other man seemed to be filling up a syringe with a blue liquid. I kicked as much as I could; trying to throw them from me, but all my effort seemed pointless.

"What is that? Get the hell away from me" I screamed, but there was nothing I could do, before I knew it the syringe was in my arm, and then darkness descended across my eyes.

When I woke the woman was gone and so were the men, I found myself leaning back in a chair gazing at the white ceiling, one single light in the centre of it and white walls, I was inside a box it seems, white walls above and around me. I lifted my head forward and gazed across the room, there was one table in it and two chairs. One for me and one for the man staring at me on the other side of the table, smiling.

"I take it that blue liquid wasn't any of the good kind of drugs?" I could barely talk, I felt so weak and tired. The man started laughing.

"No, I am afraid not, it was supposed to wipe your memory, but it appears to have failed again" he replied, still smiling.

I sat up, my eyes wide.

"Oh I get it, this is some reality television show? It needs work, this couldn't be any more ridiculous if you tried" I said with a grin on my face, I had cracked their stupid plot.

"No Leo, this is not a TV show, this is real, for the first time in your life" the man replied, now staring right at me, looking straight into my eyes.

"Where am I?" I nervously sputtered out.

"Welcome to Vala Leo." He said, standing up and walking around the table and myself, still talking, my eyes followed him throughout the room.

"Earth, is nothing more than the dirt on the ground, not a planet, not a life. You are 22 years old now, and for those 22 years you have lived in one of these" He finished talking and raised his right hand to a device on his left arm, he looked to be typing something on a keypad located on the device. Once he finished he turned around a looked at the wall in front of me. As he clicked the device one last time the wall turned into a window, not even that, just nothing, glass or air, but the wall was either no longer there or was see through like a window. I gazed out through the invisible wall and looked upon the endless room.

The room was dark, other than a light above every box within it, pathways between them and men walking around holding devices like the nurse had, if she really was a nurse. There were thousands of boxes, white boxes like the one I was in now, only mine appeared to be above the other, higher so I could see across the endless sea of them.

"ACW's, that's what we call them, artificially created worlds, although you call it home, work, earth, life." He said, still walking around me.

"Am I dead? Or dreaming? I drowned, this isn't possible" I couldn't believe my eyes, there is no way this is possible, I still don't understand what is going on.

"There are people, just like you, living the same life you did, in the same world you did, but you never met them, no one in your life was real, your girlfriend, Wayland, they are nothing more than a computer programme we created." He continued talking.

"Of course your life was different to theirs, not exactly the same, small differences and big ones in some cases."

"Do you expect me to believe this? I know what I lived, I said it was fake but I never believed, deep down I always knew it was real, what you say is impossible, nothing but another lie." I said interrupting him.

He huffed, and then starting talking again

"Are you hungry?" He said, raising his hand to his arm again, hovering it steadily over the device.

"Perhaps some Sugar Puffs?" Laughing as he said it and pressing a button on the device. Suddenly on the table in front of my eyes there was a bowl of Sugar Puffs. I looked at the man and just stared at him.

"Try it" He said, turning around to gaze out of the now see through wall. My eyes returned to the bowl on the table. I hadn't eaten in a while; I could feel my stomach rumbling and hear it as well. Deciding to try it, I reached out towards the spoon in the bowl and began to bring a spoonful of Sugar Puffs to my mouth. They tasted perfect, the sugar balance and the milk, everything. I began eating the rest as quick as my hand could bring them to my mouth, forcing them down, enjoying every bite, every swallow, every second of this moment.

Suddenly the taste changed, and the texture, it didn't taste like Sugar Puffs, but like some sort of bland, mouldy food. I looked down and the bowl, and suddenly jumped out of my seat, launching the chair across the room and spitting out the food, this can't be real.

"What is that?" I screamed at the man, looking back at the bowl now full of maggots and other insects, bugs. The man started laughing and continued pressing buttons on his arm, whatever that device was it seemed to have control of these creatures, the bugs starting growing and changing shape, they turned into some sort of animal I had never seen before, I backed myself into the corner, my eyes fixed on the bugs. They began to grow wings and started flying around the room, buzzing around my head and landing on the table, I was so afraid and confused.

They continued to grow, fixated on them I didn't know what to do, how does someone react to something like this, there must have been ten of these creatures flying around the room, as big as my torso, orange and green, scales, not fur or skin but scales all over their body, six legs and four eyes, resting upon the table right in front of me. I could see the door behind it, next to the man, as I looked at the door and prepared to try and escape, placing my hands on the floor and bringing my feet closer to my body, the creature launched forward, flying towards me, this winged insect, like a giant dragonfly, what could I do except shield myself from this approaching attack. I raised my hands to defend my face and braced.

As I sat there, confused and afraid to open my tightly shut eyes I felt time slow down, as if I myself had pressed a magical button and frozen time, something in the room felt different, there was no longer loud noises of buzzing and this heat of wind from the flap of these beasts wings smashing me in the face, like someone was standing in front of me holding an open oven. I opened my eyes and gazed at the back of my arm, shielding my face, my arms moved down and my eyes continued to open their selves. The room was still now, the man still there with his hand on the device, smiling away in the corner of the room now, but we were not alone, not yet, because resting a few inches from my hand on the cold, hard floor was this creature's wing, just barely touching the ground. I followed the wing with my eyes and saw this insect exactly where it was before I closed my eyes, only now it was not moving, the air was still around it, and even the saliva dripping from its mouth was frozen in mid-air. It had hundreds of sharp teeth and inside its eyes was an army of many more staring into mine, looking at me, hungry and waiting, patient, as if I was dinner served up to it, and it already knew I belonged to it, I was its dinner.

"Kusak" the man said, I looked over, he was still smiling with that devilish grin, just that smile alone was enough to unnerve me, reminding me that he knows so much more than I do, he was in the corner of the room, but walking forward to me now, taking long, sturdy strides, the other bugs around the pale white room all started to fade and fizzle into nothing.

"The creature before your eyes is very real, in a matter of speaking, it is called the Kusak, they live in the forest not far from here, violent little things, I suppose they are very similar to wasps or bees that you are accustomed too." He said, now sitting back on the chair, crossing his legs and stretching his arms behind him, his suit perfectly ironed, not a single crease in it, white and not a single faded patch or speck of dirt to be found anyway upon it.

My eyes drifted from him back towards the bug, everything about this creature was amazing, you see things in movies and you never think about how it would feel to be the person in that movie, seeing these things through real eyes, not the artificial eyes of a television set. I slowly lifted my shaking hand and reached out slowly towards it, as my hand got closer I could feel the heat from its body warming my palm, as if I was placing my hand in a hot bath full of water, but as I edged closer and finally touched it, I found myself not feeling its scales, not resting my hand on its back, wing or any part of its body, but instead watching my hand fall straight through the creature, as if it was not even there.

"You're very lucky, very lucky indeed, these creatures usually travel in packs of thousands, all you had in front of you was one fake one." He carried on explaining, my eyes gazing into the Kusaks eyes as it faded into nothing.

"But of course they are nothing compared to the Neatas, Grazers, Figmen or the Mangto, never seen one in person, don't even have a hologram, which is odd considering their amazing size and destruction, they can even breathe in space, usually a swarm of Kusaks means one of the Mangtos is near, but no one has really seen one and lived, imagine that, a creature in space being able to breathe." He continued, I looked up at him and began to stand.

"Well you call it space, it's known here on Vala and the Federate planets as the Abyss, because most of the planets are unknown and unvisited by us, but infested with creatures, even the abyss its self has things even I am scared of. Even Vala used to be infested, we changed that." He stopped, I stared at him and that uneasy smile slapped across his face.

"What is this?" I whispered at him, my eyes in an half open haze; my mouth remained open with awe.

"This, this is a testing room, located in a facility near the Forest, outside the Valtoorian City, you wanted proof that this was real right? He paused again looking at me, leaning forward, his smile changed, his eyes full of anger.

"I just gave it to you, welcome to the real world." After he finished he laughed, and carried on laughing, it echoed through this tiny room, bouncing off the walls around me.

"Why? Why do you do this to people, trick us, there is no point in this, or is it just me? A trick on me." I sputtered out.

"A trick? This is not some game, some magic spell; you are a guest to one of the biggest cooperation in the Federate Nation." He stood up and gazed out along the endless rows of cubicles and continued.

"Have you ever wished to know what you could have done to be rich? Or just wished someone would guide you, even for a week, just have a dotted line before your eyes telling you where to go, what to say and it would be the best possible outcome. You ask yourself how can I become famous, get the best girlfriend, or get the girl you love. What can you possibly do to gain all this? Live longest, spend the most little, basically be the best possible person anyone can ever be, know all the answers all the outcomes to everyone choice, every decision anyone ever makes, you know what they will be in the future because you have seen it."

He stopped again and turned to look at me.

"We have been doing this for years, learning the future, writing it like a book; imagine that, just for a second, what would people do for that advice? To know how to live longest, how to avoid diseases and get all the ladies, money wealth and fame, become intelligent. With this information we can control everything, everyone and shaped the Federate Nation into the greatness it once was, with this power we can learn the future, change the world for the better." He turned back to looking out the window, smiling again, the wrinkles pressed to his ear, as if the smile was going to pop off his face.

"This is wrong, who are these people? Who am I? The idea of what you are doing defeats the purpose of living, if certain people know how to manipulate the world, and change everything, people who can't afford that information will become nothing, everyone will fight to be on top, and the ones who lose will be doomed by people like you. Learning the future is one thing, but shaping a world with what you learn is different, and doing this to people to get there is wrong!" My voice thickened, you could hear anger in it now. He turned to look at me, raising his wrist and placing his hand on the device.

"You are nothing, everyone in there is expendable, your parents die, or you are orphans from birth, homeless, nothing to anyone and we save you, give you this life, and this is what you say?" His eyes flickering like fire, lips tight.
"You said all possible outcomes, what sort of lives do other people live?" I quietened my voice.
"Ones that you enjoyed watching so much on your TV, you loved horror films didn't you, they may be fake in your world, but in theirs, they are as real as the air entering your lungs as we speak, every possible outcome means EVERY possible outcome! Death at young ages, some

were raised with those creatures you just saw, some on other planets, you had it easy with your fake world, girlfriend and job and yet you complained and searched for the truth?" He shook his head after he finished.

"Regardless of what I did, how can you do this to people, real people like you? Butcher them, torment them and through them into these fake lives, horrible lives." I was out of my seat now, confronting him.

He laughed and looked at me again; even his eyes now seemed to be grinning.

"Because you and your people are nothing like me and mine, you are like the bugs you saw before you a minute ago, and we'd kill every last one of you for us, not everyone may agree, but that is irrelevant. For the good of the Federate Nation, we will just have to keep going and going." He placed his hands on a button now, at the top of the device. I looked straight into his eyes, those grinning eyes staring at me.

"You could have lived a nice fake life, now you only get to live a very short real one, goodbye Leo." He pressed the button and out of the device came a small dart, I barely saw it leave the device but I saw exactly where it landed, between my eyebrows, god this pain, this dizziness, am I dying? The room started to shake, at least it looked like it was shaking, the ground below my feet moved like it was breathing, expanding and dropping, as I looked up instead of seeing the man in front of my eyes, I could see the ground, cold and hard greeting me as if it was falling on top of me, rushing towards me and there was nothing I could do but lie there and except it, I could barely move, barely breathe, I should of stayed in bed today, my fake comfy bed, with my fake girlfriend, if I am not dying maybe I am dreaming, feels to real to be a dream, but then again you never know until you wake up. I can't take this pain, god my head hurts, a thousand knives digging into my skull, pressuring my brain and popping open my mind, this wasn't a headache, it was death. Please wake up.

"Please wake up."

Chapter 5

Endless Sleep

"**Leo, Leo honey**, are you ok?" I soft voice echoed from the darkness.

"Come on, it's time to get up, wake up Leo, wake up." The voice repeated, it sounded familiar, my mother maybe, I haven't heard her voice in years, if it was her I don't even know if I'd be able to tell, however it sounded younger than I remember.

"Wake up Leo, wake up" The voice was changing, the tone and deepness of it was becoming less familiar and more, new, unusual and frightening.

"Wake up!" I felt an itch, somewhere on my face, a small itch, then another not far from the first, it was my eyes, I could feel them.

"I'm not dead?"

I muttered out, the pain was still shooting around my body, making it so difficult to do something as simple as speak, move or even breathe.

"Wake up kid." The voice said again. I slowly opened my eyes, it has never been so hard to open to small parts of my body before, it was as if they were being pulled shut, fighting against me as I struggled to regain control of them. A blinding light suddenly shone through the tiny slit I made between my eyes lids, as I opened them wider I could see the ground still in front of me, only this time it was moving differently, it was as if I was flying above it, moving forward slowly, watching all the cracks between each tile appear then disappear behind me and every few seconds the ground would light up, my eyes hadn't adjusted to it yet which meant when it did I could feel a horrible burn pain, burrowing at the back of my eye sockets.

I could hear a noise as well, what was that, and sharp grinding noise, the sound of something plastic being dragged against something, a bag or box perhaps. As yet another light appeared and then vanished before my eyes I realised what was happening. It was a reflection of the ceiling lights in the floor, shining back into my face as if the lights themselves were mounted to the floor below me, and the noise I could hear was me, not a bag or a box but me. I decided to try and look up, Jesus lifting my head hurts, this pain was unbearable, but I had to see, and looking up I saw four hands on me, attached to these thick, pale hands was a black sleeve, and then two large men, the same men who drugged me earlier, dragging me along a tiled corridor floor. There were no doors, no windows, not even a picture on the walls; the corridors were exactly the same as the room of which I had just left, only longer.

"Where are you taking me?" I said to the men carrying me.
"TOPC" One replied, not even looking down at me, they both just carried on carrying me as if I hadn't even spoken.
"What's that?" I spoke again. Hoping for any answer at least.
"Termination Of Programmes Centre" The other one replied, their voices almost identical in sound.
"Why?" I asked with a shaky voice
"You are an inefficient programme, termination is required." The same man answered. I don't really see any point in asking yet another question, when if the answer means what I believe it does, I don't want to find out anymore, I do however find it funny how this is now the third time today of which I thought I was going to die, when all my life this is what I wanted and now I just want to wake up from this living nightmare. Even though this had become the topic of the day, believing I was going to die, I had a gut feeling this was going to be the last time where I would be proven wrong.

Today started with me leaving my torn apartment, saying farewell to my stuck up girlfriend and is now going to end with me being called a programme and having to be terminated, that sounds ridiculous and yet I could feel my eyes welling as tears started to appear within them,

I don't want to die, not by the hands of these two monkeys, not here in this facility, if this is real and there is a whole new world outside of this building I want to see it, I want those people who are just like me in those containers to see it, my story cant end here, not now, a few hours ago I would of excepted death, now I've never been so afraid of it, I can feel the tears sliding down my check and dripping off my chin now, I don't know what to do, no matter what I think of, no matter what I say, there's nothing I can do.

As I moved in the arms of these two men slowly down the corridor, I found myself slowing down, and eventually we stopped outside of a doorway. It was almost impossible to see, blending into the wall and the relentless dullness of colour that seemed to be the only colour within the whole building, even though everything looked the same, it didn't feel familiar, even this flaccid door somehow felt new to me, and I had already passed over ten of them now. The corridors seemed to go on forever, I wish they did go on forever, I would never have to die.

Both men began simultaneously typing on the keypads either side of the door that now was right in front of my nose, so close I feel like I can smell my approaching death beyond it. There was a noise on my right, turning to see what it was I could see yet another door, this one was open however. As I carried on staring at this other door I saw a man walk out of it in what looked like some sort of working outfit. Maybe it was the fear of death, maybe it was the fact that I was about to die and have never seen the outside of this new world I have just been awaken into, or perhaps it was the very fact that as that man came walking from the other side of that door carrying an object in his hands which appeared to be heavy by the fact that he was using to hands to manoeuvre it. Whatever it was, it filled me with a warm feeling of hope. The whole walk down this corridor I had two hands on me, I was a heavy object apparently, however now, I could see their other hands typing on this keypad, and it hit me, if that man carrying that object removed just one of his hands, would he still be able to hold it?

The air felt warm all around my face; even though I couldn't see my breath I could feel every exhale from my mouth hitting the door in front of me, in what felt like a life time I looked up at the two men and then again to my right, the door was still open, this was it. I rested both my hands on the floor and tensed up, finding strength in my legs that I didn't even know I had, the air was silent, even the sound of the buttons being pressed seemed to disappear amongst the tension, I could hear and feel every thump of my heart, breaking its way through my rib cage. As the men finished typing I took my one shot.

Both of my arms launched right, I used them as weight to throw my legs behind them, I could feel their arms losing grip from my shoulders as I slung my body from the floor to a running stance, my feet kicking the floor, my hands scratching and banging the hard surface trying to bring my body up as quick as I could, everything must of happened within the space of a few seconds but when your blood is up it feels like you can see everything in slow motion. I was out of their reach and now running, I could hear both men stumbling behind me as they attempted to reach out towards where I was, trying to grab hold of me again before pursuing me. The distant corridor before my eyes seemed to be stretching, loud bangs and slaps filled the air with noise as we all ran through the endless maze.

Approaching the door I quickly turned my head to see how far the two men were from me, they had stopped running and began walking now, both looking at me with this empty face, not filled with worrying or panic that I was now out of their reach, just emptiness. My head quickly darted back to the door that was now within reach, but as I reached out to wrap my hand on the inside of it and slingshot myself around into the other room I noticed something.

"No" I mumbled. The door was closed, both my hands clashed with the cold surface and rested upon it, as I went to run again down the corridor I notice two more men almost completely identical to the ones that had been carrying me, strolling towards me with that same empty look, I looked back to my left just to make sure they were not the same men, but there they were, still marching towards me. My hands on the door in front of me, my heart suddenly sinking, they weren't running and didn't look worried because they knew I wasn't going anyway, the door had already closed, now I'm here with a closed door before me and four angry suited tanks walking towards me.

"Shit" I whispered, placing my head upon my hands.

As my head hit my hands I found myself falling forward, stumbling and struggling to remain standing I gazed to where my hands had been resting to find a confused looking man staring at me through what appeared to be a gas mask, holding a crate in both his glove covered hands he just stood there, shocked by the fact that I was standing in front of this door way, I was surprised as well, where this closed door had been there was now a man blocking me instead of a grey sheet of a door. My eyes dashed left and right at the way, for whatever reason, I'm not staying here to find out its true and I'm going to die.

As my mind descending back into reality and from the train of thought, I could no longer see white painted walls and was not greeted with the sight of another bland corridor, but in fact in a room filled with machines and steam, bronze rust and pipes, my mind told me to stop, analyse where I was and where I had to go to escape, but my body wouldn't listen, it kept running, I was pushed forward by the overwhelming fear that the four men were now probably looking right at the back of my feet jumping into the air one by one and pursuing me as fast as they could themselves, I had a feeling they were much faster than I was considering the fact that they were built like a house, I didn't dare to turn and look in case I lost even a slight bit of speed or advantage.

The ground below where I was running was increasing in volume, what was once hard concrete floor was now railing and metal framing, I gazed down into what looked like an endless pit of machines and workers, fire and smoke, it felt like I was in some sort of hell re-enactment, the heat from mechanical devices burning my face as I dashed onto the platforms in front of me, moving past one worker and then another, ducking and diving through the corner and arms that seemed to be reaching out to me. One man dropped a steel plate as I ran past and screamed below to alert any people of its decent, clanging and ringing as it fell from where the man's hands were still located as if he was still holding it, hovering in mid-air, grasping nothing but the palms of his gloves within his grasp. All I saw was him turn around after losing his grip and screaming to warn the others as he failed to catch me, reaching out and letting yet another object slip through his grasp.

It felt no longer than a second that I had been running along these metal scaffolds and grates before I reached a problem. My hands attached their selves to the rails of the walkway, peering forward and then down into the deep abyss of machines and fire, sweat dripping off my body and my cloths now hugging me as if they were freezing cold and needed warmth, the sweat stuck them to my body, my mouth wide open breathing in the hot air all around me, looking back up and ahead I realised that there was nowhere to go, I was at a dead end.

CHAPTER 6

Open Door Through A Closed Window

Panic, nothing but nauseating, gut wrenching panic filled my aching body as I peered across to the other platform, after a few seconds of mindlessly gazing at it I decided to look for another way across. Turning around I could see the four men running at heavy speed through the walkways behind me, the clattering of their shoes hitting the metal grated surface getting louder and louder as they got closer and closer, becoming more easy to see, there was no time to look for another way across, I had to do something now or surrender to these men. My head rotated back to looking across to the opposite platform, my hands tightly gipped the rails attached to it, I pulled my lifeless body up onto the rails, worn and destroyed from the run, I felt as if I had been hit by a bus.

Gazing through the steam rising from below me, standing on top of these rusted rails, I reached up and brushed the sweat away from my forehead and paused just four men who had now stopped dead in their tracks and were dauntlessly staring at me, mouths open completely shocked as we all were. I looked back at the man carrying the box in front of me; he didn't move an inch, taking one quick glance at the men who were still in shock about the timing of this opening door, I realised that I had to act quick.

Feeling the tingling shooting down my arm, my fist tensed and my hand rose. The man in front of my eyes, beads of sweat dipping off my chin, he knew exactly what was happening. I pulled my arm back and raised it to behind my head, locking it into position like a rifle about to fire, the wind broke around my knuckles as I threw it forward, every ounce of energy behind my shoulder and wrist, filled with adrenaline I barely felt my knuckles connect with his face, striking him like a bat, the box flying into the air and landing behind the man, following the box to the ground was this empty shell of a person, completely lifeless as if asleep, plummeting to the ground, nose opened up and face covered in blood, as the man received my fist and the floor greeted him I leaped over the body and box that were now keeping the ground below company and proceeded to run as fast as my legs could carry me into the doorway.

I wish I could tell you that I believed in the deepest corner of my heart that I was going to escape, or even get close to leaving this god forsaken place, but if I did, I would be lying to myself, as I darted through the doorway I found myself hitting this wall of no hope, this empty feeling of despair, I would never leave this building, I would never see the outside of this world, perhaps I was asleep, lying within the protected warmth from my lonely, broken bed with the duvet over me in a corner of a sleep, perhaps this was not a dream but I had been kidnapped for some sort of ransom or to be experimented on. Believing that the thing you have believed for a year is true, is not as easy as it seems, when reality is exactly what you thought it was you find yourself questioning its realism more than ever, and right now even though I didn't think I was going to leave here, I didn't even know what here was and if anything that man said was true, or if I'm running into conciseness to find my bed and baulshit apartment at the end of this dark nightmare I appear to be living, either

for a second. My chest raising as I took what could be my final breath, the world seemed to pause with me, not daring to turn and see how close the men now were to me. I bent my legs and looked forward, pausing again and then extending my legs to their full length, launching my body forward, using my hands to push off the rails extending to the walkway above the one I had been standing on, the air flustering my hair and blowing the sweat from my worn face. My hands were now fully extended in front of my face, reaching out for the other walkway, however I could see it moving up and out of my reach as I dropped down into the abyss, my hands catching nothing but air in front of me, kicking the air with my legs and arms, desperately trying to reach forward even an inch more and catch the bottom of the walkway, the air was now coming at me from the bottom, dashing up my t-shirt and my hands still fully extended in front of me, wishing to grab the bronze, metal platform but touching nothing but air as it faded into the distance and I began to fall.

Is this it? After all this effort I fail to escape from my own attempt to jump from one walkway to the other, it was either that or except defeat, perhaps I made the wrong choice, I could feel the fear all over my body, my heart pounding, death by falling is more scary than anything I could imagine, your body drifting through nothing, clashing with the air and no matter where you reach you can't grab anything to stop your appending death, all you can do is watch it approach you slowly, like you're nothing more than a helpless animal crossing the road in front of a truck plummeting towards you, as you turn to face the headlights and realise it's too late to dodge out of the way.

"Gotcha" A voice shouted from beyond the mist. I found myself moving left and right slowly, ascended above the machines below with one arm extended above my head, it was caught on something. As the steam started to fade I could just about make out what my arm was now caught on, it wasn't a rusted loose bit of metal, or a walkway, but a hand, a soft gentle, yet very strong hand was wrapped around my wrist, holding me tightly, a few seconds passed and I could see another hand join the other and grasp my wrist, my body twitching and jerking as they struggled to pull me up. I reached out and grabbed the hands gabbing me, trying to find something to put my feet on, kicking nothing but air, and then a metal clack came crashing through the air as my foot hit something, I placed my dangling leg upon it and pulled myself up through the air and under the bottom rail of the walkway, hitting the hold grates of it, lying on my back trying to exhale every last drop of air into my lungs, my chest pounding up and down as I struggled to find the oxygen in the air around me.

As I lay there staring into the tunnel of machines above, looking at platforms and walkways surrounding me all around, I began to worry that maybe the person that caught me was one of the men chasing me, before I could even move the hand grabbed my wrist again, and my view of the area above was now blocked by this figure. I tried to move my other hand to rub my eyes so I could make out who this person was, but as it began to raise I found myself stuck on the ground by yet another hand grasping my wrist and this person now hovering right above me, one leg either side of my waist, practically sitting on top of me, as I closed my eyes tighter and then opened them again I could see the facial features more clearly now, the light from the fire was flickering and bouncing across their face, as if dancing across the checks and chin of this person.

"You're a woman" I sputtered out with what little breath I had left.
"Can you walk?" She replied in a soft, yet demanding voice.
"Not with you on top of me" I answered, smiling a little, the last person I expected to grab me was a petit woman, she wasn't dressed in work cloths, she looked normal, and well dressed.
"They will be here soon, keep up and stay right behind me" She said standing up and pulling me up with her.
"Take this" she continued as we both found our feet, holding out a little orange, round pill in front of my face.
"What is it?" I nervously replied to her, hesitant to take a random pill from a random person who I could barely see through the uprising steam and smoke.
"It will help with the fall you just took, trust me" she said, her eyes as green as a field on a hot summers day, gazing into mine, honestly if I wasn't so in shock I probably wouldn't have taken the pill, but the fear of the men approaching me soon and capturing me, got the better of me and I just wanted to get out of here as quickly as I could. Grabbing the pill I chucked it into my mouth and swallowed it, gulping as it went down my throat and into my stomach.
"Come on" She yelled, grabbing my wrist yet again and pulling me behind her as she ran through the steam across more walkways.

Running with this person I noticed no one else around us over this side of the machine room, I couldn't see any workers and the steam began to get weaker as we both trekked through it and across the metal grates, I could make out a door frame in the distance, hope I thought to myself, we were finally going to be out of this steam and fog, endless heat and fire. The noise got louder from our feet hitting the metal below as we picked up speed and headed straight for this door, but just as hope came, it left. The door way was no longer visible, all I could now see where the door way was, was this beast of a man smiling, holding a thick baton. I assumed the woman was going to drag me another direction, or stop all together, but all she did was increase speed, dragging me behind her, thundering straight towards this mountain of a man, he had no hair, was covered in grease and had very yellow teeth which you could see through his thick smile and the steam.

We approached him quickly, and as we got closer his arm raised with the baton tightly grasped within his palm, ready to pull it down straight into our skulls. We were now within arm's reach of this man, he started to descend his arm towards us, but as he did the woman raised hers, she moved it so quickly up all that I could see was the blur move up through the air towards the man and then down again, and we ran straight past him with no problem, she carried on running as if he wasn't even there, heading towards the door. I peered over my shoulder back at the man, just to make sure he was actually real, and as I turned I didn't see him standing there, but instead heard a loud thump and saw him hugging the floor, the baton above his head, he was just lying face down on the metal grate below, steam brushing up past his head and into the air above. As I heard yet another bang I turned my head back around and saw that we were now at the door and the woman had lifted one leg and kicked it open sending it flying back and smashing against the wall, still dragging me behind her, she ran straight through where the door used to be and into yet another white room.

No more running, I was now thinking to myself, my legs were aching and giving way, there was no way I could keep this up any longer, she didn't look tired or achy at all, not even out of breath, and she had me to drag along each walkway, and pulled me up from mid-flight to the ground. The white room was now all around us, and she carried on running, this room was different however, it had a chair and table in it and there was a double opening door in front of us, it was smaller than the ones I saw before, as I gazed around at everything in this room, the smartly painted table, the neatly placed chair, I started thinking about how just beyond the door behind us was a devils playground of fire and ash, and in here was the complete opposite. Even though I was looking around she was still pulling me along towards the double opening door, just as we reached it she stopped, didn't turn around or even speak, just raised her other hand, not the one that was still tightly grasped around my wrist, and pushed what looked like the wall, but was a button, as she pressed it, the sides lit up blue and it made a ding sound. She turned and smiled at me, looking me up and down. Then just as I was about to speak, the door opened and inside was an even smaller area, not a room but an elevator. There were different lights on the wall, organised in a three by eight grid and a red one just located at the bottom of the grid, she went into the elevator pulling me behind and pressed the third to bottom button, the doors slowly closed and then we just stood there, waiting for the doors to open, anxiously, nervous and scared.

Looking over I could see she was completely calm, and was still holding my wrist tightly, a walking contradiction really, most guys would assume it was because she was scared that she was holding it so tightly, I knew it was because she was afraid that I would get hurt, not her.
"Are you ok?" She asked, her eyes still locked on the door. I was panting and sweating everywhere, and she looked fine, as if she had just woken up or something.
"I'm alright" I mumbled out. Just as the words finished leaving my dry mouth I found myself on my knees, both hands on the floor in front of me, the whole elevator felt like it was shaking around me.
"It's ok" She said, standing in front of me and descending to my eye level. "It is the pill, it's entered your blood stream now, in a few seconds you will feel better, stronger, I promise." She said in a soft voice, almost a whisper, and her hand now on my shoulder.

The floor was shaking and so were my arms, I was struggling to even keep my head up, I forced my aching, heavy head up to look at her, and saw her smiling at me, my lips quivered as I began to smile back. Just as she took her hand off my shoulder the door behind her opened up, she was still level with me staring at me, but her eyes were now much wider, fear filled them. She darted her head as quickly as she could to try and turn around, but before it even moved slightly, she was pulled from my face straight out of the elevator onto a concrete floor, I reached out to grab her as she was being pulled through the air, but my hand only found the sole of her shoe and brushed it before I fell forward slightly, dropping my hand back to the ground of the elevator trying to stay on my hands and knees, looking back at where she was now lying. There were four men standing around her, different from the four that were chasing me earlier, but dressed roughly the same, the only difference was the colour of their suits, these men had grey suits, neatly dressed and ironed, the ones before had black.

    The area around appeared to be a car park, as it was filled with vehicles, none that I recognise, but by the shape and body of them it was easy to assume that they were vehicles. My eyes fixed back on her as the men began to move towards her. The first one that got close to her was tensing his arm and squaring a fist in line with her face, throwing it down towards her, she threw up her arm from the crawl position she was in and stopped the falling punch from hitting her skull, her legs jumped out and slid around the floor striking the side of the man's calf and sending him down to the ground where she was, her arm arched she dropped her elbow onto the man's throat and just as she rose it for another drop she was stopped, two of the other men had grabbed her arms, and pulled her off the ground to a standing position. They both held her in front of the third man, while the fourth one was on the floor below, not even moving now.
    "Katherine" the man said looking at her, raising his right hand too her cheek. "Oh I'm sorry, I mean Doctor Taylor, what are we going to do with you?" He continued, walking around her now, like a predator stalking its prey.
    As soon as the word doctor left that man's lips I suddenly realised who the woman was, I recognised her, we had been running so much I didn't have time to actually look at her, and in the machine room the steam covered her face most the time. The woman was the nurse from earlier, well doctor not a nurse, I am now assuming, she was there when I woke up on the bed. The man threw a sharp punch at the woman as he circled her, sending blood launching out of her mouth and splattering on the hard ground, she was limp now, but still somehow conscious.

    My arms began furiously shaking as I tried to pull them forward out of the elevator, the more I pulled myself forward the more strength I found I had, I didn't understand it, but I felt as if my body was waking up, becoming self-aware. All I kept thinking was the fact that I could not just lie there and watch this man beat the woman who saved my life, he swung two more hard punches at the woman, one hitting her chin, bruising it almost instantly, the other striking her rib cage, a loud crack filled the air as she yelled out in pain.

"You bastard" she cried at the man. He paused, his hand resting on the side of her bruised face, and began to turn his head towards me helplessly crawling towards them, slowly finding my feet, shaking as I began to stand a few feet from them.

"You're like a baby who has just been born, struggling to do simple things, such as stand" He said looking at me, laughing.

"Why not sit down and wait until I am finished, or are you so anxious to have my attention? Don't worry, we will start with you next, no one escapes the N.E.S.T" he finished, no longer laughing, but a look of seriousness filled his eyes, and anger. No words were spoken for the next few seconds, anticipation flew through the air, you could feel it on your skin, making it crawl, taste it on each breath leaving your mouth.

The man looked at one of his colleagues holding Katherine, his head nodded, as if to give the man some sort of approval. As soon as his head returned to normal his eyes drifted from me and back to Katherine, raising one hand above his head, preparing to strike her yet again. I stepped forward to stop it, I felt this adrenaline fill my body, my eyes widened and locked on to the man now walking towards myself, his fist clenched like a hammer he was about to swing. As we approached each other he began to raise his hand and pull back for a punch, my hands did not move, they stayed perched by my side, this was not a choice, my mind was screaming at them, telling them to lift up and get ready to defend from this punch, but they did not move an inch, my eyes still locked on the man now launching a fist towards my face. What was going on? I couldn't move any body parts at all, I felt as if I was not even controlling my walking now, and yet I felt like I was completely in control of the situation somehow, I wasn't scared and at the same time I was terrified, the feeling is impossible to explain.

Just as the man's fist reached the air surrounding my head, feeling the warmth of his fist against my nose, I felt my head drop, my whole body fell down into a crouching position, and the man stumbled as his fist greeted nothing but thin air, as he stumbled behind where I was now crouching he turned to strike again, pacing quickly towards me, I slowly began to stand again and as the man closed the gap between us again my whole body leapt forward one step and my leg jumped into the air, striking his chin and knocking the man completely unconscious before he had even hit the floor, his body nothing but a lifeless corpse as he fell backward to the ground, as if lying in mid-air, the loud crack from his chin smashing into pieces filled the air, and as he met the floor so did my leg again, returning to its normal stance. I was never a fighter, the ones I was in I found myself always losing, there was no way I could have won a fight against someone who was trained in a million years, even though I now had a cocky grin slapped across my face, I was still petrified at the fact that there was still two more men behind me, three if I included the one Katherine had knocked onto the floor, and perhaps this was a fluke, a lucky hit, if so there was no way I was going to stand a chance against the other men, I had no hope if being able to help Katherine in anyway, but I knew I had to try.

Still shocked by the fact that there was now a man lying on the floor with a pool of blood surrounding his head, I turned around to gaze at the men holding Katherine, they were both staring at me now, red faced and filled to the brim with burning anger and hatred for me. The main man in the different suit darted his eyes back at Katherine and opened his mouth to speak.

"You bitch; you gave him the pill, didn't you?" He screamed at her, you could feel the anger flooding into the air, she began to laugh, blood dripping from her face, still on her knees, just as quickly as she began she was soon silenced again by the man raising his fist and striking her furiously three more times, throwing her down to the cold, hard floor and turning to stare at me, both men's arms locked to the side of their tensed body's, their fists clenched so hard they looked as if any second they would burst through their palms. This time there was no pause, no time to catch your breath or analgise the situation, it was just me and them, with nothing between us but the heavy air filled with anticipation, my eyes darted from both men, sizing them up, seeing if there was anything distinctive I could use to my advantage, even though I feel as if none of this is me actually fighting, the very possibility that this could have been a fluke meant I needed some way of winning.

Screams suddenly bounced from the walls around us, as the men began charging towards me, eyes locked onto me as if they were heat seeking missiles approaching their target. Again I did not move, my legs were part of the ground, it would have been easier to try and remove one of the pillars in the car park holding up the ceiling then try to remove my legs from this spot, they were locked and not moving. Or so it felt, but as the men got closer, and my eyes jumped from them to Katherine, bloody and unconscious on the floor, at least that is what I hoped, it could be worse than that, she wasn't moving at all. As soon as I looked back at the two men I realised just exactly how close they now were, my body felt as if it was waking up, preparing itself, honestly I have no hope of this situation ending well, I never believed id ever be able to win a fight, even against one person it just seemed like something impossible, and now I was going to have to fight two men, both taller and much stronger than me, I wanted to help Katherine, I wanted to leave this place, but as they got closer all I felt was more and more upset by the fact that there was nothing I could do, it must have been a fluke.

I could of reached out and touched the men now, they were very close, their arms in the air prepared to strike me down, and I still hasn't moved an inch, but just as my eyes began to slowly close, excepting the beating I was about to receive, I felt awake, charged, even full of adrenaline I still did not believe I could win, that was just going to make the beating less painful, but it wasn't the feeling that was surprising me, more the fact that my body started twitching, moving on its own again, it was as if I was some helpless prey with a self defence system, I don't know how to describe the feeling, having someone or something else control you, your mind thinking a million different ways to win a fight you're in, or escape it, everything felt possible and I was filled with this hope that I had the power to make it all happen, this feeling came from nowhere, much stronger than before, just as my eyes closed, they reopened, and were now staring at the men in front of me, my smile grew yet again.

The area around me seemed perfect for a fight, lots of vehicles, pillars and room to move, I could clearly see that they had planned to catch us here from the moment I escaped, because if we struggled or tried to escape no one would see us and they'd have an advantage. The walls were as dull as the rest of the building, but it all looked very similar to the car parks on 'Earth' with grey tall walls and clearly marked spots for the vehicles to stay. The only real difference was the fact that there was some kind of mechanism attached to the back of each vehicle spot, and no vehicles in them other than the occasional odd looking one.

Four fists blocked my view suddenly from the surrounding area, my mind drifted back into the situation I was currently in, although I do not believe my mind has anything to do with what my body does, I am not in control. Their solid fists approached faster than the man before, however just as they reached my face I found them drifting away, not from me moving my body out the way this time, but from my hands flying from my sides and hitting their arms directly up. The leader of the group lost his balance and stumbled to my side, struggling to keep his stance while he quickly turned back around to re-join the fight, the other man in the grey suit already began to throw punches, one after another aiming for any part of my body, his arms bouncing all around the air surrounding me, each punch he threw was dodged until after throwing a punch he brought his extended arm into the side of my head, delivery a mighty blow and knocking my head to its side, I was now looking directly at the ground, the cold grey concrete soon was replaced with a grey suited leg quickly raising for my head, I lifted my arms to shield my face and pushed the leg back down onto the floor. Instead of the leg staying on the floor however, it bounced on the floor and came jumping back into the air to strike yet another kick, I was standing up straight and this kick still managed to reach my head. Just before the kick delivered its blow my body dropped to the ground and began to quickly rotate, my leg fully extended, it slid along the floor, I could feel the heat coming from the friction that was being cause by my leg grinding along the hard concrete ground. My leg struck the man's ankle and a loud snap echoed around us, and almost as quickly as the snap happened, the man dropped and screamed out in a high pitched wine of pain. My leg stopped and kicked back into the ground lifting me sharply from the ground, my arm extended, as I raised from the concrete I saw four thick lines flying towards my face, they looked like chunky chards of meat, it was the other man's fist plummeting towards my skull, my extended arm swung round and knocked the other man's fist clean out of the air, my other arm grabbed his wrist tightly and spun his body around, his back now facing me, my leg swung back and then came crashing forward straight into his the back on his kneecap, sending him to the floor, my arms quickly extended forward, my left resting sharply on the side of his neck, my right drifting in front of his eyes towards my other hand, stopping just before I reached my other hand and landing roughly on his cheek.

There was a slight pause in the air, the three men nothing but bumbling corpses now on the floor, broken limbs or just knocked unconscious, the only one still moving was the one resting between my hands, the pause lasted no longer than a second before my hands again moved, so quick this time I didn't even see it myself, all that I saw happen was the man become lifeless in my very arms, and hear the loud snap as my right hand twisted the man's head from the left to the right quicker than any action I've seen a human body do in my life, his neck snapped so quickly even if you were watching it you wouldn't believe it, and just like that, as quickly as the fight begun, it was over. The man's body fell to floor and didn't move again, I just stood there staring at the carnage I had just caused, suddenly realising why this had all begun, why these men were injured or dead on the floor below my feet.

My eyes turned sharply to gaze at Katherine, now sitting up staring at me, blood dripping from her face, her nose clearly broken, she looked as pale as the walls in this building, her thin arms barely holding her body in a raised sitting position. I stared for a few seconds and then began to walk quickly over to her, my eyes fixed on her on the cold ground, she was looking right back at me, her eyes barely open from the bruising. Just as I approached her and reached out towards her to make sure she was ok, my body dropped to its knee, I felt fine, awake and exactly like I did before, but my body was not responding to my thoughts, as I tried to stand again I found myself staring at this grey slab of concrete, the ground I was just walking on, and before I could even look up to make sure Katherine was alright, there was this sea of colours flooding through my mind, every colour I could imagine was before my very eyes, dancing like flames on a fire, darting left and right and changing texture, I could no longer see the ground, nor Katherine, all I could see before me was a dance of light, I felt like perhaps I was dreaming, maybe it was the effects of the drug I had been given, or I could have just been hit on the back of my head by one of the guys and this was my mind in an unconscious state, or worse, I was dead, and if that was true, Katherine would be dead to.

CHAPTER 7

First Born Steps into Reality

My body was lifeless, gliding through the air, flying high above anything and everything through this ocean of colours and light. Each second that passed seemed like a lifetime, and suddenly my view changed, I could see something through the colours. It appeared to be Katherine, I was looking up at her and she seemed to be carrying me, there was no look of struggle in her eyes, she did not find me heavy. Her eyes were instead filled with nervousness and worry for me, she had bruising and blood all over her face, her chin was swollen out, her long dark hair ripped and damaged her hazel eyes bloodshot and scared. For a small girl she had a great amount of strength that you would never believe she had just from looking at her.

Just as quickly as I saw her through the colours, she soon disappeared back into them, washed away into the sea, and I was again floating, soring alone through this haze of hallucination. It felt like a few seconds had passed before I saw yet another image through the clouds of my imagination. Katherine was not in this one, instead there was just a view of the ground, still grey and concrete in appearance, but I only saw it for a little while, and then instead of it being washed away like before, it changed to this dark grey, practically black colour, a thin layer of blue metal and then what looked like a chair, I recognised it straight away, we had entered a vehicle.

She roughly placed me into the vehicle and I heard her slam shut the door and walk quickly around the vehicle to the driver's seat. For a few seconds I was alone, slipping in and out of this conscious state, seeing the front dashboard through the haze of colours that was projected in front of me, it felt like being high, smoking some sort of insanely strong drug that you wish you never even touched to begin with. The driver's door opened and she climbed in.

"Engine on" she quietly whispered to the vehicle.

"Destination" The dashboard spoke back to her, there were some cars like this on Earth but perhaps not this advanced.

"Home" She replied.

There was no rumble of the engine, I couldn't even feel us moving, if I couldn't see out the front window I wouldn't have believed we had actually left the vehicle storage building, or car park as it is known on Earth, I'm just not sure if they are called the same thing on Vala. I couldn't hear her breathing anymore, when she was carrying me she was panting a lot, I could feel the heat from her breath on my face, moving my hair, but now she was silent. It didn't worry me, her injuries did not look life threatening and she had been able to carry me, so I came to the conclusion that she may have just fallen asleep, could the car, vehicle, whatever, drive itself?

Sitting here, with a headache that would make even the strongest man I knew cry, staring into a stream of colours slowly fading into the reality I had now been born into. I don't know what I prefer, my fake life, or this apparently real one, I defiantly missed my bed and my home, my takeaways, didn't even realise I was hungry until I thought of that, sitting on my sofa, with my girlfriend in one arm and my remote in the other, moments like that were something perfect in my eyes, I argued with that girl so much and we would always fight, break up and then do things we regret, but at the end of the day every time I saw her id smile, I'd feel happy and forget all the bad, now I will never see her again, for Christ sake she wasn't even real! The person I love was nothing more than a programme, I wish I never asked questions, never left her or my piece of shit apartment, I want it all back, I want my life back. I miss her.

As I sat here drifting off into a train of thought of sadness and depression I realised my sight was coming back to me. I could see the dashboard where my hands were resting upon and then a few seconds later I could see past my hands, still hazy with colour, but my eyes were working well enough to make out my surroundings. The car window seemed dark, blacked out for some reason, was it night time? I reached forward to touch the front window, it was freezing cold and so smooth, it wasn't glass.

"Don't worry". A voice said from behind me. I turned around to look into the back seat where the voice had come from.

"Katherine" I said looking into the shadows of the dark seat behind me, she leaned forward and placed her hands on the head rests either side of the vehicle, her hands bruised still and bloody, one was wrapped in a bandage, the other seemed to be a failed attempt to wrap a bandage on.

"The weather on this planet is extremely; well hostile to the weather you are used to. That is what the shield is for". She explained pointing at the window.

"That thing is to protect us? I thought it was night outside, it doesn't look like a shield". I replied, she laughed a little then continued.

"How are you Leo?" she said, bringing her eyes from the window to mine. I could see bruising all over her checks and around her eyes, she appeared to be shaking slightly as well.

"I'm fine, what about you? You don't look so good." I answered. She tilted her head forward and looked down.

I'm sorry, for everything, but why did you help me? And what was that pill? Also we need to get you to a hospital like now! You don't look too good." I continued as she looked up at me.

"I mean, you look good, just you urm, you're hurt. I wasn't saying you are not good looking or anything." Muttering I realised perhaps I should shut up; I stopped talking and turned around back into my seat, gazing ahead.

"Awakening" she said from behind me, I turned to look at her again.

"The drug I gave you is called awakening." She finished, still staring at me.

"What did it do to me?" I replied turning around again to look forward, remembering what I had done to those men.

"Those men we ran into work for H.I.V.E, they created the pill." She paused for a second.

"Their experiments give them all the answers to outcomes; I believe you already know that? The director would have told you himself before he terminated you, am I right?" She asked me. I did not reply, just sat there and gazed forward.

"He's so proud of his research, believing it's the future for our kind, stealing all those innocent people and placing them in those chambers." She paused again.

"The drug, Awakening, does exactly what its name suggests, it awakes your brain, but not your body, it strips your body down to the most basic of impulses, survival and escaping danger, eating and breathing." She jumped forward back into the driver's seat of the vehicle.

"From all the knowledge they have gained through thousands of experiments, forcing people to live fake lives that they control, they have been able to develop a basic version of this drug, the mind part they are hoping to change soon, giving the person control over their own actions, but for now they haven't got that far yet. Anyway it cause your brain to basically see into the future, you see as many possible outcomes as they have created to the situation you are in, and your body will automatically act on one of those outcomes, the ones that usually assure survival for that individual. She again paused and looked at me.

"This is all very confusing Katherine" I said to her. She smiled slightly and then continued.

"Ok, right let me simplify it for you." She said looking at me. I just smiled back as a reply.

"They give these pills to each member of their staff to insure the best work outcomes, but they give lower doses so that each person can still control their body and mind, then they sell the rest, as you can understand this makes a lot of money. The companies that buy them will usually come to the factory to see how the pill works and see the people in the complex working at 100% efficiency and buy as many as they can afford. Basically acting like the opposite of an adrenaline rush, causing the workers heart rates to slow right down, and let them think things through, see the outcomes, but your mind in a relaxed thinking state."

She paused again, only this time she reached over and placed her hand on my knee, I looked at her hand then back at her.

"The higher the dosage, the less control you have, but the more outcomes you can see, the more you can do, the better your body is, your body can run longer, fight harder and it will push itself to the absolute limit, any movie you have ever saw, any fight, every outcome from a situation, a punch thrown or a conversation had that you have seen, your body will remember and it will act on that basis, unfortunately there are two main side effects."

We both sat there for a few seconds, her hand on my knee, staring at each other, she looked down and began to speak once more, I already know what she is going to say, the side effects were obvious.
"As your body is pushed to the point where you cannot take anymore, you pass out after its effects ware off." She said.
"The other is the most dangerous part of this drug, the stronger your dosage the less control you have over your body, they still haven't figured out how to reverse these effects. I gave you full dosage Leo, when you were walking to me at the end of the fight; it wasn't to help me, even if that's what you were thinking you were doing."
I placed my hand on hers after she paused again.
"You were going to kill me." She whispered.

"I am drawn back to my question, why did you help me? And why on earth did you give me a drug that would make me a mindless zombie, you put yourself in danger, do you have any idea what it's like to have no control of your body, I've never been in a fight in my life, yet I went through those men as if they were children, I could of hurt you, couldn't you of given me a lower dosage at least?" I shouted at her, even though I didn't know this woman that well, I did not want to hurt her, she saved my life.
"You're not on Earth anymore Leo, and if I gave you a lower dosage you would have been equal to the men you were fighting, you needed to be stronger, faster and smarter than them." She looked at me again, I just realised that the car was either driving itself or we were parked up somewhere, hopefully the men wouldn't find us if we were.
"And the reason I gave you the full dosage is because I was hoping you would run away, it is supposed to give you basic instincts, survival should have been the first thing on your mind, I still don't understand why you didn't run." She continued. I spoke again before she could continue.
"If I ran you would have been killed, you were going to die for me? Why?" I asked her. She smiled and began to speak again.
"They would have not killed me, I work there remember, I get the drug on a daily basis just like the other workers, but they would have probably tortured me, and the reason I helped you, in case you asked

again, is because we have never been able to get a person who has lived in one of those lives before, you're different to other people, we need your help, we need to see what effects the machine has on your body and your mind." She finished, this time letting go of my knee and returning back to the correct position in the driver's seat, placing her hands on the wheel.

"Shield, driving view and control" she said.

"Driving view and control" the vehicle said back to her, lowering the darkness on the protective screen in front of her, I could now see that we were moving, but due to the window only changing colour on her side, I could not make out where we were, not that I'd know anyway.

"So Katherine what you are asking is for me to become your experiment after just escaping one? And who the hell is we?" I frustratingly said to her.

"You are not going to be an experiment, I am asking you to help us, join us. And we, we are the only people who care about the innocents like you, the people born in Vala and placed into a machine for their entire life, when we tried to tell the public the H.I.V.E shut us down, wiped almost all over us out. Now we are just known as the Rebels of Vala, traitors and scum." She breathed out and then quickly glanced over at me, sitting in the passenger seat of this odd looking car, I still couldn't hear or feel it moving, and even though she could see out of the window now, I couldn't see a damn thing, it was barely different to mine, only slightly less tinted.

"So Leo" She said,

"Will you help us?"

CHAPTER 8

FRIEND OR FOE?

THERE WAS NO noise, no lights slowly sliding their way across the surface of the interior of the vehicle, indicating that another car of form of transport was driving past us, no sound of another person, street or care coming from outside the vehicle, the windows were completely darkened out other than the small hole Katherine was looking through. Only she wasn't looking out the hole, her eyes were fixed upon me as she waited for my answer, her lips half open, not as though she was about to speak, more as if she had just finished speaking and expected me to answer straight away.

"I have just woken up from a very long sleep, and since waking I have almost been killed and I've been told that everyone I loved, every part of a life I thought I had lived was nothing more than an experiment, I don't know where I am or who I am, but I do know what I want to do." I said, pausing to look out the window, realising it was nothing but a black sheet of glass I turned my head back to look at her, my eyes meet hers.
"I'm in."

The vehicle fell silent for a few seconds, I did not know what to say and I guess neither did she, after everything that has just happened perhaps a bit of peace and quiet was just what we needed.

"Get some rest Leo; it's a long journey still, I will wake you when we are there." She said to me in a soft, calming voice.

"I've been asleep my whole life, I think maybe I should stay awake this time." I said with a slight chuckle. However even though I wanted to stay awake, there was this overbearing feeling of tiredness and aching filling every bone, every inch of my body, and before I knew it I was out cold, the echoes of the last words I spoke filling my head.

"I've been asleep my whole life, I should stay awake, I think, maybe, maybe I should."

Being inside my head is confusing even to me, so much had just happened and I am yet to process the fact that I am on some planet about to help this rebellion, how can I help others when I don't even know who or where I am? This felt like the first time I ever slept, only I could think so clearly inside my head, my brain didn't feel like it was switching off, maybe it was a good thing that I was thinking about exactly what was going on, but maybe it would have been better if I just fell into a deep sleep and let my mind relax for once.

Time went quick again, and before I knew it I felt a cold hand grip my arm and start to shake me.

"Wake up, wake up Leo, we're here!" Katherine whispered to me. I started rustling and moving around, just as I was sitting upright I began to open my eyes and before I could even ask where here is exactly I found myself being dragged out the vehicle and a sharp kick struck the back of my leg, sending me to my knees. A bag or sack was quickly placed over my face, I would have struggled more but I was so tired, my body ached from all the running and the long journey. That was until I heard something, Katherine was screaming.

"Wait, he is one of us, STOP!" she carried on, something about her screaming, her voice seemed to sink into my skin, waking up every bone in my body, kick starting my adrenaline, I felt stronger, and scared, but not for my safety, for Katherine's, I needed to know she wasn't being hurt . . . . And then I felt it, the same feeling I had felt earlier, the loss of control, the gain in power, strength, my mind open and closed to my thoughts at the same time, I could feel my body shake, it felt like the whole floor itself was shaking along with me. They had just finished tying my hands, the material was not metal, but it still felt strong, too strong to break, however at this point I didn't even realise my hands were tied, I had only one thing on my mind.

Katherine's screams slowed down to almost a blur as I began to move, my hand reached up and grabbed the arm holding me, I lifted the hand with ease and slowly stood up, the steel toe caps of a boot smashed into my stomach, but I could hardly feel it, I carried on raising my body and began to sense the movements of the men around me, the second kick was pushed away back to the ground by my hand, and as I was fully stance a punch was thrown directly to my right check, I raised my right hand to meet the fist, my left mindless following it, sending the hard struck fist flying in the opposite direction and regaining my thoughts to prepare for the second man's attack, I could hear fast footsteps from behind me, as the second man through a punch, I did not deflect this one but instead side stepped and grabbed this man's arm, holding it by his hand and elbow, bringing him towards me and then launching his body back behind me to where I heard the footsteps. There was a loud fumble after I let the man's body go, and I could tell from the noises that they had hit each other, hopefully sending each other to the ground, just as I raised both my hands to block yet another punch a voice interrupted.

"Enough" A woman shouted, I recognised the voice straight away, it was Katherine, she was high up from the direction of the voice, but not far.

"Take that off" A man's voice followed. The sound of Katherine saying enough somehow calmed my body, I wasn't tired like before, I felt as if I was on standby, still awake but more in control this time. I tensed as I heard footsteps coming from both sides of me, and then I was suddenly struck by a blinding light, it might as well have been a fist, the pain would have been equally the same, my eyes took a while to adjust to the sudden change in contrast, until I could make out three shadows on what appear to be a guard tower with a fierce spot light located behind them, I couldn't make out the faces, just the shapes of the body. We were in some sort of court yard, I looked around at the men around me, there were five men and two women, all glaring at me, one had a broken nose, I could tell from the blood dripping down his face, I assumed I did that to him, he was a big man, broad shoulders, at least 6ft 5inches, face like a scrunched up piece of paper, eyes like daggers staring straight at me.

"Sorry" I said to him nodding, I was smiling slightly though, this must have angered him as he began pacing slowly towards me with a look of fury slapped upon his face.

"Stand down" The man's voice said again; another man in the courtyard placed his hand on the big guy's chest.

"Dude, relax" He said, the big guy stopped walking, and just glared at the man, then back at me. I looked back up to the guard tower and could make out the three shadowy figures walking from the guard tower to a staircase on the side of it, slowly making their way down to the courtyard. I lost sight of them behind the light but could still hear the clattering of their feet hitting the metal grates below.

It seems everything about this world is strange, just the way people act seems alien, everything feels like a movie I had watched, or was watching, maybe that was it, maybe I had just fallen asleep on my couch with my girlfriend in my arms, watching some action film and was having just a crazy dream, any second now she'd wake me and we would go to bed together and sleep, I hated that crazy bitch but god damn I really do miss her.

"Sorry about that" A deep voice murmured from beyond the shadows just under the tower, I could see the figures coming into the light, Katherine was the first, her face lit up from the light, a smile from ear to ear, I couldn't tell if she was happy to see me or just happy in general.

The second person I had not seen before, he was a younger man, glasses and a normal looking face, whatever that means, he wasn't smiling, just writing something on a clipboard, he had a pale white jacket on and his eyes never really moved from whatever it was that this man was writing. The third shadow came into the light, a smiling man, he was wearing a rugged shirt, it looked a bit battered, he had styled hair and a very worn face, he was slightly older but still not that old.

"Welcome to Vala" He said opening his arms pointing around us.

"Are you okay Leo" Katherine said, she wasn't smiling anymore, just gazing at me. I was too tired to talk back so I looked over to her and just nodded, my hands were still tensed and my body was still in a tense stance, ready to fight if anything happened, I felt strong still but this time in control, it was as if Katherine talking had not just clamed me back to myself, but just gave me control over my body, of course there was no way of actually knowing this without fighting, for all I know I could back to myself, weak and about as good as fighting as a fish could fly, but then again if this is a different planet I guess a fish flying isn't that unusual, in fact it would be the most normal thing I would have seen today.

"I am fine Katherine, what the hell is going on?" I snapped at her with a harsh, sharp tone in my voice. But before she could reply to me the man stepped in front of her and began to talk.

"You're Leo Cathrey, and this is Vala, that's all you need to know for now." He said smiling.

"You're kidding right? I just woke up to find out that everything I believed, every second I lived and every god damn breath that entered my lungs was simulated, and you think I don't need to know more than my own name and the name of this planet?" I replied to him. He was still smiling

"I assume Katherine told you everything already, what is the point in repeating words already said and telling you things you already know?" He continued.

I didn't know what to say to that, I mean he did have a pretty good point, if Katherine had already filled me in on everything then surely him going through it all again would be stupid. However the way he was talking to me, smiling and glaring at me, gave me a feeling of worry, I didn't trust this man.

"Leo we need your help" Katherine whispered quietly to me, my eyes darted back to her for a second then they dropped to gaze at the floor.

"The world you know is not real, Vala is real and it is in danger, I didn't get you out of there for nothing, you're the key to stopping this." She paused; I assumed she did it to help the last few words she just said sink in.

"Oh Katherine stop being so dramatic, Leo you have a good set of skills, thanks to us, and we need them, so help us or go back to the facility and your fake world, with all your lovely fake flowers and your fake girlfriend to enjoy your precious FAKE LIFE!" The man barked at me.

"Henry stop it" Katherine demanded.

"We don't have time for this, he should have started hours ago, take him to the induction chamber, help him learn, teach him whether he wants to, or not." He replied. Before I could even blink a man was approaching me, pacing towards me, he was holding an electric stick of some kind, the blue light at the end was shooting sparks, bouncing off the ground and walls, it lit up the man's face a glowing bright blue, his face got bigger as he got closer.

"What is that? STAY AWAY FROM ME!" I began to shout, just as the words poured out of my mouth, a sharp pain entered my body, it began at the bottom of my back and travelled up my spin, piercing my skull, then shouting around my legs and arms, I could feel it pulsing like a heartbeat through my veins, oozing around my blood and muscles, then suddenly, as quick as it began, the pain was over and I was asleep.

CHAPTER 9

LESSON 1

IT SEEMS LIKE this has happened a lot today, I'm constantly being put to sleep or falling asleep. There were no dreams, no thought going through my mind as I slept, to be honest it was not really sleeping at all, I closed my eyes and they opened, as if I just simply blinked, and when they opened I was somewhere else. It was a dark room, there was two men standing in front of me around a table, fiddling with some tools, I could hear the clanging of the table clashing with the tools that they picked up and placed down again upon it. The room was bigger than a normal room, however most of it was filled with computers, some of the monitors had cameras on them, streaming feed from all around the base, some had writing, and others had constantly changing images. The room itself was black or dark stoned, even the ground was the same colour as the walls themselves, there were no windows, the only light appeared to come from a single light imbedded to the ceiling above my head and the reflecting light from the computer monitors, my cloths seem to change colour and flash from the monitors darting from image to image. Looking down at my clothes I realised that they have changed as well, they were now pretty standard looking, I was wearing a black plan top with rips all over it and a dirty beige shirt that appeared to have no buttons to connect either side together, it was constantly open, my trousers were the same material as combats were pitch black, and I was wearing something across my wrist, I could feel it rubbing as I struggled to move my arms, it was thin and silver but had a blue light glowing from it, as I struggled to move one of the men turned around and smiled.

"Hey, Leo right?" The man said, he paused as if for me to reply, I continued to sit there, silent, gazing at him.

"OK" He said stretching his words as if to sound awkward by me blanking him.

"Look I know how you feel" before he could finish he looked at me as my head raised and starred at him straight back.

"Alright I don't, but come on who does? What you went through, being a potato in bed for your whole life, then waking up and being smacked in the face with this whole Vala crap, I mean I've had bad days, woken up and missing a sock, maybe out of milk, losing keys . . . I could go, but you look like you've heard enough bad news for one day without hearing more from me like that we're out of milk, so I will just get to the point." He finished, sliding a chair across the floor behind him, placing it right in front of where I was lying, the scrapping noise piercing my ears, he sat on the chair back to front with his legs either side of the back of it.

"See these screens?" He asked pointing behind at one of the flashing monitors, my eyes darted from him, to the screen and then back.

"Those are images of Earth" he continued.

"They are not real, they are in your head, that new sexy accessory that you have on your wrist there, that allows us to see inside your head, don't ask how, we are way move advanced then what you're used to, of course the Federation are more advanced than us which is a bummer." He turned to the other man and shrugged then continued on, my eyes wandering around the room now.

"Look, first things first, we need to make sure that you realise this is real, and those" he said pointing at the images.

"Are nothing more than memories of a fun virtual reality game you once played."

"A game?" I replied, my eyes slowly moving from the monitors towards him, my palms tightening, his face changed, his smile weakened.

"That was not a game, I lived every one of those moments, it was as real as us talking right now, and no part of it was easy or fun, every day I worked, I argued with my girlfriend, I spoke to my friend, I went shopping, I LIVED!" I yelled at him. The room fell silent after, my head dropped as tears fell from my cheeks. The man leaned forward and placed his hand on my shoulder, his head was right next to mine; I could feel his warm breath on my ear, moving my hair.

"You call that living?" He whispered and leaned back. He starred at me as I raised my head back up.

"Leo I can see in your head, the only person you are lying to is yourself, I know you doubted any part of that life was real, you hated your girlfriend and I even know about your little trip to the roof, you weren't living, you were dreaming a nightmare, and now it's time to wake up." He stood up and walked over to the computers, sliding his chair behind him as he walked and then dropping back into it.

"Time to get started" he smiled and started typing, the images stopped and all changed to some sort of text, there was a picture of the device on my wrist, it was sectioned into different parts, each section was blue but they were all changing between red and blue one by one. As if the red was going round each bit in a circle.

"Deep breath" He said as he pushed a button on the keypad, the other man was just standing exactly where he was before, not moving, just holding a notepad, writing. As the first man pushed the button, the red on the screen stopped in a part of the device and began flashing, without a warning I could feel my wrist suddenly burning, as if someone just stabbed a boiling hot needle into the top of my wrist and twisted it into my flesh, I let out a scream but the burning only just got worse.

"Stop! STOP! Please!" I kept shouting.

The burning continued as my screaming increased, the man pressed another button and the burning stopped. The pain was completely gone, as if it never happened, I felt fine.

"WHAT THE HELL WAS THAT?" I yelled through my fast panting, struggling to catch a breath. The man stood up and walked over to me, clapping his hands once and smiling, he let out a little laugh.

"My friend that was the same equipment that the Federation used on you, that is the power of a human mind, your mind to be exact." He paused and smiled

"It's fake Leo" The other man said, I looked up and saw him gazing at me, I couldn't make out any features on his face, but I could see the direction his head was pointing, just from that I could make out that he was staring at me.

"It's all in your head, the pain feels real but I wasn't, you were in no real danger, it's not real." The other man continued.

I could see the point that they were trying to make, it's amazing what a human mind can accomplish, but just because the pain was in my mind, it does not mean that I don't feel it, it doesn't mean that it's not real.

"OK I understand, I get it, it's not real, can we move on?" I whimpered, I was completely terrified and just wanted it to stop.

"Nice try" the man at the computer said, winking at me.

"When you come to realise that the pain is in your mind it will disappear, and only then will you truly believe Vala is real, we can't have you running around believing everything you see and touch is fake, although you say you believed your old world was unreal, we can see into your mind, you never truly believed it, you just thought you did." The man with the clipboard said in a harsh, firm voice.

"So to sum up, pain fake, world real, realise this and we can move on." The man at the desk said, when he finished talking, he turned around and placed his hand on the desk above the button, his head turned to the other for approval, he nodded, and just like that, the pain began again.

It felt like someone had hold of my arm, I could not move it at all, and this person with pushing their fingers deeper and deeper into my skin, piercing it touching the bone beneath. But this persons fingers were not ordinary, as if that wasn't enough, they felt as if each finger was made out of glass, each piece was just pulled from the furnace after it was heated to an insane temperature to transform from the sand it previously was into the glass that was currently piercing me skin, causing my lungs to exhale and my throat to shake as my voice got weak and the air around us was filled with an echo from my endless screaming.

This felt like it lasted for about 10 minutes, the constant pain, until finally it stopped, just like before as if it just faded into nothing, exactly how I was before.

"Did it work, did I do it?" I muttered under my voice.

"Sorry Leo, we just thought you and our ears needed a break from this." The man at the computer chuckled.

"How is this funny to you, I'm sitting here screaming, you're torturing me do you know that? Just stop, let me go" I replied, struggling to get my words out. The man with the clipboard stepped forward out of the light, I could make out his face now, only it wasn't a man, it was a woman, she had a rugged face, dark brown eyes and a pony tail with brown hair, her face was sagging and her eyes had bags, she looked as if she had been awake for weeks. She knelt down next to me and began to talk. I imaged she could be better looking if she just slept and wore some makeup.

"I'm sorry we have to do this to you, you don't understand how important it is that we hurry this along quickly, we need you out there, not in here on this chair, this is the quickest method we have to insure that you are no danger to us and to yourself, you need to know we are real, you can keep telling yourself that we are, but deep down a part of you is holding on to Earth, let go, the pain is as fake as that world, it's not torture because it's not real." She finished placing her hand on my arm.

"Feel this? This is real" she said looking at her hand.

"Feel this?" She whispered, slowly moving her head towards mine, I could feel her breath getting warming, warming up my face, her lips gently touched mine, opening slightly, she began to kiss me. For some reason all I could think of is how this kiss felt different from others, how warm her lips felt, how cold her tongue felt, and I found myself wishing it was Katherine kissing me and not this woman, I felt myself smile just thinking about her, as I did the woman closed her lips and pulled them away from mine, she stood there and looked at me for a while.

"That pain you felt Leo, those feelings you felt in your world, dig deep down and remember, did any of them feel like my touch? Or our kiss, what feels real to you?" She finished and walked back over towards the light, I only realised now that there was two lights in this room, one above my head and one right in front of me, strange how I had not noticed that light before, it was covering her face this whole time. As she began walking over, moving her clipboard from one hand into both her hands again, I looked up and said to her.

"If that's true then that means I just had my first ever kiss?" She turned and looked at me; she smiled and then continued walking.

I felt confused and yet somehow I felt like I wasn't, my mind was working a hundred puzzles at once, a hundred different stories I could tell about my life faded, they were just memories, like a dream I had once, they were never real, I could feel myself begin to cry, tears dripped down my face as I realised my best friend, my girl, none of it was real, I wasted so many years of my life lying down and living in a dream world, a fake world, I had told myself this since I got here, and a year before that, but I only believed it now, I never truly believed before, I just wished for it. I was looking at the floor again when I heard her speak; she had a deep voice, husky and quite masculine for a woman.

"Continue" She murmured.

I had a million different images running through my mind, I had a horrible headache and I was just about to experience the worst pain I have ever felt yet again, I sat there and waited for the shock, for the burn of the device on my arm, but nothing happened, I carried on waiting, just lying there with my eyes closed, imagining so many things at once, but nothing continued to happen, no pain, not a sound came from either person, the room was silent for a few minutes. I opened my eyes and slowly lifted my head to gaze upon the two people in front of me, the man at the desk had turned around on his chair and was looking at me, the woman had walked a few steps forward out of the light so I could make out her face clearly now. They were both just looking at me, and they were both . . . . Smiling.

CHAPTER 10

REALISATION

"**You did it**" those three words as sweet to my ears like sugar to my lips.

"Leo you did it" She said again smiling at me, the man at the desk still patently sitting there smiling as well, I could tell this man wanted to continue on fast, he was tapping his foot slightly and still had one hand on the keyboard, however I just wanted to savour this moment, no more pain, then it hit me, this is only the first part, what is the second? There is no way I can endure another round like that, I've never experienced pain like that before, I know it wasn't real but considering I lived around twenty years of a fake life, thinking it was real, feeling what I thought was real pain, feeling it all again then felt as real as every scratch I had ever gotten, every scar on my body, wait a second. I thought to myself as I began looking around my body, at the back of my hand.

"When I was twelve I put my hand in an oven to pull out a pizza and a friend of mine mad me jump, my hand went straight into the top of the oven" I said to the two of them.

"I had a scar, right there on the back of my hand." I continued, all the while still gazing at the perfect, un-scarred hand.

"Every bump, bruise or scar that you had was a simulation of the mind, you are in perfect health Leo, you have no marks on your body from your past, other than when you were escaping from the facility of course." The woman replied to me. I was still staring at my hand; I could see the scar in my memory as if it was still there on my hand.

"Leo, have you even looked in a mirror since you woke up?" She asked me, her voice quiet, I could sense worry in it and general concern.

"Why? Is there something wrong with me?" I asked with a slight quiver in my voice. She walked forward and put her hand on my shoulder.

"Let's take a break; we can get started with stage two after you've got cleaned up, and had something to eat. OK?" she asked, I did not reply with words but instead gave a small nod, I was tired and aching all over, even talking seemed like wasting energy I needed to keep.

As she began taking of my restraints and releasing me from the chair I was bound too she started talking again.

"My name is Jane by the way and that one over there" she said shaking her head in the direction of the man at the desk, indicating she was referring to him.

"That's Reggie" she explained, I looked over at him and saw him give a slight wave in my direction.

"Everyone just calls me Magic Man" he said with a smile across his face.

"Magic Man? Whys that?" I asked.

"How do you think it is that the Federation haven't found us here, that this all powerful, all knowing organisation cannot locate a few random rebels?" He replied to me, I did not answer, just looked at him.

"Magic" He said, pushing his hands out from him into the air, he chuckled and then turned around again in his chair and began typing at his computer. He was a small guy with some facial hair, between a scruffy beard and stubble, his hair was medium length and curly, but more of a bushy curly then actual curls, he had thick eyebrows and a simple face. His cloths were grubby, he was wearing brown trousers and a top close to the same colour but a bit darker, he had a shirt jacket over it all but it was ripped and torn so much that he might as well of not been wearing it. He was slightly overweight and had stubby legs, there looked like there was random food stains all over his clothes as well.

"Fair enough" I said, standing up after Jane had removed my last restraint, rubbing my wrists, I always wondered why people did that in movies after someone took off hand cuffs or something similar, now I knew, it's because when you've had them on for so long it still feels like their on even when they have been taken off. It's just a way of proving to your mind that they are well and truly off your wrists. At least that's why I did it, but my mind is so messed up right now that I may be thinking that's why I did it, but really I just had an itch.

    I looked around the room, as it was still pretty dark in there I could not see anything new, I turned and looked at Jane.
    "Come on" She said, turning around and walking towards a bulk metal door, she pulled the handle up and a loud clank echoed throughout the room as she pulled the door open, I could feel a rush of cold air hit my face, as if she had just open a window and not a door. On the other side of the door was a long corridor, the walls were thick concrete, all unpainted and a bland colour with cracks and dents, there were metal doors all the way down it on either side, every single one was closed. I couldn't hear a single sound; something sinister was in the air.

    "Where are we?" I asked Jane.
    "We are in one of the Federation's old Hives." She replied
    "Hive?" I said looking at her with a look of confusing, she seemed to forget I did not know anything about this place, the Federation or Vala for that matter.
    "Sorry, I should have explained, a Hive is like" she paused, "you know what a military base is? Or a bunker? That is like a Hive, when the Federation first inhabited this planet they placed Hives all over the surface, little stronghold points that they could use for ammo depots, or storage of fuel." She continued, we began to walk down the long corridor, our footsteps echoing as we moved.

    "You see Leo Vala is not our home planet, the Federation have hundreds of planets, most of us do not even know which one is our original, we can guess but that is about it. The Federation ran out of resources very quickly on our home planet, they were the business powerhouse of everything, so they used as much of the world up as they could without destroying themselves, then they built Ships and moved on to another planet, most were un habited, others were full of life." She paused again, this time stopping and looking at one of the metal doors.
    "It didn't matter, the Federation treated every planet the same, they followed guidelines, first you scout, then you build the Hives, then you look for the resources and depending on how much there is you either

leave and move on or a city like Vala is made." She continued walking again.

"Vala? I thought that was the planet?" I asked

"Vala is the city and the planet; the planets only have numbers when they are first discovered, if a city is built on the surface of a numbered planet whatever it is called becomes the name of the planet also. The Federation could not always build cities, some of the planets were deemed un-fit and sectioned off, the most famous one being planet 451." She finished as we came to a door at the end of the corridor, I turned, for some reason all the lights behind us appeared to be off, they were on when we walked down, but now there was no light, I could see past my hand, and I wouldn't even be able to see that if it wasn't for the red light above the door we were now standing in front of.

She stood in front of the door, just looking at it for a few seconds, her hand on the handle, she turned towards me.

"Leo we need you, you're the first person we've ever met from one of those machines, I just want to warn you that the younger ones will have a lot of questions for you, then again, we all do." She said opening the door; the handle released a loud clank as she pulled it down, pulling it towards us, opening the large metal door. There was a big dim room on the other side, it had concrete pillars scattered throughout it, and each looked as if it had been ten rounds with a sledge hammer. The ground was grey, it looked like a smoothed down hard surface with the occasional hole or dent in it, there were small concrete walls, about half the size of me, I guessed they were once walls for rooms but over the years have been eroded down into small stubs darted around on the floor, barley standing on their own. The room itself was warm, but dark, only lit up by a few small lights and candles it seemed, it was much larger than the room I was in before, which was odd considering the other room was colder, you would think the bigger one would be harder to heat up.

Looking around I could easily tell why this room was hotter than the other, it was because it catered for a large amount of people, each warming the room with their body heat and warm breaths. There looked to be around fifty people in this room, some families hugged together, reading to each other. Others were on their own, just sitting on a small camp bed, most were sleeping, other than the children who seemed to all be playing some kind of game, running around chasing each other and shouting, yet the others slept soundly. Everyone was wearing tattered and torn clothing, it was all dirty and ripped and looked as if they had never been washed, the beds they were sleeping on were also tattered, each one had small holes poked into it, and there was no duvet covering it, but instead there was a grey materiel, like a rug, it looked very rough and uncomfortable.

"Who are all these people" I asked Jane as we stepped through into the large room.
"This is Vala's frontier, we call ourselves Dreamers" she replied.
"Each woman and man here, every children even the pets, they all have dreams, we all dream of a free Vala, one where new born babies aren't stolen from their cribs and experimented on their whole life, never breathing an outside breath, a dream we hope to make a reality." Just as she finished talking there was the sound of cluttering and fast steps coming from in front of us, I looked down and there was a group of young children standing in front of me all gazing up towards me. I nervously peered back.
"Young ones, this is Leo" Jane said to them, they did not reply, only continue to stare.
"Hello" I said slowly leaning down. None of them moved, they were all just standing there quietly, until one of the smallest ones stepped forward and held his hand out towards me, he just held it out in front of me, and then he lifted his other arm up and held it out in front of me as well, it became clear what he was asking for, the little boy just wanted me to give him a hug. He was a small child, his cloths as dark as the ceiling above, his eyes however seemed to be a dim blue, his hair was a light brown, almost blonde, he was holding a ruined teddy in one hand, the teddy was peculiar, looked to be some sort of animal with a few arms missing.

I paused for a brief moment before smiling at the young child and opening my arms, he walked forward and embarrassed me, I hugged the boy back. While I was hugging the kid he leaned in and whispered something in my ear.
"Are you here to help us?" He said in the faintest murmur, I pulled my head back and starred at him. At that point a woman called for the

children, the young boy let go of me and turned to run with the other children, they all quickly ran in the opposite direction, beyond one of the small walls past the woman who appeared to have called them.

It's time for dinner, go and find Price." She said to them all as they ran past her, I recognised her voice almost immediately, standing up and looking over to where the voice was coming from, I could only make out the shadow of her body and her hair as the room was so dully lit.

"Katherine" Jane said walking over towards the shadow, they approached each other and began to talk; I couldn't really make out what was being said, nor see them very well. At this point my mind began to wonder, I hadn't really spoken to her since the car, then my mind wandered towards the thought of the facility, and I remembered her on the floor after taking a beating from those men.

"Are you ok?" I asked her, interrupting the conversation she was having with Jane, walking over towards them both, the thought of her injured severely still fresh in my mind. She looked over Jane's shoulder at me and smiled.

"Yes Leo, I am fine, how are you feeling?" She replied, hearing her soft voice again made me instantly smile, I felt like some childish school boy, how could I be this smitten about some like this, I suppose when two people save each other's lives in the space of an hour, you realise just how much you and that one person have been through together in the short time that you have known each other, maybe it was something else that made me like her so much, I really didn't care, I was just happy to see her again.

"I'm much better now" I answered smiling at her. Jane looked at both of us and just began to laugh; Katherine hit her lightly on her arm to get her stop.

"You must be hungry" Katherine asked me. I didn't say anything, my thoughts were still elsewhere, I just gave an awkward smile in reply to her question, implying that I was.

"This way" she said waving her hand in a gesture telling me to follow, all the while still smiling, it made a nice change to see her smile, the only other times that I had previously saw her she always seemed to look upset; I can't really blame her considering she was fighting, arguing or running away from someone.

Her and Jane led me through the larger room, past a few beds and broken walls, most people were in a family group, reading to one another, a few were on their own sleeping and the rest were either couples huddled up on the beds or children playing games, it looked very run down and poor, there was no electronic equipment other than the monitors and computers I had seen in the other room, everything was lit by candle light, with the exception of small lights attached to the walls or the occasional lamp by a bedside. The smell was very musty, like warm air and hot bodies, sweat and unclean clothes; it wasn't necessarily a bad smell, just made the air seem much thicker than the air I was used to.

We walked towards a big open door; it looked more like a hole than a door as there was not actually any door attached to it, just an opening into a well lit room with what seemed to be canteen tables. This room was much better lit than the previous ones, I could clearly make out everything, had to rub my eyes because the lights were so much brighter than what my eyes were now used to, there was big lights all over the ceiling and about ten big tables with chairs, at the back of the room was a serving station with two women behind the counter serving a few of the children that Katherine had sent in here earlier, they were all holding small metal bowls and were standing in a scruffy line presenting them at the two girls. Most of the tables were empty, there were two that were full up and the others had a few people sitting on them, all eating from the same small metal bowls, the room wasn't very loud considering they were all talking and there were a lot of children, most people just seemed to be having quiet conversation over their meal. At least that was the case, until I walked in the canteen.

Everyone stopped eating, even the women at the counter stopped serving and looked over at me, the children with their bowls still raised turned their heads and were now gazing at me as well. I looked around the room slowly, at each and every one of them, some were smiling and some looked angry, there were a few men who didn't even move their heads from their food. After looking around gazing at the people staring at me I looked at Katherine, only to see that her and Jane were also staring at me, Katherine looked slightly upset, she turned to the other people in the canteen and coughed loudly.

"Back to your food every one, don't be so rude." She said in a demanding voice towards the others before grabbing my hand.

"Come on" She said, pulling me along with her, the majority of people had gone back to eating their food, but there was still the occasional person staring mindlessly at me as if I was naked or had a giant head, they seemed to have this looked of shock and happiness in their eyes, along were fear and nervousness.

We walked over towards the counter; the children had all received their food by now and were running past us back to one of the empty tables.

"You must be Leo" one of the girls behind the counter said as we approached it.

"Yeah" I replied quietly. She didn't say anything, just stood there smiling at me, holding a ladle in one hand and the other gently resting on the pot, it appeared to be full with some kind of soup, there was no lumps in it, it looked almost exactly like gravy.

"Some spice?" The other woman ask, also holding a ladle with a pot in front her.

"Three please Helen" Jane replied. The woman grabbed three bowls from a stack beside her and began to pour the gravy looking substance into each bowl, placing them upon a tray on the counter in front of us. She finished filling up the last one while the woman beside her began to talk.

"Katherine have you seen Henry this evening?" The woman asked her.

"No, I heard he went on retrieval" Katherine replied.

"Yeah he did, he went with Oscar and the other young ones." She said sharply.

Katherine didn't talk, she just looked at her bowl and then muttered something quietly to herself, I could easily tell there was some hostility between Henry and Katherine, my guess was that Henry ran this place; he seemed like the man in charge when I met him earlier, not the greatest first impression.

"Thank you Helen" Jane said, picking up the tray and turning around, Katherine smiled at both the women and then followed.

"Urm bye" I said to the women nervously and began to trail behind Katherine, her and Jane were walking towards an empty table near the far side of the room. Jane went to the other side of the table and placed the tray on the table as she sat down. Katherine joined her on the other side of the table, just opposite. It wasn't hard to choose where to sit; I slowly sat down next to Katherine and waited patiently for my food.

"Eat up." Jane said, slapping down this grey metal bowl full of the gravy looking soup. I could see the steam coming out of the bowl, feel the warmth hitting the bottom of my face, it smelled like a homemade stew, like the kind my mum would always try to make in the kitchen with leftovers from the days before, it never worked, she'd throw in almost everything, one time she even put in Cereal, they always came out absolutely disgusting.

"You're going to need all the energy you can get." She finished.

"Not torture again, is it?" I said quietly, lifting my eyes from my bowl to her.

"Look Leo, regardless of what you think that wasn't torture, I'm sorry you felt like you had to go through all that pain, but it was the equivalent of a bad dream and nothing more, can you imagine what would happen if we sent someone out there into Vala with your skills, believing that everything they see and touch is nothing more than a figment of their imagination?" she snapped at me, her eyes lock on mine, she had a look of genuine anger, her lips were tense, eyebrows raised and her hand steady with a spoon in it balancing above her food.

I didn't say anything, how could I argue with that, she made a pretty good point, if I went out into the world trying to get home to Earth, not only would I stand out to everyone, including The Federation but I would probably go insane when I found out there is no way of actually getting home. Instead of trying to argue with her I just lowered my head and picked up my battered spoon, it was freezing cold and slightly damp but I really didn't mind as I was starving, hadn't eaten anything but that pill in what felt like days. I slowly placed the spoon into the bowl and began to scoop up some of the brown liquid, raising it to my lips and taking my first taste of the substance. Just as it touch my tongue I found myself spitting it out, launching the soup like food across the table from out of my mouth.

"What the hell is that?" I Yelled at Jane, they both started laughing, looking around the room I could see other people staring at me, a few laughing as well.

"It's spice Leo, all the herbs and vitamins a human body needs to survive" Katherine answered me, Jane still laughing, she was trying to hide her mouth by using her hand to cover it, her spoon tightly gripped in it.

"Do you have anything else? A sandwich? Or bag of crisps? Hell even some fruit?" I asked them both. They paused for a second and then answered me simultaneously

"What are crisps?"

CHAPTER 11

TIRED AND HUNGRY

IT HIT ME like a bullet, the sudden horror, how could I ever consider to live like this, how could I go on?

"You've never heard of crisps? Do they not exist here?" I nervously asked them.

"Leo there is going to be a lot of difference between here and what you were previously used too." Katherine answered.

"Oh Jesus" I said, placing my elbows on the table and dropping my head into my hands.

"Right, this is a serious question, I want you both to think about this for a few minutes before answering, O.K?" I said to them both. They looked at each other before nodding in reply.

"Is there such thing as pizza here?" I asked, looking at them both, there was nothing but silence for a few seconds before they Jane answered.

"Yes"

"Really?" I asked in anticipation

"No" she answered, her and Katherine both let out a laugh.

"What is pizza?" Katherine asked?

"Imagine a crunchy base, with a soft, smooth centre and a creamy top. Then throw all your favourite meats and vegetables all over it, mushrooms, ham or bacon, extra cheese and then some sausage of chicken, maybe even a few meatballs. All of these combined together to create a taste sensation in your mouth, and for a few seconds as you look at your bitten slice and see a the rest of this delicious masterpiece behind your hand, you realise, I get to experience that feeling with each bite over and over and over again." I finished, my mind imagining a slice of pizza in my hand, cheese dripping from the sides.

Looking up I noticed both girls with massive grins across their faces, stretching from ear to ear.
"What?" I asked, looking down I realised my hand was raised to my lips as if I was eating something; I dropped it back down and placed it upon the cold table.
"We have spice" Jane said, pushing the bowl in front of me right up to my chest.
"Now eat up Leo, you have a long day ahead of you." She continued. I gazed into the brown goo inside this bowl below my noise, the smell rising into my nostril, I could still taste it at the back of my throat, it was clutching to the end of my tongue, my stomach refusing to allow entry to something so revolting, staring around the room I could see everyone else eating theirs, even the young children were eating it, some were even walking back over to the two women behind the counter asking for seconds, my eyes wandered back to Jane and Katherine, they were also both eating the food, no flinching or bad facial expressions, they all appeared to actually be enjoying it.

Maybe it really wasn't that bad, maybe I just wasn't used to the flavour, I never believed myself to be a fussy eater, but then again this is the first real meal I have ever actually eaten. I picked up my spoon again and placed it into the bowl, the spoon filled up with the spice, lifting it out of the bowl and bringing it to my mouth again, I could see my hand shaking slightly, come on Leo don't be such a baby, I start repeating to myself, it's just food, not poison or molten magma. I opened my mouth and brought the spoon into it, releasing the food onto my tongue once more, it was still just as horrible, I wanted to spit it out again but I was so hungry I knew I needed to eat something. My face scrunched up and my eyes started to water, I have never tasted something so bad, it tasted like mustard and rotten eggs. I looked at Katherine and Jane again, they were both looking at their bowls but I could see them sniggering, their backs rising up and down as they tried to hold in their laughs, I swallowed it, it felt like hot oil going down my throat into my body and they both looked back at me.

"It's good" I sputtered out through my watery eyes and scrunched mouth, I must have looked like a just ate a raw lemon, both of them burst out laughing, so did a few other people around the room. Lucky me, I still had a whole bowl full of this stuff to finish.

"That was more difficult than the first test" I said, wiping the sweat from my forehead, and placing my spoon in the empty bowl below my hand. Listening to my thoughts I realised how pathetic this all sounded, but that if so disgusting, maybe I would eventually get used to it, but for now I am not eating that again for a while.
"Come on slugger" Jane said with a sniggering tone, standing up and turning around to walk away.
"We have to get back to work" She finished and began walking over to the doorway. I didn't follow just yet, but instead I sat there with Katherine, we were both quiet, our hands resting on the table, both looking down.
"Is it going to hurt?" I finally said. Katherine looked up at me and smiled.
"No Leo, however this next step is going to take the most time." She stood up all the while looking at me.
"You'll be fine; I'll see you when you get out." She said still smiling. She began to walk over towards the counter, but just as she was halfway there she turned around.
"O.K?" She asked.
"Yeah" I nervously replied, I didn't want to go through any pain again, not like last time, but I trusted Katherine, if she said there wasn't going to be any then I believed her. Still not sure why it is I trust her so much, guess saving my life has this effect on me.

I stood up, taking my hand off my spoon and leaving it placed in the bowl. Before walking anyway I stared around the room, trying to find where Jane had gone off too, I managed to make her out standing by the doorway, she was talking to a few younger children, they all looked young but none looked the same age. I left my spoon and bowl on the table and began to walk over towards Jane, passing through the tables and the chairs, and sliding pass the people sitting down, still eating their food, I still could not rap my mind around the fact that they all seemed to really enjoy the spice, it tastes so revolting, I must be the only person in here who does not like it.

Just as I passed one of the tables I felt something tug at my arm, I looked down to see what was stopping me walking over to Jane. To my surprise there was a young girl holding my arm with both her hand, they were dirty and had cuts on them, her face nearly black from where she hadn't washed in a while, she had long, dark, curly hair that covered her eyes, I could barely make them out under it all, it looked as though it had not been brushed in a while. Her eyes were a dark brown colour, with a hint of yellow in the middle of them.

"You're Leo?" She quietly asked in a squeaky voice. I leant down to be on eye level with her, placing on hand on her shoulder.

"I am, and what is your name?" I replied to the young girl.

"I'm Teara" she answered.

"Teara? That is a very pretty name." I said to her, just as I finished my sentence a woman stood up from the table behind her and walked over. She was tall and thin, with short, dark hair.

"Teara come on, your food is getting cold." The woman said holding out her hand.

"Bye Leo." The little girl said as her mother lead her back to her table. I stood up slowly and turned my view from Teara now eating her food at the dinner table back towards where Jane had been standing. To my surprise she had moved, and was now standing right in front of me, it may be jump slightly backwards.

"Jesus Christ" I said in a hushed panicking voice.

"Let's go" she said demandingly. This time she didn't just start walking away without me, she grabbed my hand and started pulling me along with her, like when a mother is angry at her kid.

"I can walk on my own" I said trying to pull away my hand as she dragged me along.

"Apparently not" she replied all the while tugging me through the canteen doorway.

We walked back through the room, past all the battered down nubs of concrete where the walls used to be, and all the people sleeping on broken beds being held up by bricks and boxes, past the children playing with odd looking toys, and back to the steel door which we came through earlier.

"Are you ready" she asked me.

I replied with a nod, and with that, she opened the door, it made a loud creek as she tugged it half open, she indicated for me to go first as she held the door for me. I walked through nervously and turned to wait for her to follow. She proceeded and closed the door, releasing a thundering echo as the door slammed shut, I suddenly felt very scared again.

We walked slowly door the long corridor as I silently thought to myself. What if it does hurt again? What if I can't complete this one like before and I'm just in pain for hours? Or I'm stuck in there for days trying and can't help these people? But the one main question I found asking myself was . . . what is the test going to be? As we approached the door at the other end I grew more and more nervous, the sound of our footsteps seemed to echo more quietly with each step, until the only thing I could hear was the sound of my own heartbeat, thumping away in my chest, the surrounding noises were shut out from my head, and I was left alone with my thoughts and nothing else but the occasional pound from chest, I knew it was beating fast, but it seemed slow motion, the walk felt like it last a life time.

Jane placed her hand on the door, there was no pausing this time, she opened the door and walked straight in, I couldn't see in the room, from where I was standing it looked pitch black inside. I heard talking from inside, I slowly peered in the room and followed Jane into the dark room once again.

"Leo my man!" Magic Man said, quickly changing the subject from whatever it was he and Jane were talking about as I walked into the room. I could see the computer screens again and the retractable chair squatting in front of them, Magic Man was standing up next to them with Jane a few feet in front of him. He was smiling at me.
"You ready for round two?" he asked me, pointing at the chair, walking back over towards his and sitting down upon it, sliding in front of the computer screens, he frantically began typing.
"And . . . . Done" he said bringing his hand down and pressing one last button on the keyboard. Jane was just standing in the same spot, the room was colder than I remember, it still seemed insanely dark, the light that was in here before seemed to be gone, the only light that was now lighting the room was the reflections off the computer screens, it barely lit up the chair that I previously sat on, I could just make out the shadow of Jane, in fact the only thing I could see clearly was Magic Man who

had no turned around and was staring at me, Jane was looking at the monitors from what I could make out.

Magic Man let out a quiet laugh and then leant forward slightly towards me, he was now leaning far forward on his chair with his hands on his knees.

"So, shall we begin?" He asked me.

CHAPTER 12

Lesson 2

SITTING IN THE chair again I was struck suddenly by the fear I had previously felt sitting in this same chair earlier today, the panic rushed through my body. My palms began to sweat as did my forehead, I could feel myself getting hotter and hotter despite the cold temperatures of the room. I did not gaze around but instead just patiently sat there, on the surface I looked much calmer than what I was actually feeling. Both Jane and Magic Man were at the monitors, staring at something on them, Magic Man was frantically typing, his eyes darting from him keypad up to the screens every so often. Jane turned around and look at me, the sound of taping from the keyboard was the only noise filling the dense air, Jane walked over towards where I was sitting, she had a rather blank expression in her face, I could not tell whether she was worried or happy, sad or angry, it was amazing how she could keep her cool like that, I did not harbour such a skill, although I felt as if I was acting normal or even looking normal I could tell that both Jane and Magic Man knew my true feelings.

Jane placed one hand on my arm and the other on my hand. She didn't look at me, or even acknowledge I was there at first, she just pulled a thick leather strap from under the chair and wrapped it over my arm, binding me to it. After she finished with one hand she slowly walked around me to the other side and did the same, binding both my arms.

"Do not panic, this is just so you do not fall from the chair when Magic Man starts the session." She said to me in a calming voice as she finished tightening the second strap, I did not speak in reply, I just looked up and waited for her to make eye contact with me, she looked up from my hands towards me, her eyes barely visible in the light, I just nodded slightly to clarify that I understood.

"Magic Man" she yelled, looking over to him, he turned his head to the left and looked at her through the corner of his eye.
"Begin" she finished. With that Magic Man turned to his computers, raised his hand and brought it down, pressing one button with a sharp click.
Almost instantly I felt my body jolt with a shock, and sling back into the chair, my chest raised into the air, and I let out a slight moan of pain. But the pain only lasted a short second, and before I knew it I felt perfectly fine, I was just sitting here in the chair. But this time I felt different, I felt full on energy, it was pumping through my veins, my heart was palpitating through my chest, I felt so awake. I raised my hands and they simply snapped the braces clean off.
"Leo" Jane yelled at me.
"Stay still!" She continued. But I did not listen, I was full of too much energy to sit still, my whole body was buzzing with this amazing power, this strength, it felt like I'd been asleep for years and each bone had been rested and at the same time gained the full amount of muscle it was possible for a human body to receive.

My eyes slowly looked forward; they locked onto the steel door we had come through. My body shaking as I began to stand up, and as I did time seemed to pause, the air around me stood still, Jane was balancing on one foot, her other foot was raised behind her back as if she was running towards me, one arm was stretched out, reaching for me. Magic Man has his head turned to me, his mouth open as if to be speaking, but they were not moving, his lips, Jane's legs, nothing but my eyes were moving. It felt as if everything had been caused by a remote, the whole room was still. I found myself able to see everything, the room was lit up so brightly now, I could make out the expressions on both their faces, Magic Mans was a look of shock and surprise, Jane's was a look of worry and concern, she was good at hiding her feelings from her body language, however this time it was quite obvious what she was feeling.

No one could move, not even me, I stood there, frozen in time for a few seconds, my body building up with this massive amount of energy, it felt like I was going to explode from the rush, my mind was open, I could see a million pictures at once, from my life and from television, from anything I had ever personally seen. And then it stopped. The images faded instantly from my mind, the room still frozen, but this time I was not. My head turned to Jane, slowly moving through the frozen air, and as it did the room began to wake up, Jane's leg edged forward, Magic Mans lips began to tremble as he tried to speak, their bodies moving at a thousandth of a second.

Time was slowly unfreezing, and I could feel my body filling with this immense energy, it was impossible to hold any longer, with a short burst time snapped back to normal, Jane was running towards me, a few inches from my arm, Magic Man was shouting, but it was impossible to make out exactly what it was he was saying. With the sudden burst not only did time return to normal but my body released its energy, almost spontaneously I darted forward, running as fast as my legs could straight towards the metal door, Jane was now shouting as well. I reached the door and broke through it without even blinking, my arm raised, hit the door and the door just shot off its hinges and I sent it crashing down the long corridor, hitting the walls and ceiling as it bounced. I was running faster than I had ever ran, faster than anyone I had ever seen run, there was no sound, I couldn't hear them shouting me anymore, or even the sound of my feet hitting the floor, the adrenaline was now so strong that it had stopped my hearing completely.

The sides of the corridor were nothing but a blur, the ground was the same, nothing but a mash of colours, everything looked as if I was in a vehicle traveling at an insanely high speed, and was looking out the window at the objects and surroundings just shooting past my window. Although I could clearly see all the surroundings around myself, my eyes or head never changed from looking forward, I was mindlessly focused upon the door at the other end of the corridor, thundering towards it and a tremendous speed, my arm raised in front of my head, the back of my forearm facing the door, ready to strike it just as I did with the one behind me.

Only this time was different, as I approached the door, my feet pounding the ground, I noticed a glimmer from the seams of the steel door, shining through, at first it was hardly noticeable, nothing but a small beam of light, as if someone was one the other side holding a torch and pointing it directly through the side of it. But then there was more than one light, and they were rapidly growing, the closer I got the more the door lit up. Bright white light shining all around it, it was getting increasingly difficult to see the door, all I could now see was this glimmering light, I could not even tell if I was still running directly towards it.

My eyes were now filled with white, as if someone was holding a blank piece of paper in front of me, blocking my view of anything else around me. I didn't feel like I was running anymore, I must have stopped before I reached the door as it didn't feel like I had struck it yet. Trying to piece together what was going on, I noticed the light began to change, it appeared to be retreating, being pulled back into the distance, it faded and became dimmer, until I noticed the light mould into a smaller source of light, in fact it was now possible to see where exactly the light was coming from. It was Jane.

Jane was standing over me; the light was coming from her hand, a small torch to be exact.
"What happened?" I muttered, trying to move my head but struggling.
"You tell us" Magic man replied, although I could not see him, I recognised his voice coming from somewhere else in the room. Jane all the while was still standing over me, only she had now lowered the flashlight so it was not shining directly into my eyes.
"I tried to run away, or escape? Honestly I don't know, my head feels fuzzy." I answered. I saw Jane look over to a different direction, my guess was she was either looking at Magic Man or one of the monitors.
"Leo you haven't left this chair." Jane said, looking back down towards me.

"How is that possible?" I asked them both, I could now move my head slightly, I tried looking over to where Magic Man's voice was coming from, but my eyes had not yet adjusted from the light so it was very difficult to see anything considering the room was always so dark.

"The second test is one which sees how well the drug you've been given has coded with your DNA, most people can only take the pill we like to call awaking, three or four times in their life, if you take it more than that your body will usually shut down." Magic Man said.

"However some people don't die, they just slip into a comer" Jane finished.

"The pill allows the taker to see hundreds of different outcomes, well millions actually, all thanks to the Federations experiments, we don't agree with it at all, but we figured we could use all the help we could get." Magic Man continued.

"That's why I stole some of their pills when I rescued you, we had a short supply before, but we were close to running out." Jane said.

"So anyway, the taker will see all these different outcomes to situations they may be in, or could avoid, pretty much anything. For example right now you're in this chair, by taking the pill you will see thousands of ways to either escape from this chair, kill us, rest, eat or whatever, the pill will show you all these paths and choose the best one." Magic Man finished.

"It was invented as a money making tool first, to see how they could make more and more from different outcomes, different investments. But soon after that it was turned into a weapon, they encoded it into soldiers DNA, some handled it well and became super human, others handled it averagely and some just got a small improvement, it allowed these soldiers to see different fighting moves and techniques to win, which punches and hits have the most effect, which parts of the body are weakest. The Federation gave the different soldiers different colours to show which ones were the strongest and which ones were the weakest." She explained.

"If you ever see one in black, run." Magic Man interrupted.

"The drug they are given is the small as awaking however it is put into the bones and mind just to target fighting, that's all they know, how to be a good fighter and how to take orders, everything else is unclear to them. The ones in black are the ones the drug has bounded with the best, making them." Jane paused.

"Very dangerous" Magic Man interrupted again.

"We believe the one you and Katherine encountered on your way out were standard level 1 soldiers, they usually have grey suits, which

Katherine told us they were wearing. One thing that didn't make sense however was that she remembered Black ones chasing you at first." Jane said, pausing.

"What's so weird about that?" I asked in reply.

"Leo no one can out run a Black suit, they would catch you before you even started moving, they let you go on purpose." Magic Man said.

No one spoke for a few seconds, I just looked down at the floor, my mind wandering off, thinking. Why would they let me go on purpose? That makes no sense, but the more I think about it the more I realise something.

"It was too easy" I muttered under my breath.

"Leo we're not stupid, chances are that they let you go because they knew Katherine would help you and bring you here, which is why we have been trying to train you fast. You need to learn to use this gift we have given you so you can begin helping us, at the moment we are wasting time and any second there could be a knock at our door." Magic Man explained, Jane looked over at him with slight anger in her expressions.

Again I did not say anything and began thinking. It's strange, even though the machine said I believed this world was real part of me still felt like this was a dream, this dark, cold room, Jane and Magic Man, even Katherine, this world and my new life seemed to interesting, something I wasn't used to, I keep expecting to wake up at any moment in my bed back in my boring life. However, after everything I had seen and felt up until now, every ounce of pain and strength, every fight and argument, every taste and smell, the only times I felt like I was really eating or feeling, was in these last few days, my life never made sense, I believed I followed a pattern and I did, but now . . . There was no pattern, no system, it did feel different, whether this was a dream and my other life is real or the other way round, I did know one thing for sure, and that was that I'm here now, and pain is very much real here, I can't let these people die because of my, or get captured and put into one of those machines. Although my head was all over the place I knew what I had to do.

"What are we waiting for then?" I said, breaking the silence that filled the room before. Glancing up at them both from the chair I was in, opening my mouth to continue talking.

"Let's keep going".

CHAPTER 13

Running Out of Time

WITHOUT ANY HESITATION Magic Man turn around in his chair and began franticly typing, I could just about make out a small smile across his face.

"The next test will be very similar, your brain will still be thinking of a million different outcomes to this current situation, we managed to block them all and just increase the feeling of one outcome, which you have already experienced, we wanted you to see what a full dose and do to your mind, but this is not how you will usually receive the drug, you won't get it as intensely as that otherwise you'd only ever see one scenario, you will get hundreds in seconds in the future, the feeling will be much different from what we just did, and now, we are going to show you what a normal episode will feel like by not stopping any possibilities from this current situation reach your mind, non will be enhanced, this is just what will normally happen on its own when you get an episode, hopefully they won't always be random and you will be able to control it in the future." Magic Man continued talking, insanely fast; even Jane looked like she was having a hard time keeping up. He turned and looked at us both, still slowly typing on the keyboard.

"Ready?" He said, smiling, his fingers paused over one button.

I peered at Jane, she smiled back at me, and then my eyes moved over to Magic Man.

"Sure, sounds simple enough" I answered. I could hear Jane laugh slightly; Magic Man once again turned around in his chair and brought his finger down onto the button he was eagerly waiting to press.

"Then here we go" he said bringing his finger down and pressing the button with a sharp click.

Almost instantly my head began to ache, this horrible sharp pain shot through my arms and up into my brain, pulsing through them and back again over and over, until the pulsing was now darting through my whole body, I could feel it inside my skin, scratching below the surface, it felt like someone had injected me with thousands of grains of sand, gliding through my veins and scrapping the sides as they travelled throughout my body. I heard Magic Man pressing buttons in the background, the clicking grew louder as the pain in my head grew. And then just as quickly as it begun it ended, but it didn't just vanish, it changed into a different feeling, as if I was learning a million things at once, my head no longer had an aching pain but instead it felt great, all the knowledge, all the learning, I could see my future before I had even decide what to do, it was like having a dream whilst being awake, but at the same time as you were having that dream, you were having and living thousands of others, all revolved around decisions you could make in the situation you were currently in. I could see myself getting up and killing both Magic Man and Jane, taking a small weapon from the inside of Jane's leg and using it to escape. At the same time I could see myself kissing Jane, taking her away somewhere, and unfortunately I could see myself doing the same with Magic Man. Then it was small things, like sneezing or acting like I hurt my hand, weird, small things that didn't really change the outcome of the situation I was in. There were so many images and yet I could clearly see them all, flashing at fractions of a second through my mind and it was as if I was staring at them for hours and letting them sink into my mind.

Before I knew it I found my brain locking onto one image in particular, at first I thought it would skip through like it did the others, but here I was lying on this chair and my mind was still focused on this one image, and then suddenly, my body woke up again. There was a loud crank and scratching sounds as my arm lifted up, straight up, pulling the restraint's right out of the chair, I don't remember them restraining me, but I suppose it was a smart decision at the time. The restraints felt like they were made from paper, my arm ripped through them like a knife on butter, they stretched and snapped clean off, and as my arms raised up my body did too, my legs dropped to the ground and I stood up quickly, walking straight to the door, not even looking at Jane or Magic Man by the monitors, however I could feel something on my arm, I didn't look but I could feel the change in temperature around a certain position on my arms, like cold hands had just grabbed me. It didn't make any difference, a brick wall wasn't going to stop so I doubt any one holding me was going to do much either, my eyes were fixed on the door as I carried on walking towards it.

This felt almost exactly like last time, when I found myself running down the corridor, only this time I generally felt like I had control of my body, but that image in the back of my mind drove me forward, and I wanted it too, it wasn't a subconscious decision, it was my own decision to get up and go, I locked onto the scenario flashing through my mind because it was the outcome I liked the most, the outcome that gave me a warm feeling inside, I could feel a grin pressing itself into my cheeks as I approached the steel door.

The steel door was as frail as the restraints, as I approached it I simply raised my right hand in front of my body and pushed the door open, the lock snapped and the door open as normal, as I walked through the arch way I turned around to look back inside the room, my hand still on the door. Jane and Magic Man were both shouting and holding my arm, Jane had pulled the weapon from her leg and was holding it in her hand, they both looked scared and angry, screaming at me, but I couldn't even hear a slight muffle of their voices, I could only listen with my eyes and see their lips more around and their facial expressions scrunched and eyes wide open. I could still feel myself smiling as I pulled my hand away from their grasps and slammed the door shut with my other. The door flew shut, straight into the hinges, it was jammed into the wall itself, there was no way they would be leaving that room for quite some time without any help.

As the door shook slightly, the walls around it cracked and broke, shooting little splinters of rumble all over me and the floor around where I was standing, I turned back around and carried on walking down the corridor, slowly and cocky, the smile still slapped across my face, my shoulders and arms swaying with each step, in fact they weren't just swaying with my steps, but I found myself jumping slightly, I was skipping, Skipping down the corridor and humming a song

I remembered from Earth. It was a band I used to listen to called The Screamers, they did this one song that would always be on the music channels in the morning when I watched T.V and it would always get stuck in my head the whole day, it was called Honestly I just want to Sleep, the chorus was so catchy, and right now as I skipped down the corridor I was humming that catchy chorus to myself. The lights from the celling slowly approached and drifted past as I got closer to the door at the other end, but as I got closer, I got faster, and faster, until I was no longer skipping but sprinting full speed at the next steel door ahead of me, my feet slapping the ground as my spend increased, my body closing in on the door very quickly, the lights were now blinks of my eyes, shooting past my vision as I ran past them.

The door was no within a few feet, my hand raised once again as if to prepare me to knock down the door at full sprinting speed. But before I even knew it my feet stopped dead, a few inches from the door, I was completely still, just standing in front of it. My hand turned into a fist and slowly slip down the door towards the handle, my knuckles grazing the steel surface of the door itself, as my hand approached the handle, it open from a fist and wrapped around the door handle, all the while humming the song out loud, still smiling, I pulled the handle down and opened the door with ease, swinging it open, and standing in the door way.

I could now see the people inside the door, everyone in the room was staring straight at me, a few were standing up, but no one moved an inch, they just stood there staring at me, in the distance I could now hear banging, it was Jane and Magic Man banging the slammed door behind me at the other end of the dark, dusty corridor. One person in the room stood up from a bed and looked over at me, it was Katherine, she didn't have the same facial expressions as the others, they all looked petrified and scared, mothers holding their children tight in their arms, fathers standing in front of their whole family with their arms slightly raised to shield them. Katherine on the other hand, she looked generally concerned, and worried, she didn't look angry or sacred, just worried. No one moved for a few seconds, and then Katherine raised her hand and placed it on a man's shoulder to her right, nodding her head at him, as she did he moved back slightly, out of her path. She began making her way through people towards me, placing her hands upon their shoulders and arms to ask them to move out the way.

Her eyes stayed fixed on me, occasionally changing to look at a person as she asked them to move, she was a few meters away now, no one else was between me and her, just a few concrete walls and nubs on the ground. As she approached me I didn't not move at all, I steadily stood there, humming the same song and smiling at Katherine, my eyes never left hers. She stopped just short of my reach, and gazed into my eyes for a bit, before stepping forward and raising her arm slowly to my shoulder, placing her cold hand on the top of it slowly, my head turned to her hand, then back to her.

"Leo, what's wrong?" She asked, not a single sound was in the room other than her soft voice. So many people and not even the children were making a pep, the tension was so intense, not for me, I was completely calm and still smiling away humming this song, but everyone else looked tense from my point of view.

A few moments after she asked me the question my arm began to raise, and suddenly wrapped itself round the back of Katherine, flinging her towards the floor, however my arm never left her back, instead of striking the floor she was suspending above it with my arm firmly placed behind, supporting her, I was staring into her eyes and she was staring back at me, her facial expression had changed, she looked scared now, still worried, but a different kind of worried now. My eyes darted from hers, to her lips and then back to hers, my head edged forward, and my lips opened slightly as they approached hers, they were dry and cracked but were still able to be used for kissing when they needed to be. As my eyes began to close I could see her expression change from worried to something else, but I wasn't quite sure what. My eyes firmly shut as my lips pressed against hers, my arm wrapped around her suspending her in the air, my lips opened slightly releasing my tongue into her mouth, her tongue greeted mine as it entered, I could feel her lips moving, kissing back, our dry lips soon becoming wet from our mixing saliva. To be honest I was very surprised she was actually kissing back, I expected her to push me off, or just not kiss back in general, my hand raised behind her head, gripping it gently, I could feel hers do the same.

I could feel the kiss coming to end, our lips slowly closing, tongues returning to our own mouths. Our lips still touching as our heads slowly pulled away from one another's. My eyes were locked onto hers as hers were locked onto mine. I couldn't help but smile slightly. We both stood there for a moment, just gazing at each other, until I decided to break the silence, and end the fear of the people still shaking behind her.

"I kissed Jane" I sputtered out, I don't think there is a single sentence that could have been more inappropriately timed then the one I just said, a look of confusing struck Katherine's face, and before I knew it, her face suddenly started fading, turning into a mindless blur, her features all scrambling together, my head felt faint, as if someone had stuck something in my ear and was filling my brain up with hot air.

"Leo?" Katherine asked her voice anxious and worried. That was the last thing I heard, everything went black for a moment, her face faded into complete darkness, her voice echoing throughout my mind. Was it another simulation? Was I about to wake up in the chair again?

"He's dangerous, breaking down that door, what kind of person can break through and slam shut a steel door? Even a Wraithier would have a hard time doing that!" A man's voice was shouting at someone, it started quietly but got slightly louder, I could tell he wasn't standing close by, perhaps a few feet behind me. I was lying down somewhere, my eyes still could only see black for now, but I could hear just fine.

"We knew there would be risks with this kind of operation, but Magic Man says they now have a diagnostic on whether or not the pill has encoded with his DNA properly. We won't have to put him through that again, the danger is practically over!" A woman replied, I recognised her voice straight away, it was Katherine.

"And? Did it?" The man asked anxiousness in his voice.

"No, not fully" She answered, I heard a loud huff come from the man, as if to sigh annoyance at what he had just been told.

"But it hasn't not worked either, the pill works better with him than anyone I have ever seen, he has only taken one dose and yet he is still able to access the effects of it, the only problem is that it can't be properly controlled, the pills effects are activated when Leo experiences an increased adrenaline rush or it can be complete random, however before you say anything about danger, the effects won't be like last time, it will be a normal reaction next time, Magic Man had to induce enhanced effects to see if the pill worked, so next time he will not be able to tear steel doors off walls, his strength and body should be normal, he will just know how to use it better."

Katherine finished. There was a moment of silence; no one said a word, until a slight whisper came from the man.

"He is your responsibility, I want he fit and ready for his mission in thirty minutes, wake him and send him to me straight away, we are running out of time Katherine, we needed him days ago, the Federation could be here at any moment." The man explained.

"We need more time, he's not ready for combat yet, we still don't know how well the pill worked or if we can make it work better." Katherine stated.

"I gave you thirty minutes, I wanted him ready yesterday, that's twenty four hours and thirty minutes more time then you already had. Thirty minutes left Katherine, hurry up!" as the man ended what he was saying, I could hear the sound of footsteps take the place of the two talking. One heading in a distant direction and just as the sound faded, another sound of footsteps started, this one closer and lighter footed, my guess was these were Katherine's, they were increasing in volume, getting closer. And as they approached me they stopped just behind my head, my vision still darkened.

There was a slight tapping sound coming from behind my head, as if Katherine was typing on something. Then she spoke,

"Time to wake up Leo" She whispered under her voice, her voice nervous and cracked, she sounded upset. And with that, there was a loud click and then a weird robotic sound, like wires moving or cables. A light appeared in the distance of my darkened vision, it was like looking down a pitch black tunnel, seeing the exit at the end, only the exit was coming towards me, I was not heading for it, the light grew more and more, I could make out a lamp now, and the ceiling behind it, but the light was so bright it was hard to see anything else, seeing the ceiling behind the light itself was a struggle. As my vision increased and returned back to normal I could make out a shadowed figure standing over me. It was Katherine, she wasn't smiling, she looked upset, there were tears on her cheeks and her eyes were bloodshot and red, she looked scared.

"I hope you're ready for this Leo, I really do" She murmured through the tears. Why was she crying? What was wrong? And why did that man want me, where was I going?

CHAPTER 14

THE TUNNEL BOARS TUNNEL

THE REST OF the time I had left was spent getting ready, I was given a new set of cloths, these were all dark colours, a black T-shirt, black over jacket, dark navy blue jeans, a newer pair of trainers that adjusted to my size automatically when I put them on, I was also given a pair of gloves and a mask of some kind, the mask was pitch black but when I tried it on white patches formed across the front of it around my mouth and eyes, they weren't perfect circles or anything, the white patches looked like splattered paint, I must admit the mask did look pretty cool although that was the last thing on my mind, I was more worried than happy at the fact I was being given all these different clothes, the fact they were all dark, and the very idea behind a mask intends that I'm going to be doing something where no one is supposed to see my face.

As I finished getting dressed and placing the mask and the gloves into my pockets Katherine entered the room I had been sent too to change.
"Are you finished yet?" She asked quietly. I looked up at her and nodded, she wasn't crying anymore but still looked very sad, my assumption was that she did not think I was ready for this and needed more training. However that was not the case of the man clearly in charge around here. Henry, I don't think I liked him much, him and his big goons seemed to have a different attitude to Katherine and Jane, they came across and more aggressive, but then again they keep telling

me there isn't much time, maybe they really are in serious danger, and if that's the case, how much more time do they actually have left? I've been here for days now, how much time have I actually wasted?

"Come on" Katherine insisted. "We need to take you to the equipment room to everything you need for this mission. She continued, waving her arm at me as if telling me to get up off the bench I was sitting on and go with her.

"Katherine I want to know what it is exactly that I am doing? What mission? I don't even fully know what these abilities are yet that you all say I have, how can I possibly help in any way?" I said to her, my head dropping into my hands, resting gently on my palms. I could hear her footsteps approaching me, and then feel her had touch the top of my shoulder, as it did I raised my head from my palms and looked up at her.

"You will learn how to use it in time Leo, and you're not here to help, you're here because no one else can, everything else will be explained by Paul and Henry in the briefing." She explained to me. My head dropped back down, gazing at the floor.

"Just trust me Leo, in time you will learn to control this ability, come on, we need to go." She finished, her hand slid down my arm, brushing against the surface of my over coat and reaching my hand, she grasped it and pulled me towards her, lifting me up to and stance.

We stood there looking at each other for what felt like a life time, I didn't want to leave this room, just stand here and stare endlessly into her eyes. She jolted her head towards the door and starting to turn around walking towards the door, pulling my hand behind her, leading me along with her, dragging behind. The next few minutes past quickly, we walked slowly throughout the building, passing through broken doorways and damp corridors, climbing slippery concrete stairs and the occasional ladder. For a futuristic world this base seemed older than what I was used to on Earth, it appeared to come across as an old military base of some kind. We approached a steel door at the top of a stairway, we had climbed a lot of stairs by this point, I imagined we must have been climbing a tower or tall building. Without hesitation Katherine opened the door and walked through, still pulling me behind her.

The room we entered looked familiar, the broken down pillars and bed sets darted around the dusky room, candle light dimly lighting up what dark corners that it could, still making it hard to make out the ground or anything below the waist. I didn't say anything but I guessed that this was the same room from earlier, the one with all the people sleeping in, only this time it was different. There wasn't a single person in the room anymore, no one sleeping in the beds, no noises from the young children playing and running around, play fighting and giggling at one another, or angry parents telling them to be silent, just an empty room, quiet and cold, the stained concrete walls flickering with the candle light, dancing across the walls around the room like a hundred people dancing, the walls darkened and relit as the light changed direction from the candles, must have been a cross breeze from somewhere, that would explain why it was so cold in here, how could anyone sleep in this cold, they must be freezing, even the bed sheets were worn out and torn to pieces, yet the children run around laughing and happy, sleeping in rough, scratchy sheets and eating that horrible, revolting mush that they call food.

"This way" Katherine said, she let go of my hand and began walking around the side of the room, I noticed picture frames of people on dark wooden boxes next to the beds, the occasional wrapper, or small box would be placed next to the pictures as well, maybe a memento of some kind, or just leftover rubbish from a type of food they had, perhaps they keep it to remember the food that they used to it.

Katherine walked around the side of the room, moving to dodge the broken down pillars and lifting her legs over the concrete nubs, her trousers were ripped and ripped even more as she raiser them to stretch over the debris on the dark floor, I clipped them and accidentally tripped a few times, it was impossible to make out anything on the ground, I don't know how Katherine managed to see it, you'd need cats eyes to be able to see anything clearly in this room. We past a few more bedsits and came to an old door, this one wasn't made out of steel but instead it was made from what looked like wood, a mud brown colour, it was a double door and looked like it had been worked over with a hammer, parts of it that had been beaten or battered were covered with small metal grates to hide vision into the next room. Katherine stood in front of it, her legs slightly apart, her arms dropped down by her side. There was a loud clank, followed by creaking as the wooden doors in front of us began to pull open, Katherine began walking forward, I followed cautiously behind her, we walked into the room, however the light was much brighter in the next room, my eyes were not used to it, all I could see was a white and yellow sheet covering my vision as my eyes struggled to re adjust to my surroundings.

When my vision started to come back to me, I pulled my hands away from my eyes and stooped rubbing them to try and speed up the process of regaining vision. I could make out Katherine standing in front of me and a few men behind her, I recognised them almost straight away. Henry was there, standing on her left with the Man dressed in white from earlier. On her right were the men who I had got into a fight with when I first visited, I don't remember their names. And there was also a young woman standing next to them, she had a rough face as did the men, she had short brown hair and cuts across her cheeks and forehead, her eyes were empty and yet she seemed to have a small smile, her nose was slightly tilting to one side, her lips dry and splitting, she looked as if she could have been a beautiful girl if she tried, instead she came across as someone who had seen too much combat to last a lifetime.

"So, the gangs all here" I sarcastically muttered, still rubbing my eyes occasionally to help see a bit better.
"Leo" Henry began talking.
"I believe you already know Katherine, the man next to me is Jonathon our lead science and weapons engineer. The two gentlemen over there are Nogla, the little one, and the big one with the broken noise I believe you may know a bit better, that's Hank." He explained, pointing at the two men on the other side of Katherine.
"Hello Hank" I said smiling and given a slight wave towards him, his face filled with anger.
"The woman standing with them is Trax" Henry Finished.
"Trax?" I said confusingly.
"It's a name" she answered, her little smile still across her bruised face.
"Fair enough" I replied. Henry stepped forward, passing Katherine, he began talking again.
"So you know why you are here" he asked with a sharp tone.
"I have a guess" I answered. Straight away he continued talking
"You are here to help us Leo, the drug you have been given"
"Awakening" I interrupted.

"Yes, awakening, the drug that is now in your system, passing through your blood and veins, pumping around your body allows you to do so much more than a normal human can, your mind is open, your body can be used to its full potential, and the fact that the drug itself has bounded with your DNA, meaning you never have to take another one so long as you live!" He passionately said, all the while walking around me and passing throughout the room.

"Hopefully one day the pill will be active longer and more efficiently then it is now considering unless you are hooked up to a machine like the one earlier it only activates randomly, which as you know can have troubling consciences." He paused for a second, glancing over my shoulder.

"However it's not all bad, we are hoping that eventually your body will naturally pick up some of the effect from the Awakening drug, for example you will be able to fight better, have better eye sight, your IQ will be raised, basically you will become a human 2.0" He placed a hand on my shoulder

"Just wanted to tell you not to worry, your body is changing but in a short time you will be better than you could have ever have dreamed of being." He finished, turning around and walking back towards the other people.

"But before that Leo, we need you to help us first, with your new skills, your talents, you are essential to this mission. Jonathon will explain." He said waving his hand towards the man in the white coat.

Jonathon stepped forward, he had a syringe in his hands, he paced slowly towards me, lifting it up and holding his other hand out, reaching for my arm.

"Do be afraid" he whispered.

"You will only feel a slight pinch for a second." He finished. Jonathon was a tall man, his white coat, despite the grubbiness of everyone else, remained neat and tidy with no stains, however there was a slight tear where the pocket was; as if someone cut the bottom of the pocket open. He had a small stubble beard, with a few scratches hidden underneath, his face was skinny, you could make out the bone structure below his skin as if he had not eaten in years, his eyes were blood shot and wide, gazing mindlessly at my arm as he grabbed it and gripped it tight, his eyes still wide with this mad gaze, not blinking, just flickering, jolting from side to side but only by fractions of an inch, his hair was just touching his shoulders, it was greasy and damaged, a mixture between blonde and light brown, no exact colour in his hair.

Suddenly I felt this sharp pain in my arm, I looked down at it to see the blood filled syringe pulling out of a small bleeding hole in the side of my arm now, the blood seeped out and dripped down my arm, a dark thin stream of red.

"You may want to put so pressure on that" he said quietly as he walked backwards towards Henry. His voice was quiet and wining, but deep at the same time, the pitch went up and down with each word, if I'm being perfectly honest I found this man to be a bit creepy and fascinating at the same time.

"Now that's over, Jonathon" Henry said sharply, slapping Jonathon on the back, not a hard slap of intended pain, just a friendly slap to urge Jonathon to do something. Although Jonathon jumped slightly, he looked worried and edgy when Henry's hand struck his back.

"Explain" Henry finished, looking at Jonathon as he glanced back to look Henry.

"Right, yes." Jonathon muttered, trying to find his words.

"I invented a device that will allow us to gain all the information we need on the Federation to help us find out a few of their weaknesses. I believe that my device, once entered into their primary core and activated, will download all the information on their system into the device itself, which we can then upload onto our own database to use to our own advantage. Now the device is inside the city already, we had it moved a while ago for this mission, we were just waiting for the right time, now we have you we believe the right time would be now."

"Do you not think you are all over estimating me?" I interrupted.

"I mean come on, a few days ago I was waking up in a bed, no fighting skills, no great intelligence, nothing unique about me, I was a nobody. And now because of this Awaking drug I'm suddenly better for this mission than any other trained person on this base. This is ridiculous, you all know I don't know how to control this drug, at any time it will randomly kick in, who knows what will happen when it does!" I shouted at them all. My body tense, my breathing increased but remained steady. They all stood there, staring at me for a few seconds before Henry stepped one step forward.

"Leo, if you get into a fight and that drug kicks in, you will win and escape, if you get captured and that drug kicks in, you will escape, if you are returning to base and that drug kicks in you will return quicker, if you are running you will running faster, if you are talking you will talk better, no matter when Awaking kicks in, no matter what you are doing at the time it will help complete this mission, do you understand? As soon as you leave this base you are the only one who can come close to downloading the data and returning here because at some point in that journey the drug will activate and you will do whatever it takes to complete the mission." He explained, walking one step back again, his eyes locked on mine, I was speechless, I thought they were crazy for sending me over everyone else, but I couldn't think of any reason why they shouldn't now.

"Jonathon, continue" Henry said, still looking at me.
"That's it really" Jonathon said, looking at the floor.
"Oh one more thing, if you run into a Black suit, I would run, unless that little orange pill has kicked in, they will tear you apart. Trax blurted out.
"Now gear up she said, jolting her head behind towards a large metal container, she bent down and brought out two black rucksacks, she threw one at me, it struck me in the chest, I let out a slight whimper, but managed to put my arms out and catch the rucksack before it fell to the floor, it was very heavy and freezing cold, it smelt of gun powder and smoke. I looked up, they were all moving around now, the two men, Nogla and Hank were trying to open a door with Jonathon watching over them, the door was small, about half the size of a person, and was made out of a sheeted metal of some kind, like something people on Earth would have on top of a shed or in an old army bunker. Henry was talking to Katherine I couldn't make out what they were saying, but I could see both their faces clearly, Katherine looked scared and worried, were as Henry looked angry and stern. Trax was standing on her staring at me, when my eyes finally reached her she smiled, not a happy smile, it looked like a confident smile, the sort of smile someone would give before they were about to fight and knew they were going to win, or someone who had just played a video game and beaten the high score. She didn't say anything or even move, just stood there, with her arms behind her back. I hadn't noticed her hair earlier, it was short, shorter than mine but with a fringe that dripped down her forehead slightly.

"Leo" A voice called from over where the three men were. My eyes went from Trax to the door again, looking for the person who called my name.

Jonathon was standing there looking at me, so I guessed it was him who called me as the other two men were still fiddling with the door which they had now got it open. I walked over towards Jonathon, passing Trax, whose eyes were following me as I walked, I guessed she was here to make sure I did what I was told because the way she was watching me gave me the impression she was told too. As I walked past Katherine and Henry I heard only the fraction of a sentence Henry was saying
"Then you know what to do, don't hesitate" he said harshly to Katherine, I saw her look up from the floor after that and catch my eye as I walked past, I could make out a single tear sliding down her check, he eyes were red and tired. I looked forward as I passed them back to Jonathon, I approached him, he seemed different now, he had a little smile, and was bouncing around slightly like he was excited.
"I must say this is a real pleasure, I have never met anyone from the Earth simulation before" he said with great excitement reaching out for my hand, gripping it and shaking it in a greeting way.
"I have so many questions I want to ask you when you return, well if you return, not that you won't, although the odds are not very good that you will as no one ever has, but then again no one has ever reacted with the drug like you have." He continued, spitting out words so quickly that they began hard to understand. I raised my hand and placed it on his shoulder. He stopped talking and focused on me.
"It's an honour to meet you too Jonathon" I said to calm him down and stop him from frantically talking.

He smiled and then coughed awkwardly, then began talking once more as I removed my hand from his shoulder.
"Right, yes, the mission" he said, spreading out each word in length.
"There are a few things you need to know, firstly when you climb the wall you need to make sure your body stays close to it, the wall was built to defend the city from the harsh weather conditions that surround it and of course the creatures that live in the uncharted forest and ocean that make up the rest of the planet, so staying close to the wall will stop any of those creatures spotting you and also stop the high winds from getting

in between you and the wall and therefore pulling you straight from it." he paused looking up at me.

"Secondly the equipment in your back pack is only really supposed to get you over the wall; there are no weapons other than a climbing knife to cut the ropes if you need to. Once you get to the safe house inside the city you will be given the equipment you will need to get inside the Federations tower, you will also be briefed there on what it is you will be doing to make that happen and to breach the tower." He paused once more, this time to catch his breath.

"Lastly there is another pill in your back pack" he said with nervousness in his voice. "This is a last resort pill, do you understand?" He asked me, his bloodshot eyes piercing my own. I didn't understand at first but then it hit me. The pill was a suicide pill in case I got captured, that way the Federation could not use me to their advantage. When I figured it out I just gave Jonathon a slight nod. He smiled and slapped the top of my shoulder, the way Henry slapped his back. After doing it his facial expression changed.

"Sorry" he said, I looked back at him confusingly.

"We are ready Henry" Jonathon shouted.

Henry and Katherine came over to where we were all standing, along with Trax trailing behind.

"Hank, Nogla, good luck." Henry said to the two men. They both nodded and then stood in front of the door. It was then that I realised the door wasn't a door at all, it was more of a garbage shoot, it was no more than a dark long tunnel, I couldn't see past the entrance, the rest was pitch black, in the distance of the darkness I could make out a faint orange light, possibly the other end of the tunnel. Nogla placed his hands on a small railing that was in front of the door way, he gripped it tight and pulled his legs up, throwing himself into the darkness and disappearing. Just as he did Hank stepped into the same placed Nogla was just standing and did the same thing, disappearing.

"Leo" Henry said, pointing towards to small dark passage way.

"You're kidding right" I replied.

"It is the quickest way to get to the wall from here, and the less likely to draw the attention of the Federation or anything else." Jonathon answered for him.

"Hank and Nogla will be waiting on the other side for you; I will be right behind you." Katherine said. I looked at them all once by one, I could feel my heart beating in my chest, jumping into a dark black hole was a fear I did not want to have to experience. Looking at the hole my feet began slowly walking towards it, one by one, each step bringing me closer to this darkness I had to embrace.

I reached the hole and placed my hands on the railing above it, staring into the abyss, exhaling my breaths loudly, I could hear each one echo through the tunnel. My head turned back to the four behind me. They were all just standing there staring at me, Trax still had that cocky smile, Katherine was still teary eyed, Jonathon was looking at me with amazement and wonder and Henry, he didn't really have an expression, he looked at me with no emotion, just blankly. My head turned back to the hole, I lifted up my legs, my arms frantically shaking as my legs raised and disappeared into the darkness, I couldn't even see them in front of me, I could just make out above my knees, everything else was nothingness.

"Leo, don't fail us" Henrys deep voice said from behind me. I did not turn around, instead I just gazed into the tunnel, I exhaled once more, closed my eyes, and feeling my heart beating through my chest I released my sweaty palms from their grip of the railing.

CHAPTER 15

DESCENDING, ASCENDING

MY EARS WERE ringing with the thundering of the material I was sliding down on, it was cold and hard. It rang louder the faster I went; I could feel my hair flappy in the wind my speed was creating. My hands were across the front of my chest, my body completely straight. I was falling through the tunnel for a few seconds before I began to see the glimmer of the orange light I saw earlier, I felt a sigh of relief leave my body as I saw the light gaining strength and becoming brighter. Suddenly an orange light on the ceiling darted past my vision, and the light faded once more. It wasn't an exit light at all, just a ceiling bulb barely lit. I continued falling, still gaining speed, I couldn't lift my head anymore, or my hands from my chest, the force was too much. I was stuck to the floor of the tunnel, falling through darkness.

More and more orange lights passed my vision, I counted eight now, and they all seemed to be the same distance from one another, about twenty two seconds to be exact although the number of seconds between them did decrease as I gained speed. But it did mean that I had been falling for eight times the twenty two seconds or less now, another light went past as I thought that to myself, nine now. My body began to ache, the speed was so fast now that I couldn't hear anything but wind, my ears popped from the pressure, and it was now getting increasing hard to breathe, I couldn't breathe through my mouth at all, instead I had to breathe through my nose. My ears felt like they were going to explode, the pain was unbearable, more lights passed, I tried to focus on them instead of the pain, I now counted fourteen.

Number twenty seven had now passed, I was starting to think I was never going to come out of this, I could move at all now, barely breathing, I couldn't even open my eyes without them hurting, the pain was ripping through my body, piercing every part of me, everyone inch, every bone when suddenly I found myself struggling to breathe even worse now, I tried to take in some air but it was like there was just no air to breathe in, I was holding what last of my breathe I had left inside my lungs. The pressure was pushing down on my chest, forcing the air out of me, I couldn't hold out like this much longer, the pain was now so intense I could no longer feel it, all I could focus on was the fact that I could not breathe, I lost count of the lights now as I was keeping my eyes closed to avoid even more pain.

Digging deep I managed to gain one more breath of oxygen inside me, it didn't change anything really, I felt no better. Almost instantly I found myself freezing cold and wet, I was out of the tunnel and shoot straight into water, I dropped down deep into it, my eyes opened and I tried breathing in on instinct, swallowing nothing but cold water, my arms flailing around, trying to push my body up ward toward the surface, I could see two white light in the distance of the water above my head, they were moving around, changing direction through the water. I closed my eyes and put all my strength into my body, kicking my legs as hard as I could, they shook with each kick, my arms pushing down and then dragging themselves up to push down again. The water was intensely cold, the temperature was like a blister under my skin, only it wasn't just in one place, it was all over my body, draining my strength. I didn't know how close I was to the top of the water, I did not dare open my eyes to find out, if I saw I was still far away I would lose hope and that was something I just couldn't do at the moment, I had to believe I was close, or getting close.

My lungs and body weakened now, I had already swallowed a lot of water, I was starting to feel dizzy from the lack of oxygen my head was receiving, my limbs were barely moving through the water now, they were only just pulling me up, I opened my eyes and looked up just to see if I was even gaining height, it felt like I was swimming for hours. As

I stared up my eyes hurting, not due to the water but the blinding light they were now looking at, I was staring straight at one the two light I was looking at earlier. My head pierced the surface of the water and my mouth shoot open, gasping for air, my arms rose as they pushed through the last of the water. As soon as I reached the surface I was lifted straight from the water and dragged out of it on to land, the ground was hot compare to the water I had just been in. I turned from my back to being face down, placing my hands on the ground to raise my head as I threw up the water from my lungs, coughing and spitting it all onto the floor, choking on the oxygen at the same time. Once I finished getting it all out of my lungs I turned back onto my back and felt this wonderful feeling of no pain, there was no strain on my body, lack of air entering my lungs, I was lying there and I had never felt so relieved in my life. There were two lights shining bright in my face, I could make out Hank and Nogla behind them, they were both laughing at me.

"You should never land in water the way you did at those speeds mate" Hank said through his laughter.

"You were like a dart; it sent you straight down into the depths. Your legs and arms should have been open, not close together." Nogla explained.

"No one told me there would be water at the bottom" I sputtered out followed by coughing.

"If they did I would have worn my swimming gear and brought a towel" I continued, all the while coughing up occasional splatters of water. Hank and Nogla laughed at my joke, pulling me to my feet.

"Your bags floating on the water" Nogla said, pointing to the small area of water I had just climbed out of. I walked over, my head still dizzy from the lack of air, stumbling around I dropped to my knees next to the water and reached in to grab my backpack. As I grabbed it and pulled the dripping bag from the ice cold water I heard a loud thundering sound, I looked up and saw Katherine shoot out of the small dark hold in the wall above the water and dive straight into it. Nogla and Hank walked over to the side of the water and shined their lights into it like they did with me.

"You should have a light too Leo, check your bags front pocket." Nogla said. I looked down at my soaking wet rucksack and un-zipped the front pocket, pulling it open. Inside wasn't just a small light, but also I damp chocolate bar of some kind, and also a small book and as well as the knife Jonathon had told me about I could see a little green squared item.

    I pulled the light out and turned it on, as I brought it down and shined it on the water Katherine's hand suddenly flung out of the dark surface and rose up, water flew everyone, splashing all over the front of my body, I forgot how cold it was for a second, I was now brutally reminded. Shortly after her hands exited the freezing depths her head quickly followed. Reaching out I grabbed her hands and pulled them up, Nogla and hank also grasped her, pulling her from the water. She was only under the water for a few seconds, when she exited the tunnel her legs and arms were out from her side which probably would have stopped her from going as deep as me. She didn't fall to the floor like me either, she stood straight up and looked at us three, not even coughing she began talking.

    "What happened to him" she said pointing at me.
    "He darted the fall" Hank replied
    "How long was he under?" Katherine asked.
    "Sixty six seconds" Nogla answered.
    "You ok?" She said looking at me. I nodded in reply.
    "Good, let's move then" she said, flipping her bag from the front of her to her back. She turned and began walking through the new tunnel, Nogla and Hank followed behind, I placed my bag on my back and began pursuing them.

    "At least this tunnel is bigger" I said to myself looking around the area. It looked almost exactly like one of those sewers you see in the movies, the walls were covered in green slime, there was a small stream in the middle leading to and from the pool of water we had been thrown into, the tunnel itself was rounded and had two pathways each side of the little stream. We began walking away from the pool on the left walkway, there were no lights other than the small torches we all had, Katherine lit hers up and lead the way. No one said a word, just followed her as we began walking.

    The ground was hard and slippery; there were drips of liquid coming from the ceiling that would every so often hit me. I was falling behind a bit so I started gaining speed to try and catch up.

    "How many times you climbed the wall?" I asked the three in front of me. At first no one replied to me, but then I saw a light shine back from one of the two guys.

"Hank and I have never climbed the wall." Nogla replied

"Katherine on the hand has climbed the wall hundreds of times" He finished.

"You guys nervous?" I asked them, my torch shining on the floor to watch my feet, making sure I wasn't going to walk into anything, occasionally id lift it up to make sure I was still on the right track and could still see Nogla, Hank and Katherine.

"Excited" Nogla replied.

"We have never seen the city outside of the pictures we get shown, we grew up outside the walls, this will be the first time we have ever had a chance to climb the walls, I can't wait to reach the top and look at the city for the first time." Nogla explained, I hadn't thought of it that way, most people are born in the base I saw and I guess they die there too, of course Katherine would have seen the city as she was undercover in the Federation, I imagine that is why she was coming with us, because she knows the city better than anyone, if this planet has one city I can imagine it is bigger than anything I have ever seen, without Katherine we'd never find our way round. The more I thought about it the more I became excited as well, seeing a futuristic city for the first time, what would it look like? What would be in it? And I was intrigued to see how big the city actually was, maybe I would be able to see this forest I've heard so much about from it, or a creature that I was warned about. Then I remembered what I was told.

The extreme weather could rip me from the wall, the creatures that dwell around it could kill me, and they had put all hope into me, suddenly my excitement turned to fear, if this city is so big, big enough to cover up a good amount of the planet, then the wall I was just about to climb must be taller than anything I have ever seen as well, and I was going to have to scale it.

The walk became heavy and slow, although we were making good pace my mind was thinking in slow motion, the drug had not kicked in but I was still seeing hundreds of different possibilities, hundreds of ways that could go wrong and as soon as we reached the end of this tunnel I was going to have to face all those possibilities and try and conquer them, hundreds of ways I could die, only one that will let me live and that is me making it to the top of the wall. I'm not a strong climber, never did rock climbing as a kid, never did anything that involved heights really,

I've always had a rather big fear of them, which made me avoid them as much as I could. The air was steady, all I could hear was the sound of footsteps echoing around us, the ruffling of rucksacks moving from side to side on our back, the stench of faeces and urine in the air, my only guess was this was the city's sewer tunnel, if that was the case then the water I had previously landed in was not water at all, and I swallowed it, all that human waste was now in my stomach being dissolved into my system. I suddenly felt very sick, the intense smell wasn't helping, I realised most of it was coming from my clothes not my surroundings.

"Right lads, this is the last service passage before the wall, get ready!" Kath said as we approached a small ladder leading up through an opening in the ceiling of the sewer. Hank and Nogla gathered around the bottom of it, placing their rucksacks of the floor in front of them, we I caught up with them all I placed my on the floor the same as them.

"Pick it up." Hank snapped at me. I looked at him puzzled in reply.

"The reason we have put ours on the floor is to get our weapons out, you don't have a weapon so pick yours up." Hank explained.

"Can't I have a weapon?" I asked.

"Sure if you tell me how to take down a Raptor with a knife then you can heavy a weapon" he answered.

"A Raptor? Like the Dinosaur?" I asked in reply. He laughed loudly; you could hear it bouncing off the walls around us, going down the tunnel.

"No not a Dinosaur, it's a big winged creature, similar to your Earth Eagle, only this creature is very skinny, usually runs but can fly and instead of a beak it has a large jaw, they are twice the size of us and they hunt alone around the outside of the wall." He finished, Nogla and Hank then pulled out two big machete like weapons, they both slid them into a holster located on their thighs.

"Leo, both these men have killed these creatures before, you haven't, you are essential to this mission so all we want you to do is run as fast as you can in the middle of us, don't leave our sight. It's a long run to the wall and if we lose you we will never find you again." Katherine said, placing both her hands on my shoulders, they were freezing cold I could feel the temperature of them pierce my jacket. She then removed her hands and lent down inside of her bag, pulling out a similar machete to what the guys had pulled out, she didn't place her in a holster, she just held it in her left hand and placed her right on the runs of the ladder, her right foot was raised and placed on a run as well. She turned and looked at us all.

"Leo you follow me, as soon as we reach the top we will be running, keep your rucksack close to your back so the wind won't take it, Hank and Nogla will be right behind us, do look back, just look at me and do exactly what I do." She said, she didn't sound afraid or worried, just calm and steady, I nodded in reply and with that she began climbing the ladder.

She was moving fast up the ladder, I picked up my rucksack quickly a threw it on my back, trailing after her, I placed my right hand on the bottom of the ladder and gripped it tightly, my left hand followed a bit higher and then my feet one by one, I looked up and saw Katherine was almost near the top already, she was very strong for a woman and very fast, it was strange considering the fact that she was so small and skinny, I wouldn't take her for the athletic type. My hands hit each rudder with force, pulling my body up as fast as I could so I could catch up with Katherine, my feet was jumping from one step to the next as fast as my hands were. Suddenly there was a fierce wind, it shot down the passage and nearly knocked me clean off the ladder, I looked up quickly to see the hatch above my head wide open, the wind was coming through it, striking me viciously. I gripped the rudders even tighter and continued climbing after Katherine, trying to keep my body close to the ladder so that the wind would not get between me and it and pull from the rudders straight back down to the floor. The wind was so intense, it was almost exactly like falling down that tunnel into the pool of waste, only this time every item of clothing I was wearing was flapping around and my back was hitting my back hard and pulling away from me before striking me again.

I felt my right hand grow extremely cold, I looked up to see Katherine's shadow in the darkness gripping it, I couldn't make out any features of her, her facial expression or even clothing, just a black shadow grasping my hand, it could have been anyone to be honest, but I knew it was her. I had reached the top of the passage, I was still looking up at Katherine, trying to find my footing, the wind was even stronger now, and as well as the darkness there was a sheet of white fog surrounding us. I looked down at my feet, placing them correctly or the rudders, I looked back at up at Katherine and saw a bigger shadow standing behind her, it was much larger than her and was right behind her, not moving an inch. I yelled to warn her but the wind took my words away with it and carried them into the distance. Suddenly the larger shadow darted forward, and both Katherine's and the larger one disappeared from my sight, I felt shear fear for her safety, my eyes wheeled up, my heart thumbing.

Pulling my self-straight out the whole into the wind above, I darted my eyes around the see if I could see Katherine anywhere close by, or the larger shadow. It was so dark, and the fog made it impossible to see anything, I looked up at the sky for a second, only there was no sky, just white fog, my eyes fell back down to the ground around me, and began searching for Katherine once more, I was throwing my head left and right, rotating my body completely trying to find her.

"KATHERINE!" I screamed at the top of my lungs, I could barely hear my own voice, just the muffle of my words in the strong wind.

"KATHERINE, KATHERINE! KATHERINE!!!" I continuously shouted, my eyes still searching for her, my chest now hurting due to my massive raise in pulse.

"Katherine! I shouted one last time, I turned fast around to see if she was anywhere to be seen, the wind striking me hard, each breath more difficult than the last to take in. when I turned again I saw a shadow standing in front of me, it wasn't large like the one I saw behind Katherine, however it did appear to be growing rapidly, and becoming larger and larger, whatever it was it was getting closer to me. I couldn't help but stare at the shadowed figure as it grew beyond human size, it must have been no more than a few feet in front of me now.

As the shadow approached me and seemed to be within touching distance it was immediately thrown to the floor, a smaller figure seemed to have tackled the creature and was fighting it on the floor, I couldn't make out who, or if they were winning against the creature, however a fierce scream suddenly filled the air, a man's scream, it was loud a pierced the wind. I once again felt the cold on my shoulders; it pulled me to face away from the two shadowed figures fighting on the ground below me. When my eyes were averted I saw Katherine standing in front of me once more, she was standing right in front of me, her cold hand on my shoulder, I could see a dark red colour all over her face, it was falling down her cheeks and covered her forehead, it must have been blood. She leaned in even closer, her head touching mine, I could feel her warmth breath on the side of my face, she grabbed me tight and screamed in my ear.

"RUN LEO, RUN NOW!"

CHAPTER 16

The Wall

The shadowed figured of Kath grabbed my hand and pulled me straight behind it, dragging my through the wind and screams of me, only it wasn't just men screaming I could hear, there was a fierce screeching sound everyone so often, it was high pitched and surprisingly loud considering the fact that the wind made it impossible to hear even the louder noises unless they were right next to you. I could see anything other than the back of Kath's shadow pulling me fast behind her, I struggled to keep up, she was very fast, my legs were hitting the ground hard, hurting my feet, my breathes became heavy and quick, what little air I could receive felt like it wasn't making it into my body, I became dizzy and tired very quickly. As much as I wanted to give up I couldn't, Katherine was to strong, every time I felt myself slowing down I felt her pulling me along speeding me back again. The screams of men had now stopped, I wanted to turn back and looked to see if there was anything following us, one of those creatures or Hank and Nogla, but I didn't, I did as I was told and carried on running forward, looking forward and staying right behind Katherine.

We had been running for a while now, the sound of those animals screaming and the wind were the only things I could hear, the ground was now wet and soft, it felt like damp grass, not concrete. Our pace had slowed, but we were still moving quickly, I couldn't help but wonder how much further we had to go, and also if there was anything behind me, the fear of something being there was too much to take, I turned my head slowly as we ran I looked behind us, there wasn't two figures there, or even one big one but instead there was around twenty shadowed figures, all much larger than humans, they were only a few seconds behind us and were gaining us quickly, I couldn't tell if any of the figures were Nogla or Hank as there was so many, one appeared to be much larger than the others, about ten times bigger than myself, I stared at it with amazement. As I did I saw two dark red lights appear from the top of the creature, they were looking right at me, they were its eyes! The creature was staring right at me, chasing us. A horrendously loud roar shot through the air, it shook the very ground we were running on, a few of the smaller shadows began disappearing as the larger one got bigger, as it got closer, it appeared to be crushing the smaller ones in front of it, it was running much quicker than them and us. All I could make out was its shadow and red eyes gazing into mine.

With nothing but fear driving me forward I turned back to looked at Katherine, my pace increased and I found myself running beside her, our hands locked tightly in grasp, as we continued running forward I could feel the ground shaking below us with the footsteps of that creature behind us, catching us up. Regardless of our tiredness, or the pain of our limbs and the lack of air we were receiving due to the intense fog and winds, we carried on running forward when suddenly there was a bright red light in front of us, not like the creatures eyes, this was a larger red light, could it be a bigger creature than the one following us? Surely not. I tried to slow down but Katherine thundered forward, dragging me along with her, pulling us closer to the red light. Then there was no longer just one red light, but three, then seven and the number kept increasing as well got closer to them, they were all in a straight line stretching across my vision. Then it hit me, realisation, I gazed up to see this dark figure standing strong in the sky, the wind striking my face, hitting me repeatedly. The dark figure grew larger as we got closer, I couldn't see the top of it, just it disappearing far into the sky, it was the wall!

It was magnificent in size, it was a black as the sky above it, the fog hid it well and if it wasn't for the red lights darted all around it, it would be impossible to see until we were standing right in front of it, touching it. The fog above it swallowed to top of the wall, the giant structure that we were going to have to climb. My eyes scaled it before my body, looking at every part of it that I could make out through the mist. When I looked at the bottom of it, now very close to where we were running, I could see two small figures standing there, they appeared to be looking at Katherine and I as we got close to them, they were much smaller than the creatures that were previously chasing us, I could not feel the ground shaking anymore either perhaps the creature had given up on catching us, that wouldn't make sense as it was gaining on us, a few more seconds and we would be in its grasp.

We quickly approached the Wall, I could see the figures more clearly now, it was Nogla and Hank, Hank looked rough, he was covered in blood from head to toe, I couldn't tell which was his and which was the creatures. Nogla on the other hand look remarkably untouched, he had no blood or tears in clothing like Kath and Hank.
"Go quick" they both shouted at us, Katherine let go of my hand and grabbed a small rope that was dangling in front of us, it was in between Nogla and Hank, Katherine scaled the rope quickly, pulling herself straight up the wall, where did she find all this energy, my body was fading now, I felt exhausted from our run, I just wanted to sit down and relax for a bit before beginning this climb, I couldn't even see the top, we were all going to climb into the fog above, how much higher could it be, it was high enough to pierce the sky above, and for good reason I suppose, it kept people like the Rebels out as well as the creatures that surround the city. My hands gripped the rope tightly as I got close to it, I darted my eyes at Nogla and received a nod, he was telling me to go quickly, so I did. I pulled with all my might, dragging my body off the ground and placing my legs on the wall, my feet struck it hard and began walking up the vertical climb as I quick as I could so that Nogla and Hank could follow, this was it, we had begun the climb of this unbelievably massive, pitch black structure.

Looking up I could see Katherine was already high up the wall, she was scaling the rope quicker than anyone I've ever seen, I turned to look back down to make sure Hank and Nogla had both made it up the rope, they were further down but were both now climbing behind me, catching quickly. I pulled my body up with my aching arms as best I could, struggling to keep the wind from getting in front of me, it had already gotten between me and my backpack and was slamming it into the centre of my back and pulling it out, making it insanely difficult to keep the correct balance as I continued climbing the rope.

The wall was like nothing I had ever seen, in my mind I expected it to look like an ordinary brick wall just on a much larger scale, but it was nothing like that. There were no bricks or anything that suggested it was built piece by piece, it appear to be one large black metal slate, it was covered with red lights, some of which were flashing and had the occasional indent where something had struck it with enough force to damage it slightly. Other than that it was nothing more than I black sheet of solid metal, this would of course be the reason for the rope, there was no way we would be able to scale it otherwise, it's too hard to use climbing boots on or any equipment to dig in the side of the wall, and it was too perfect to use bare hands and feet on, with no real places to rest your hands you would not be able to climb it like that at all.

Looking up I could see that Katherine was now much further ahead, but she appeared to have stopped as the more I climbed the closer I seemed to be getting to her. My arms were shaking with each pull, the run we had just overcome had drained all the strength from my body, my legs kept slipping from the wall, the material made it hard to keep them constantly placed on the side of it and the fact that I was continuously growing more tired made it increasing difficult to keep climbing the wall. I looked down once, the wind throwing my head around making it hard to turn back to look down at Nogla and Hank, they had now caught up and were scaling the rope behind me, I was going to shout to them to see if they were ok but I knew they would not be able to hear me in this wind, behind them all I could now see was the fog, there were no creatures in sight climbing the wall after us, but whether or not they were waiting for us at the bottom if we fall, that was a different story.

As we all climbed, grasping whatever strength we had left from the core of bare bones and muscles we started to approach Katherine. I looked up at her to see why it was she had stopped, she was holding on with one hand that appeared to be bleeding slightly, and was using the other one to check her equipment. As she finished doing the last of her checks she turned back to look at us, it was difficult to maintain constant vision with her by looking up due to the constant high winds, I had to keep closing my eyes and opening them again slowly to try and gain a better sight of what she was doing. Her head moved up and down slightly, I assumed it was a nod. As soon as she nodded at us she turned back to face up the wall, her left hand reached up and grab a crack in the side of the wall, she pulled her body to the left, dangling from her left hand alone, she reached up with her right hand and gripped yet another crack in the wall, then I noticed what she was doing.

The rope we were using to scale the wall had ran out, we were all now at the part where the rope had connected into the hard surface, we now had to continue climbing as best we can without the rope, Katherine was now free climbing without any harnesses. I knew I was scared but I didn't feel scared, my body was so physically drained and tired that it was hard to gain any more fear, also we had experienced so much in so little time that fear had now become normal on this journey, from escaping the creatures, to sliding down that tunnel into a pool of waste and filth, and now climbing the wall with nothing to support us, just our weak hands and legs to now rely on, I hadn't even considered the fact that Katherine and Hank were injured and were still managing to climb this beast of a structure.

Katherine had now steadied her body and was carefully moving upward, she didn't look back once after she had begun free climbing, she must have been in deep concentration on the task at hand. I raised my hand and gripped the open crack in the side of the wall, my right hand was still fiercely wrapped around the rope, even though I was tired I could feel my heartbeat gradually increasing again, I didn't look back at Nogla behind me or Hank behind him, my eyes didn't stop looking at my hands once, they were completely fixed, all I could focus on was moving my right hand to the next crack scratched into the dark surface of the wall, but I couldn't stop thinking about the fact that as soon as I did this my whole body would fall from the rope, all my weight would be placed on aching hands, I didn't have the energy. Kath did, I wasn't trained like the two men behind me, this wasn't something I could do, I couldn't help but think about the lack of prep I received on this mission, I was not told about the creatures until the last minute, I was not told about climbing the wall without harnesses or the drop into water, even how long that tunnel went on for, I understand that due to The Federation closing in on their position they needed to send me on the mission quickly but surely they could have taken ten minutes to explain to me in a bit more detail on the tasks I was going to have to overcome on this horrific journey.

I felt myself getting angry at the thought of them sending me on this mission as ill equipped as they had, in knowledge and also in the very fact that I did not receive any weapon to defend myself against these ferocious beasts that wanted nothing more than to rip my limbs from body and drag me off into the dark, cold night. I decided to use that anger, the last bit of fuel I needed to make this climb, I stopped looking at my hands shaking, one grasping the rope the other barely hanging onto the small crack in the wall and starting gazing at the second crack, the next indent that I had to reach, my body began to tremble with the rush of adrenaline, letting out a mighty scream I removed my right hand from the tattered rope and flung it up towards the grove.

My hand slipped into the crack, my nails snapped and bent on the surface of the wall, ripping out of my fingers, however they were frozen from the cold temperatures and high winds that the pain was completely numbed, it felt uncomfortable having blood and loose nail in my gloves but there was no pain, no feeling at all. My legs threw themselves backwards and crashed straight into the side of the wall, my knees bashed on the hard metal, my feet soon followed after, striking the surface as well, the wind pulled them back out towards the ground below but my hands stayed locked into the cracked of the wall, the wind was not going to take me from this position. I steady my legs, there was nothing to place them in, no groves or indents, I just had to bring them as close to the wall as I could and let them dangle below me, gently flapping in the wind as I struggled to keep control of them. Still I did not release my grip, I brought my legs up close to my body and darted my eyes up to the next indent in the wall, as soon as I got there I'd be able to use my legs to help make this climb, until then the weight of my body rested entirely in my hands and busted, bloody fingers.

I could feel each breath leaving my body but could not feel a single one going In to take the place of the ones leaving my lungs, my head was dizzy for the dramatic increase in heart rate, my hands and feet shaking, I could taste blood in mouth and smell the damp metal of the wall in the air, the fog around us was dampening the wall itself making it even more slippery and dangerous than before, my eyes were still looking directly up, I couldn't see Kath anymore, had climbed higher than my vision could, I realised I would have to spot the indents myself instead of being able to see which ones she had reached for to make the climb. I found one that appeared to be just out of reach, I would have to jump for it if I wanted to make it to the next one, I had to act fast while I still had the rush of adrenaline in my body, when my heart rate once again slowed it would make me increasingly tired before eventually I would not be able to make this climb. I dashed my eyes back to my hands, and back then back to the next crack, once again raising my legs to my body and placing the soles of my feet flat against the wall, I gripped the indents I was currently holding tightly and readied my legs for the jump, my eyes all the while fixed on where I wanted to go, I was focused, determined.

My hands pulled forward and my legs kicked off the wall sending my body upward slightly, it wasn't as high as I felt I was going to get, I only managed to pull myself a few feet upward and was now not gripping any section of the wall, even my feet were now in mid-air. My eyes were still fixed on the crack, now panicking I threw both my hands towards the dent, my left one stretched and slid of the side of it, falling back down towards my body, my right hand had made it equally as high, I kicked my legs in mid-air, one of them hit the wall sending me a few inches upward, just enough to slide my right hand into the third grove, I kicked my legs once more, this time sending them hurdling forward, my left foot slotted straight into the grove my left hand was just in, my right foot copied the left and drove itself directly into the second crack, they whacked the wall with such force that both bounced out again slightly, however I managed to bring them back into the wall and steady my position, I now had both feet in the wall as well as both my hands, bringing my left to join my right in the small crack, I could relax, breathe for a second before once again continuing this climb.

The wall was as cold as ice, the wind pierced my clothing like a knife through butter, digging into my skin as I struggled to scale the wall, bringing each hand slowly up into whatever split or crevice I could find in this devilish material that the wall was made from, I moved slowly but at least I moved, I did not want to make any mistake and fall to my death, even if I survived the harsh fall I would be ripped into pieces and eaten alive by the creatures that waited for us at the bottom of the structure, waiting for one of us to fail and become their dinner for the night. Kicking my legs into the slots that previously held my hands, my body climbing the wall out of nothing but pure instinct, the overwhelming willingness to survive, I was empty, my bones broken, my gloves filled with blood from my finger, my breaths turned to ice before my very eyes, tasting blood each time I breathed in and out, not that when I breathed in anything actually went in, the air felt like trying to breathe under water with your head inside a small pocket of air. I didn't know how much longer I could physically cope with this before my hands just stopped gripping altogether, each grasp I made felt weaker than the first, each step was taking longer than the last, each movement I made was costing me more and more energy, it wouldn't be long before I run out of it completely and fall to my death, I only hope that Nogla and Hank are not behind me when I finally give in and let go, otherwise they would surely be dragged to their deaths alongside myself.

Just as I felt I was about to run out of every ounce of strength that my body could muster, from every part of my body, there was that cold feeling on my shoulder once again, that familiar cold grip that I had felt so many times before, even though my skin was frozen and the cold seeped through to my bones, chilling the very blood that pumped through my veins, I could still feel the cold of Katherine's hand grabbing me. As soon as I felt her touch my body died, my hands released their grip and my legs fell from the crack they were in, my lifeless body appeared to be falling for a moment, perhaps I was mistaken, perhaps it was not Katherine's touch I felt but just a drip of ice from the wall, or the start of rain landing on my shoulder. If that was the case then I was falling through the air and I would soon greet the ground below, I wasn't scared anymore, I was so sick of this, all the pain, the torture that has been Vala, the constant worry of death and doom that seemed to be an everyday lifestyle of this place, if I was going to die now then I would finally be at peace, I could finally rest without being disturbed, without being afraid, I would be what I always wanted, I would be forever free.

The falling only lasted a spilt second, my mind processing a thousand thoughts at once, I guess it's true what they say, when you are facing death, no matter how pathetic your life was, no matter how short the moment is that you believe you are truly going to cease to exist, that pathetic life that you have lived, you will get to relive again through a short window of millions of images, all passing before your very eyes within a second, you experience those feelings, and time itself stands still just so you can remember everything before you forget it all and fall into your endless sleep. However this was not the case, I saw the images, I believed I was going to die, but then I felt the cold again, it wrapped itself around my wrist and sent my soaring into the air, before I could even open my eyes I felt a sudden thumb as I struck a hard surface, it felt like the same material as the wall, my eyes opened slowly, gazing through the fog I could just make out the tattered, black shoe of a person.

Averting my eyes from the shoe and following the leg upward until I could make out the face of the person, it was Katherine, she had made it to the top and pulled from the wall, she looked absolutely shattered, her body was slouched, she was breathing heavily and faster than I was, her eyes were completely bloodshot, there was blood dripping from her eyes, nose and the cuts she had all over her body, her clothes were torn and ripped, and yet despite all this she was smiling. She started laughing, her laugh was loud and deep, it was like a man's laugh, she stopped again and looked down at me staring at her, before she dropped to the floor and was now lying next to me.

"Let's not do that again" she murmured out through her panting breaths. She was lying face up staring at the sky, the fog wasn't as thick up here, I could see much more clearly than before, but it still lingered around.

"Did we make it?" I asked, spitting out thick red blood in doing so.

"Look" she said, barely raising her hand to point behind me. I turned my body around to see what it was she was pointing at, and that's where I saw it, for the first time I saw what people had gone their whole lives not seeing.

"Vala" I said in amazement, gazing across the city, it was like nothing I could have ever imagined, not in all my dreams, we had made it.

CHAPTER 17

Vala

VALA, IN ALL its beauty, all its uniqueness, my eyes have never seen a city like this, my brain could never imagine something as remarkable as what they were gazing upon at this very moment, at first the city appears to look just the same as any other, any on Earth anyway, but then you look beyond the immediate area surrounding the wall, which stretched much higher than any other building that was located close to it. As soon as I looked further than the buildings below the other side of the wall I noticed they start to get taller, and taller, and bigger in shape not just size, and there were more than I could count, they grew high above the wall, these grey and white buildings disappearing into the sky above, some were rounded and circled their way up, others unusual shapes, rhombuses or hexagon shapes, one was nothing more than a giant circle, you could see straight through the centre of the building, a few others were made out of clear glass, showing you all the contents of the buildings insides.

Then there was the really remarkably tall skyscrapers, these were so wide, they had the length of a large town, and they grew a hundred times higher than there width, these however were not the same colour as most, they were a rusted brown or sluggish green colour. There were five of these mega buildings that I could see from the top of the wall. The night sky caused them to light up like giant Christmas Trees, all the lights on the buildings were different and yet somehow all seemed to fit this perfectly organised structure, the buildings were very close together, most looked as if they were actually touching, but if you gazed upon them from different angles you could see that there was the slightest fraction of a gap between each one, from the distance the gaps look too small to even place your hand through.

Surrounding the buildings was an army of tiny lights darting around each one, some going up and down, others following an organised straight line further down, they were vehicles, flying vehicles! There were none close enough to get a good look at but from what I could make out they seemed to look very similar to the cars on Earth, I guess the ones I grew up seeing in that false reality were modelled after the ones here, the only difference was their rounded bodies and shapes, they all had the same blue or green headlights and were all flying on what seemed to be four yellow lights under the vehicle, jets maybe? Or something else. Most were White; however there was the occasional Black one, and then one or two Red vehicles.

"Flying cars?" I whispered through my lips, still staring in awe at the city before me.

"Not cars, they are called Mechanics, most don't work beyond the wall, see those little yellow lights under them?" She said, standing up slowly and pointing to one of the vehicles, she was groaning a bit whilst trying to find her feet once more, she had her right hand gripped to her side, you could see that she was in a lot of pain.

"Those yellow lights are strong magnets, inside the walls surrounding the city are the receiving magnets, this allows each vehicle to fly and move anyway it wants, but the receivers are only on the inside of the wall, so if you go over the top they will stop working, and then you crash." She explained, dropping to the floor as soon as the last word left her blood covered lips.

"Katherine relax for a second, just stay down" I quietly said to her, placing my hand upon hers. She didn't move for a bit, nor did she talked, she was just lying face down on the top of the wall, her eyes wide open, her breathing still heavy.

It wasn't long before we heard a grunt, I shot to my feet, and stumbled, they were aching so much, my sides hurt, my hands suddenly felt like they had been through a blender, all the pain that my adrenaline or tiredness had blocked out was now slowly creeping back up on me.

"Leo gives us a bloody hand" a voice yelled from over the wall, I found it ironic that the voice was asking me for a bloody hand when my gloves were still filled with my own blood. I managed to limp over to the side of the wall, I didn't look down, I just fell to the floor beside it and placed my arm over the incline, dangling it for Nogla or Hank, whoever it was that called me.

"Thank you" Nogla's voice called out, I recognised the tone now, a hand reach up and grabbed mine, the weight was immense, there was no way with all my drained strength that I would be able to pull him up the wall, instead I just rolled my body over on its side and tried moving my whole body back, that way using my counter weight to pull him up. His second hand appeared from the darkness, gripping the top of the wall, his ripped gloves cut open even more as he grasped the side of the wall. His hand was followed by his head and then elbow, I struggled to pull, my arm felt like at any moment it was going to pop out its socket and Nogla would take it with him to the ground below.

After he managed to bring his second elbow up he looked at me.

"You can let go now" he sputtered out, struggling to talk and hold his own weight at the same time. I released my tight grip from his hand, in doing this he placed both his palms flat on the surface of the wall, he pushed down onto his hands, locking them into the surface, he then managed to lift his whole body straight up and over the wall, he didn't lie down like Katherine and I did, instead he stood straight up and took one deep breath before saying.

"Help Hank up" he then pulled his rucksack from his back and threw it on the floor, dropping to his knees and opening it, he began remerging through the contents of the bag. I looked back over to the shear drop of the wall, I had to help Hank up, he was twice the size of any of us, I could barely hold Nogla's weight, there is no way I would be able to hold his.

"You're joking right?" I asked in reply to Nogla, he didn't say anything, nor did he even acknowledge that I had said anything, I believe he didn't really care what I thought, he just wanted me to do what I was told. I scurried across the wall to get close to the drop once again, as soon as I reached the side of the wall a voice came from below.

"Don't worry about it kid" the voice moaned. Hanks giant hand then threw itself over the side of the wall, gripping the top, followed by his other hand almost straight away, he pulled himself straight up without so much as a groan in pain despite the fact he had blood dripping from almost every part of his body, he like Nogla stood straight up and threw his backpack down to the floor beneath our feet. Both men were unbelievably strong, but Hank was two times as tall then any man I had ever met, his arms were the size of my legs, his head was square and bulky, you couldn't even see his neck, just pure muscle, he was a beast of a man, I was sure glad that he was on our side.

"So this is Vala" Hank said, gazing across the city as I did when I first reached the top.
"The city so nice they named a planet after it" He continued.
"Have you spotted the Mechanics?" Nogla asked him. Hank let out a short grunt in reply before saying
"No as impressive as I had in mind" he sarcastically said in reply to Nogla.
"The building is over there by the way" Nogla said, pointing towards what looked like an unfinished skyscraper, there was scaffolding surrounding it and it had no window or any lights on inside it, just an empty shell of a building, it seemed to be taller than the other buildings around the wall. This one was almost the exact same size as the wall itself. It was grey in colour, and looked like nothing more than smooth concrete in material.
"Alright, pick up Katherine and let's move quickly then lads." Hank said, picking up his bag off the floor and walking across the wall towards this building. I turned my head to look at Nogla, he had walked over to Katherine who was still lying face down, not moving, he picked her up as easily as he did his back, throwing her over his shoulder and then turning to look at me.
"Move" he snapped at me, indicating for me to follow Hank across the surface of the wall.

The top of the wall was thick in width; there were no fences or anything for that matter, to stop people falling off the side, Hank didn't seem to care, he was walking across the top of the wall like it was just another path, he was walking precariously close to the edge of the wall, in fact he occasionally stopped to look over the side we had just scaled, and then would walk to the other side to look down on the small buildings surrounding the inside of the wall. Nogla was trailing behind, he must have been completely drained from not only climbing but also the running beforehand, and now he had to carry Katherine on his back, even though she wasn't heavy it would still cause him great strain to his back.

We approached the abandon building, however the building itself was not connected to the wall nor was there anything leading from the wall to the building, and it was still a rather long way down, if we jumped the distance there was a possibility of landing wrong and breaking both our legs. Suddenly there was a loud whack! I looked over to where Hank had been standing and to my surprise he was now gone.
"Throw Katherine to me" A deep voice said from the abandon building, I looked down and standing on the roof of the building was Hank, his backpack was on the ground next to him. How did he land that without hurting himself? It's at least a twenty foot drop onto hard concrete, and there was a gap between the wall and building of another ten feet. I couldn't help but think that these men were much more capable to do this mission then I was, they were strong and fast and clearly knew what they were doing, something I did not. Nogla took Katherine off his back and bent down with her in his arms, dangling her over the edge of the wall towards Hank, Hanks hands were raised with anticipation waiting for Katherine to be dropped into them.

I averted my eyes back to the part of the wall we had climbed up to see how far we had walked to get to the building, it couldn't of been longer than a minute walk, I could see the small patches of Hank and Kath's blood scattered across the ground and couldn't help but think how perfectly coordinated this mission was, we scaled the wall and made it to the top at the exact part we needed to, too insure that the building we needed to get too was close by. The whole mission so far seemed the planned very well, other than the obvious fact of everyone deciding to wait until last minute to fill me in on any actual facts about this mission or what it would be exactly that I would have to do.

As I was thinking this the two men were preparing to drop Kath, Nogla was now almost leaning completely over the edge of the wall, he was hanging over a massive drop through the gap between the wall and the building and yet seemed unhinged by the fact that one slip and him and Katherine would fall through the darkness to the dark cold ground below. There was no smell I'm the air, no industrial smoke or factory smell, the air was clean and pure, and there was no sounds either, no people, no car horns or even engines, the air was still and quiet, any loud noise we made could probably be heard distinctively in anyone of the nearby buildings. I was thinking about warning the guys, however they weren't really making any noise, they weren't even talking to one another, they knew what they had to do, they didn't really need to say anything.

Katherine fell through the air as Nogla dropped her, her arms flailing around, her legs surprisingly still, she fell quickly and landed straight in Hanks huge arms, he grasped her tight and brought her close to his chest, before bending over and placing her gently on the floor, Katherine no longer had her eyes open, she was sound asleep, either that or she had passed out from the lack of oxygen, or exhaustion. I noticed Hank was still looking up at us, his arms in the same open position that they were for Katherine.

"Go on" Noglas voice said from beside me.

"Go on?" I asked in reply, confused by what he meant, he jolted his head slightly towards Hank.

"You want me to jump?" I asked him nervously.

"Yes" he quickly replied. I looked at him still confused for a moment before drawing my eyes over to Hank. Approaching the edge of the wall and gazing down through the gap all I could see was a pitch black void, no lights, not even the ground below.

"O.k" I repeated quietly under my voice.

"O.k o.k o.k" I carried on repeating all the while pacing forward and back from the edge of the wall to where Nogla was standing, I was doing my best to try and gain the confidence I needed to make this jump.

Hanks arms were open, he had them in a circled shape, they grew bigger and closer as I fell from the wall towards them, the jump wasn't as bad as I thought, I fell straight into his arms and he placed me gently on the ground next to Kath.

"You alright lad?" He asked me, standing back up and facing Nogla on the wall.

"I'm fine" I replied, sliding my bloody hands over Kath's. I looked back up at Hank to see Nogla falling from the wall and landing straight in his arms just like we all had previously, Nogla was not a very big man but he was muscly and was probably the heaviest out of the three of us that had dropped into Hank, yet it didn't faze him at all, he didn't moan, stubble or look like he was struggling at all, he caught him with ease and placed him next to Kath and I, only difference was Nogla was standing up.

"We will stay here the night to regain our strength." Nogla said, looking at Hank and then me on the floor.

"Try to get some sleep; we live for the safe house as soon as the sun rises over that wall." He continued, pointing at the wall after he finished explaining.

We were well hidden from sight, the roof of the building had concrete pillars and half-finished walls darted all around it, we walked to the centre of it and found shelter under a small unfinished roof with three concrete walls surrounding us. Kath remained asleep as Nogla carried her to our spot; we all sat down on the floor other than one of us.

"I'll take first watch" Nogla said, picking up the machete from his bag, the same one that used to be strapped to his leg, and walking to the entrance that we walked through, he stood there, steady and calm, staring out into the dark of night. Hank rolled over and closed his eyes, he fell asleep quickly, I could tell by the way he began loudly snoring, it even echo slightly throughout the building, I amusingly thought to myself that it would be the worst ending to this journey if the Federation found us due to his snoring and killed us all while we slept peacefully under the nights sky.

Kath was fast asleep still, I was lying next to her on the hard concrete floor, I had removed my black jacket and placed it over her to keep her warm, it was a freezing cold night, the temperature seemed to continue to drop the more time went past. The last thing I saw before my eyes shut and my mind fell soundly asleep, a well-deserved sleep after the day we all had, was Katherine, and watching my hand resting upon hers as I drifted away, relaxed and calm for the first time tonight, my hands still aching, worse than before, every bruise and scratch was inflicting intense pain, but it was easy to ignore when you were as tired as I was, my eyes tightly shut, the sound of nothing but snoring as I fell into my deep dreamless sleep.

CHAPTER 18

TIME TO GET TO WORK

"LEO, LEO WAKE up, we have to go!" A soft voice whispered, I could feel a hand on my arm rubbing it gently up and down. I opened my eyes to see Katherine staring at me, she was smiling. The sun light brightly shone behind her, this was the first time I had seen sunlight on Vala, every time I had been outside, or seen outside it was nothing more than endless darkness. The sun was shining through the unfinished ceiling above us and the doorway where Nogla and Hank were now both standing; talking about something, all I could make out from their conversation was a bunch of muffles and grumbles.

"Here's your jacket" Katherine said handing me my black, torn jacket.

"Come on you two, time is up." Hank barked at us. They didn't wait want longer; they just walked off and left me and Katherine there. I looked at her and she was still looking back at me.

"I bandaged your hands for you" she said smiling, I looked down and she was holding them both, the gloves were still on, but they felt so much better, almost completely healed, no pain at all.

"Thank you, I can hardly feel anything" I replied all the while staring at mine and her hands holding each other's.

"Come on, they found a ladder down to the street" she said, standing up still holding my hand, pulling me to my feet.

"Where's my bag?" I asked her, looking around on the floor to see if I could find it.

"Destroyed" she answered; I averted my eyes back to hers.

"No one is this city uses rucksacks unless you are from the poor areas, it is considered a sign of poverty, having to carry so many belongs at one time, the equipment in them was only meant to get us over the wall, when we reach the safe house we will receive more equipment, but for now all we have is this." She explained handing me what appeared to be a bottle.

"A bottle?" I asked

"Yes, you drink from it, now let's go" she answered, dragging me towards the opening in the concrete walls.

We left the roof of the building and climbed down the ladder on the side, each step on the ladder made a slight beep when I part of your body touched it, Kath said this way people would know when they are correctly placed on the ladder to continue moving. We climbed down into an alleyway off the main walkway, Hank and Nogla were standing there waiting for us, it was dark and as hidden as the roof was, there were large square bins outside doorways and two vehicles in the alleyway as well, but other than that it seemed rather empty, no people to be seen other than the occasional person walking past the entrench to it.

The people of Vala dressed very differently to the rebels, they were all tidy and clean, the men all wore their hair the same way and the women too, the men had their hair clean cut down the centre, parted to each side, on Earth I think it was called curtains. The woman all had their hair short, almost the same length and the men's, only the woman's was not styled; it went from the shoulders around to back all the same length other than the fringe, the hair stopped just short of the eyebrows. I tried not to look too much at them as we came out the alleyway.

"Try to look natural" Nogla said, leading the way. He turned left and we all followed, the sunlight shined down bright on us, my eyes hadn't yet seen the light, not for a few days, it struck them as if someone was shining a torch directly in my face. I rose my hand to cover the sun from directly coming into contact with them and waiting patiently for them to adjust, at the same time I was walking forward, I could see the other threes battered shoes walking along the ground as I looked down to avoid the sun, it was easy to tell them apart from the other people as everyone else wore the same shoes and there were not half destroyed and hanging off their feet.

As the sun dimmed and my eyes started to adjust I lowered my hand. Directly In front of us, standing tall, soaring into the sky above was a large white skyscraper, I followed it up, gazing at it in all its glory, as I reached about halfway I started to see the mechanics flying around it, they were so much closer now than before, darting in and out of buildings, and dashing across the sunny sky above, there were many clouds in the sky, the sun would disappear and then reappear as the dark clouds engulfed it, swallowing it before spitting it back out again like a child dissatisfied with its food. Next to the large building was three more exactly the same, each was connected with a small thin bridge, due to it being so high up I couldn't make our what was on the bridges but it looked like hundreds of small moving dots, people perhaps? Maybe the bridges were a way for people to travel between them easily without having to come all the way down here.

"This way" Nogla said, turning left again off the main walkway, we were trying to avoid people as best we could but there were so many all walking along the walkway, despite our scruffiness and ruined clothing no one seemed to really I pay any attention to us, or each other, they just walked facing forward, most were actually in perfect lines, only a small few including ourselves were walking from side to side as well, moving out of the way of other people whenever we were in the way. The next path we turned into was even smaller, and had less people on it, there was a small tree by the entrance of a building, and a little bridge that lead up to another entrance, each building seemed to look the same from a distance but up close they all had their own small quirks, making each one slightly different from the next.

We had been walking for at least an hour now, the buildings were gradually getting smaller in size and the colours started changing, we had passed to green tower blocks now, and one red, the red was twice the size as the greens and took twenty minutes to walk around due to the insanely large width of the building. The strange thing was that the people also seemed to change, most people near the coloured towers had worse clothes then we did, not a single one had the same clothes, most were torn and tattered, and the majority of them didn't have much hair, the ones that did were scruffy and greasy.
"How much further Katherine?" Hank asked

"Two more rights, second building on the left just opposite Tower 431" she replied

"Good memory" I whispered under my breath.

We passed the final corner and Katherine took the lead ahead of Nogla, there was another green tower on the right side of the pathway, the entrance was large and hard a few people queuing outside of it, some were holding young crying children and others were with their family holding as many things as they could carry, they all looked poor and unhealthy, most had cuts on their faces and arms, some had broken bones, I could tell because they had their arms in slings, or they were bandaged.

"For a futuristic city with flying cars and massive gorgeous skyscrapers there is a lot of normal looking people here, and poor people." I explained to Hank as he was the closest; Nogla and Kath had walked off ahead towards a building on the right side of the pathway opposite the tall green tower.

"Most of the people in the city are rich, and the majority is wealthy, however not everyone can have loads of credits and live a great life in Vala, people like these work in the factories underground, they get paid very little and in return for working they get to spend a night in one of the coloured towers, different colours for different jobs, green is the power stations." Hank answered,

"So all these people, even the young children, work in an underground power station?" I asked in reply.

"Unfortunately Leo, yes, it's a day's work for a night's sleep. If you are too tired to work then you sleep on the street, or the Federation soldiers may send you deeper underground to work the coal mines." He answered.

"I've lived around the city my whole life, I have met many people who escaped and scaled the wall to join the Rebellion, some even made it passed the Raptors, but till this day I have never heard of anyone coming out of those mines alive." He continued.

Gazing at the green building closer I could see something unusual about it, there was a small type of railroad attached to the side of the green building. A vehicle dropped down at intense speeds, it created a gush of wind that went flying in our direction, moving my hair around my face, the ground shook as the train like vehicle was swallowed by a large open hole in the ground. I could only guess that the trains led to the factories underground, it must have been an easy way to transport people from the building to the workplace without them having to work around the city, wasting time. It also means that it would be easy for them to tell who was actually working for the rooms; they could easily tell it the trains brought people there and back from where they slept. That must make increasingly difficult for the people who don't work to get a room or food for the night, especially if most people are sent straight there from their rooms. I wonder how many of these trains were in one building, they weren't very large, by size alone they could only hold a maximum of a hundred people, you'd need a lot to get everyone there quickly, considering the building was so large they was clearly a rather large amount of people that worked in the factory, which meant they'd need more than just one train to take the Valarian people there and back in efficient time.

We approached the building and stood behind Nogla and Katherine. Nogla lent forward and knocked on the large rusted red door. The building was tall and thin, parts of the walls were crumbling away and the door itself had four large holes in it, they were patched up with some kind of wooden material. The building was no taller than two hundred feet and was a dull brown colour. It was nothing like the skyscrapers we had passed to get here, and it was wedge between two much mightier buildings, both as battered as this one but they were much larger in scale by comparison. There was a loud creek as the door pulled open, behind was a small young woman, she had brown eyes and dark hair, she was very unclean but had no scars or cuts on her body from what I could see, she had small nose that was slightly crooked, and her hair was just long enough to cover her ears. She was wearing a dark grey top that was ripped down the centre; her trousers were yellow combats that looked like she had worn every day for years. The smell that came from the building was revolting; it smelt like blood urine, as well as damp and just human filth. There was a small staircase behind the woman leading straight up further into the building; there were no other doors or ways into the building other than this one staircase.

"Katherine" the woman said as she glared at Kath.
"Hi Laura" Katherine replied looking at the woman. Without hesitation the young woman jumped out of the doorway and threw her

arms around Katherine, they both embraced one another as if they were lost sister who had just been reunited.

"Quick, quick come in!" The young woman insisted, releasing her arms from around Katherine, she grasped her by the hand and began leading her inside the foul smelling building. As Katherine entered the building she shot a quick look back at Hank and Nogla, giving them a slight nod. Both men relaxed, and entered the building behind the two girls now going up the stairs.

"Come on" Hank said to me as he entered the building. I stepped nervously forward I tot the brown building, holding my breath slightly as I entered. Ironic how most of this journey I was struggling for air and now I'd much rather not breathe in any.

We walked up the wooden staircase and straight into an open room, there was a small cream colour sofa opposite the doorway that Katherine and Laura were already sitting on, it was as dirty as the house it was in, covered in unusual stained and dotted with countless holes. On the left on the sofa was a desk, upon the desk was a large amount of computer equipment with two men gawking at the four monitor screens that were resting on other equipment, stuff I had never seen before, a lot of it looked like the same stuff Magic Man had back at the base.

"Please guys take a seat" Laura said to the three of us as we walked in, Nogla turned to look at me and Hank and gave the same nod Kath gave to him. We both walked over to the second sofa just opposite the one that both Kath and Laura was sitting on, both sofas were completely identical, other than the tears and stains which of course were in different locations. Hank and I sat on it and looked over toward Laura. Nogla was standing next to an armchair in between the two couches that we were sitting on. He had his arms folded, and was looking down at us all, Laura gazed up at him and shuffled a bit, moving forward as if she was preparing to talk.

"I am so glad you managed to make it!" She said with a large grin across her face.

"I hope you didn't have to much trouble climbing the wall, many of the old routes have been patched since you last made the climb Katherine." She explained, placing her hand upon Katherine's bruised legs.

"I tried to get a message out but I received the Intel too late and knew that you would already be on your way here." She finished

"its fine Laura" Katherine replied.

"Do you have the equipment checked and ready for us?" Nogla interrupted. Laura glanced over towards him standing up.

"You know you can sit" She said to Nogla, the smile still across her dirt covered face. Nogla didn't reply, instead he just stood there staring at her, his arms locked in a crossed potion.

"Yes, there are four bags ready for each of you in the backroom, they have been triple checked and all have the equipment you specifically asked for." She explained, Nogla started walking over to the backroom without hesitation, he grasped the handle and walked straight inside, the two men at the monitors looked over at him and stared dauntlessly. Hank slowly got up and walked over as well, he looked at Laura and Katherine as he reached his stance and gave them both a small nod before walking into the room to join Nogla.

"You must be Leo" Laura said, picking up a small bottle from the table in between us, taking a sip from the lip before placing it back upon the table.

"I guess" I replied.

"I have heard a lot about you, make sure you look after Katherine tonight" she snapped slightly at me, still smiling however.

"Wait, tonight?" I confusingly asked them both.

"The mission is tonight? I thought we would be staying here for a bit longer than that." I continued. Both girls looked at each other before looking over towards me.

"No Leo, we don't have the time to stay longer, we are only here to pick up our equipment." Kath answered.

"The Federation Tower is just beyond Tower 431, once your men have finished checking your equipment you are free to go, however please make sure you eat first." She asked pointing over towards another wooden table; this one was much smaller than the one between us and had a large metal pot on it with a small stream of steam rising slowly from the contents inside.

"Thank God I'm starving" I said standing up and walking over the steaming metal pot. There were small grey bowls next to the pot, I picked one up and used the ladle inside to pour the contents of the stew into my bowl. The steam rose from the bowl and struck my nose, the smell was remarkable, it smelled like meat and gravy. I took a deep breath in, inhaling the smell into my lungs, before picking up a small wooden spoon and lifting the stew towards my mouth, taking a large gulp swallowing the hot liquid into my stomach; it warmed my throat as it poured down into my belly.

"That is amazing" I groaned through my wet lips, the stew dripped down my check onto my chin before falling onto the ground below.

"Glad you like it" She said smiling. Nogla and Hank then walked out of the room, they were each carry two rucksacks in their hands.

"Katherine" Nogla said, throwing one over to Katherine on the sofa, she reached out and caught the flying bag, standing up and placing it on her back.

"Leo" Hank said, handing me another black rucksack, I held the bowl in my left and reached out with my right hand to grab the bag, it was completely identical to the one I previously had.

"Guys you have to try this before we leave, its delicious" I said to them as they walked past me towards the staircase.

"Raptor meat and faeces, no thank you" Hank replied as they walked through the opening down the stairs.

"Faeces" I muttered under my voice.

"Come on Leo Katherine said, standing up and hugging Laura, before following Nogla and Hank down the stairs.

"Faeces" I repeated looking at Laura, she was just standing there smiling back at me.

"Thought that was gravy" I said to her, my stomach rumbled with disgust, I could feel the food unsettling inside my body, all I could picture was this pile of dung now sitting at the bottom of my throat.

"Good luck Leo, don't forget what I said." Laura called out as I left the room following the three down the stairs towards the main walkway once more, the two men at the computers didn't once glance up as we all walked out the room, nor did they say anything as we sat there talking. The room had no proper light in it, just one window above the sofa that Katherine and Laura were sitting on, and then there were the artificial lights, only one bulb on the ceiling to be exact, not sure about the other room as I never went inside it.

We walked out of the front door, I closed it behind us, Laura was standing at the top of the stairs when I shut the door behind, she was no longer smiling, she looked worried, I could make out tears streaming down her face. I imagine most people knew what a dangerous mission this was, breaking into one of the Federations Towers, most were trying to not talk about to avoid the awkward subject of almost certain death, hence why Laura must have been smiling, she was trying to hide the fact that she was terrified for our safety, the only way she could was by shielding it with a different emotion, and that one was the fact that she was just happy to see us and know that we made it over the wall safely. But now it didn't matter, however she reacted to us leaving didn't matter, we were still leaving and still would have regardless. This was something we had to do, what the Federation were doing to people like me wasn't humane, it wasn't right, and no one has any power to do anything about it, I didn't even know if people in this city even knew about it, about all those innocent people being kidnapped and placed into those machines their entire life. They were my people, I was one of them, and if getting this information from the Federation Tower was going to help those people in any way at all then that is exactly what I was going to do. Or at least try to do, but the likely outcome was that Katherine, Nogla, Hank and myself would get to the Tower, perhaps make it inside, but that would be as far as we get and the reality would be that we would never walk out of the building alive.

CHAPTER 19

INTO THE LION'S DEN

IT WAS NO longer as light as it previously was outside, the sun had begun to set, the sky above was still filled with grey clouds that would occasionally move between us and the sun, blocking our heat for a moment as dropping the temperature dramatically. The patches of sky that were not disguised behind darkened clouds were now a peach, orange colour, there were small bright lines shooting across the sky, each a similar colour, some were red, most were orange or yellow, they looked like millions of dancing firefly's, each striking one another and duelling above our heads. The sky lit up with this amazing battle of colours as the sun reflected the land below crafting this outstanding contrast of colours.

"Leo" Katherine said, she was walking out in front but she had now paced backwards to walk next to me, Nogla was leading the way with Hank only a few feet behind.

"Do you know where we are going" She asked.

"The Federation Tower" I replied with a nod, I could see the entrance to the green tower and the building we had just left disappear behind yet another large building as we left that particular street to walk down another.

"That's right" She answered.

"When we get there you will be nothing more than my shadow, stay behind me and do as I say exactly." She ordered.

"O.K" I replied to her.

"Here, put this on the right side of your chest." She asked me, handing me a small labelled badge. The words Federation would across the top of it in large black writing, there was a bar code below the writing and nothing else, the badge was no longer than my forefinger and no wider than the length of my thumb.

"What is this?" I asked Katherine, placing the badge where she told me to, looking at it down on my chest.

"The Federation soldiers will scan you as we enter the building, these badges will come up on their system as maintenance workers, will we be able to enter the building without causing them to draw any unnecessary attention towards us." She explained.

We continued walking down the narrow roads, the amount of people varied upon the size of the streets themselves. The buildings once again began changing back to the white ones we had seen before, each reaching into the sky, disappearing into the sun set, orange sky, above the clouds. It had been at least an hour since I had seen a coloured building, also they all started gaining their individuality once more, the shapes became more unusual, I passed the circle one and was confused to wonder how the building itself managed to stay standing up, the supports were thin and slender, they did not look strong to support a skyscraper of such height and unusual shape.

"Katherine I know so little about you, or any of you for that matter, this may be the last chance I get to have a proper conversation with you. Tell me something about yourself, what made you want to join the Federation, where are you from?" I asked her as we passed another turning, it was strange not having vehicles on the same level as me, you only had to gaze up and you would see the vehicles flying above your head, no roads on the ground, not even in the air, the vehicles followed an invisible street, organised and structured. Although that might have been due to the fact that the magnets controlled where the vehicles went, there was no way of changing speed or direction, the magnets were coded to send the vehicle in whatever direction was entered. At least that is what I believed; nothing else really made sense, there is no way that thousands of different magnets could each individually move around any direction they wanted, the magnetic fields would get mixed up causing a large amount of collisions and crashes, the only way to prevent this would be for the cars to enter certain codes and only go in set directions.

"I grew up here Leo, in a building a lot like the one we were just in" Katharine answered.

"One night when I was little I heard a scream, I woke up to see the Federation soldiers inside my home, I hid at the top of the stairs looking down on my family being beaten within an inch of their lives by the soldiers." She continued, I could see her eyes glisten in the sun light as tears formed inside them.

"My mum looked up at me and smiled, the soldiers took them and my sisters away from me, my twin sisters were new born, they were taking them for the machine you were in" She paused, darting her eyes over to me.

"After they left I was all alone, and that's when Henry found me" She looked up towards Hank and Nogla before continuing.

"Henry took me in and looked after me, he found me queuing up to enter a Green tower, but because I was too young to enter if I had made it to the front the Federation soldiers would have taken me to the facility to be experimented on, so he removed me from the queue and carried me on his back all the way to the wall, he then carried me down the wall still on his back" she said with a little smile across her face.

"I grew up in the base that you saw earlier, learning to hunt, fight and kill, he taught me to write and read, and hide from anyone who would do us harm. Until I hit 16." She paused again, this time she did not prepare to continue, she paused as if to finish talking all together.

"What happened when you turned 16?" I anxiously asked. She stop walking and looked at me, I too stop and starred back.

"You found me at the Federation Facility, I was there for a while, that's all I want to say" she continued walking, this time much faster, I struggled to keep to her pace.

"What about Nogla and Hank" I asked trying to change the subject and pointing at the two men in front of us, they were much further ahead now but still in sight.

"Hank was born in the base, he grew up there. He was always much taller and stronger than the other boys and soon became renowned for his fighting skills, when Henry first saw him in combat he insisted that

Hank join his private group of soldiers, Hank excepted and has been a member ever since." She explained, her voice was in harsh tone now, I could see she was upset about having to talk about the facility she was working in.

"And Nogla?" I asked, still trying to take her mind away from the previous conversation subject.

"Nogla found us, he was no older than ten when he turned up at the base, he didn't talk for years after that. Nogla has always been a naturally good hunter, he was the best in the entire rebellion, which made Henry gain a great interest in him, and since then he been one of our main sources of food, he never told us where he came from, or even his real name, Henry gave him the name Nogla, it means hunter in some languages, seemed appropriate for him." She continued, I can't imagine growing up around people who had no real idea of where I came from or anything about me for that matter.

We approached a turning in the pathway, Nogla and Hank seemed to be standing beside it, they were talking, but did not turn the corner, just stood behind the wall that was next to it. The sky grew dark with night approaching; the clouds engulfed the stars and hid them from our sight once more. There was no moon to be seen either, just a darkened sky with the city lights reflecting off the clouds. The buildings around us all slowly lit up one by one, some had white flashing lights placed on the outside of them, they were emitting a loud buzzing sound, like an alarm. People on the streets seemed to be rushing to these particular buildings, crowding around the doors, and the number of Mechanics in the sky began to shrink in numbers, leaving only half the amount that was there before flying around.

"What's going on" I openly asked as Katherine and I approached the other two standing on the street corner.

"Curfew" Hank said quietly.

"We're here" Nogla said looking at Katherine. She walked around him and glanced over to the other side of the street, around the corner was a large silver building, the first few floors were made of pure glass, you could see into the lobby and the floors above. Further up the building the glass turned into a black sheet that shielded the public's eyes from all view of inside the building.

"Jackets lads" Katherine ordered. Nogla and Hank placed their rucksacks on the ground and unzipped the top of them. I remembered what Katherine had previously stated about rucksacks being a sign of poverty in the city, which made sense why we picked ours up in the poor area of the city, there would be no attention drawn to the fact that we were carrying a bag such as ours. Both men pulled out white jackets from their bags and placed their black ones inside instead to replace the white ones. They also pulled a clipboard out, only this was no ordinary clipboard, these were electronic and bright green in colour with a red light going around the outside of them. They pulled the jackets over their clothes and tidied them up to look neat. Katherine had also done the same; the white jackets all had the same writing in the top right hand coroner. F.E.D.E.R.A.T.I.O.N it stated in clear black writing, the exact same to the badge Katherine had given me, and below the writing was a small bar code similar to my own.

"Do I not need one?" I asked, checking my bag for a white coat of some kind only to find that my rucksack was completely empty, there was nothing inside at all, how could it of been so heavy then? I starred at the empty insides of my bag with a smacked looked of confusion.

"Nope, each group that enters has a labourer and three observers; the labourer usually comes from the poor area of the city, which is why it is important that you stay grubby and unclean." Katherine snapped at me with a sarcastic smile.

"Great" I replied in a low pitch voice.

The surrounding area of the Federation building was wide open, no buildings were close to it, and every building that was in the immediate area was much smaller than the tower itself. The tower was not as large as some of the skyscrapers we had seen but still large in comparison to most of the buildings we had walked past in the other areas of the city. It was the shape of a rhombus, only the further up the tower went the thinner it got, the top was no bigger than the roof of the safe house we had visited.

"Right everyone know what we are doing?" Katherine asked. No one spoke on reply, Nogla and Hank just nodded slightly.

"Urm I don't have a clue what I'm doing" I replied to Katherine. Nogla and Hank completely ignored me and turned around, they began slowly walking, their clipboards in hand.

"Yes you do Leo, you're my shadow, only say what I tell you to say, remember?" She asked. I didn't know how to answer that, it wasn't a lot of information to go considering we were all about to enter one of the most dangerous places in the city. I didn't nod, nor did I talk, I just gazed at her in fear.

"Come on" she said, tugging my arm around the corner before letting it go. Nogla and Hank were walking in front of us, and Katherine was walking slightly behind me. Each of them left their rucksacks on the floor around the corner; I guess they got everything they needed from inside it.

As we approached the building I found myself panicking more and more, I managed to hide my fear well but I could feel myself start to sweat, and my breathing started to become heavier the close we got. The building look taller and larger the closer we got to it, it was the centre piece of four walkways that lead directly towards it, a large building sat on each corner of the walkways before the wide opening leading to the Federations Tower that stood like a monument in the centre of this open space. The building was well lit from the inside but seemed empty. There was one man behind a single desk that was on the bottom floor, there was only one door into the building which was made from clear glass, the walls that surrounded it were also made from the same material. As Nogla approached it he raised his hand and the door slid slowly open, it was a double door and opened from the middle, each section of the door went into the glass walls next to it and allowed entry for the four of us. Nogla entered without hesitation, Hank cautiously followed behind, their footsteps were at a slowed pace, I gained quickly behind them and slowed to match their pace, I could hear Katherine enter behind me and the door slide close behind her. We were inside.

The lobby was completely empty other than one man and a desk, everything was made from clear white, and there was not a single speck of dust or dirt anywhere other than on my clothing. Even the man behind the desk was wearing pure white clothing, his hair was even dyed white, he was clean shaven with no marks on his face at all, his skin was a tanned white colour and his eyes were as blue as a summers day sky, his eyebrows were neatly trimmed and white as well to match his hair, he was wearing a suit with a white tie and shirt, the overcoat and trousers were once again white. I looked around the room and realised that you couldn't see outside, the glass on this side looked like nothing more than a sheet of paper, it matched the ceiling and walls and blocked complete vision of the surrounding area. As we approached the desk the man gazed up at us.

"Hold" he quietly said in a calm voice, his eyes dropped back down to what appeared to be a monitor screen.

There was suddenly a quiet hum, I looked up to see a small circled machine flying around the head of Nogla, the machine was a tiny silver ball, it was humming as it flew around the ceiling. The machine stopped in front on Nogla and shot out a small blue light, the light scanned Nogla up and down before stopping at his bar code that was attached to his jacket, the machine held the light over the barcode for a second before letting out a slight bleep, it then moved onto Hank, the machine once again began scanning, it scanned Hank from the flow to the tip of his before resting over the bar code in his jacket, it hovered there and then let out the same quiet bleep. I was next, my heart rate rose as the tiny silver ball flew over towards me, it flew around my head twice before stopping in front of me, I guessed that the reason it flew around me was to check how large the area was that it needed to scan. As soon as it stopped the same blue light shot out from the machine and shinned brightly on my clothing, the light moved from my feet up towards my face, it scanned my face once and then slowly moved down again, however as the light started to move down it suddenly stopped, it hovered just below my neck before the light once again rose up and scanned my face. I didn't move, I didn't even breathe, I just stood there with my eyes wide open staring straight ahead, I could feel my heart beat through my chest, I wonder if the machine could also feel my heart beat, maybe that's why it was scanning me longer, it knew I was a fraud, had I just blown the operation?

The man behind the desk averted his eyes up slightly and began looking at me, this only worried my further, he didn't look at either Nogla or Hank when they received their scans, why was he looking at me. The man then caught my eye and glared at me, he looked disgusted by me, his eyebrows rose, his teeth tightened, he looked as if he was about to be sick, perhaps it was because he believed I was from the poor district, he must have not wanted one of those kind inside this building. The machine suddenly bleeped, I looked down to see it hovering over my bar code, it then flew back up toward the ceiling and over my head towards Katherine standing behind me, I did not turn around, my eyes stayed fixed on the wall in front of us, I could feel the man staring at me, and just about see him in the courier of my eye, making the same face, pure disgust. I let out a sigh of relief and felt my heart rate decrease once more.

The final bleep filled the air as the machine finished scanning Katherine, I saw it shoot pass my head and land behind the desk where the man was sitting.

"Continue to floor 717" the man said, he pressed a button behind his white desk, the wall in front of us suddenly began shaking, there was a small crack down the centre of it, the crack grew larger and larger, a bright light shone out of the small gap and created a small line across my body from the ground up. Behind the wall was a lift, there was a small area with an endless number of buttons on the far wall of the tiny elevator. Nogla walked forward into the opening and stood inside, he turned around and faced out towards us, with that Hank then followed, I nervously lifted my legs and pursued Hank into the elevator, Katherine's footsteps echoed behind me as she followed the two of us, I caught a glimpse of the man's eye as I walked into the doorway, he was still glaring at me with hate filled eyes, it made me very uncomfortable, feeling someone's hate for me pierce my skin. The air inside the elevator smelled clean and fresh, like the air inside the lobby only less filtered. I turned around as I entered and faced outside the doorway towards Katherine, watching her walk into the elevator in front of us and turn just as we had, I was now standing in front of Nogla and Hank inside the tight space and staring at the back of Katherine's head as the doors closed slowly in front of us, they made a clicking sound once shut, and before we knew it we could feel the lift begin to move up the building.

"Nogla, now" Kath said in a sharp tone, Nogla turned around and began rubbing his hands up and down the surface of the wall, feeling for something. I turned to watch him, slowly backing myself into the far corner to give him a bit more space. Hank suddenly smashed his clipboard against the wall as hard as he could, the clipboard let out a few sparks as it shattered into hundreds of small pieces. The red strip around the clipboard had fallen off and was the only part that seemed to remain intact, Hank bent down and picked it up, as he held the red strip it bent over towards the floor, he grasped it tight before whacking it against his leg, the red strip began to light up, becoming brighter, the flimsy material that it was made from seemed to harden, it became a long glowing stick, he fiddled around with the bottom of it and the top suddenly sparked, it shot small blue sparks into the air.

"What's that?" I asked Hank with anticipation.

"Stinger" he said, bringing it down beside his leg. It stretched from his hand and finished just below his knee, the whole thing was a glowing red light other than the occasional spark at the end.

"Nogla how's it looking" Hank barked at Nogla, his eyes locked on the door in front of him. Nogla had removed a panel from below the buttons darted across the wall of the elevator to reveal a control circuit of some kind. He had his clipboard wired connected to a few lose wires that were hanging out of the panel itself.

"5, 4, 3, 2, 1." Nogla counted, when he reached 1 the lift lights fizzled and then shut off, we were now standing in complete darkness. The only thing that gave off any light was the two remaining clipboards that Kath and Nogla were holding, and the weapon that Hank seemed to of created from his broken one.

"System reboot" a female voice said as the lights fizzled before turning back on, they had now changed colour however, and were shinning a bright red, as bright as the weapon Hank was carrying.

"Good job" Kath said, she too then smashed her clipboard against the surrounding wall and snapped the red strip against her leg turning it into the same weapon Hank and now Nogla, picking his up from the floor, were holding.

"Stay behind us Leo" Kath said, moving to the front of the lift, Nogla and Hank joined her, I was now standing behind all three of them, each of them had a weapon and I did not, hence why I was very glad to not be standing by the door.

"There will be two guards on each side of the elevator door when it opens, if you strike fast you will be able to naturalise them before they can fight back." Katherine explained to Nogla and Hank who had now stepped in front of Katherine and were crouched down by the elevator door. Katherine was standing in between them both slightly further back and then I was right behind her. Each of them was holding a Stinger in their hands, gripping it tightly, anxiously waiting for the door to open. My heart was in my throat, without the effects of Awakening there was nothing I could do to help them, I just had to stay behind them, stay hidden and out of sight.

"What colour?" Nogla whispered under his voice.

"Blue" Katherine replied. The tension grew thick; I could smell the sweat in the air, feeling it dripping from my forehead off my nose onto the ground below. Blue, were those the same ones Katherine and I ran into in the Facility, Katherine was almost dead, if the pill didn't kick in when it did she would have been as well as me. And now they were going to have to fight two more of them? My nervousness grew, the doors seemed to stay shut for an eternity, no one said a word, not a single person moved an inch, the air was still, all eyes focuses on the door, just watching, waiting.

CHAPTER 20

WHERE DO WE GO NOW?

THE DOOR SHOT open, on the other side was a long white corridor, it looked almost exactly the same as the one from the facility, the one where I had been dragged across the floor to be terminated, I was right next to two black suits then and I managed to escape? What they said back at the base made more sense now, the only reason I escaped is because they wanted to follow me back to the rebellion base, could they off done that? Had I lead them there? Jane was there, little Teara, even Magic Man, all those young children would end up living a life in those machines because of me. My mind wandered back to the task at hand, I gazed down the long white corridor it was completely empty, there were doors all the way up the right and left hand side, and built in fluorescent white lights shine bright down from the ceiling. The floor itself was so clean that it actually reflected the lights off them; you could see them as clearly as looking at them directly in the reflection alone. Then my eyes saw them, there was two men standing right outside the elevator, I could see their blue selves hanging out of their dale black suit jacket, they began to slowly turn around to look inside the elevator.

Before their heads could even glance towards us Hank and Nogla had shot out of the lift, Nogla threw his legs straight under the man on the right, knocking him straight to the hard ground below, Hank took a different approach to his, he lifted the other blue suit clean off the ground, charging him into the wall, smashing his head against it before throwing the man straight to the ground. Nogla had now launched his Stinger into the air, he brought it down with a mighty blow, striking the man directly across his chest, the man let out a loud moan. Nogla then picked up the man from the floor and wrapped the Stinger around his throat, cutting off the air supply through the man's windpipe, crushing it tight with his weapon, pulling tighter and tighter. The man began kicking in mid-air, his grew bloodshot, you could hear him chocking on nothing but his own tongue.

My eyes darted back to Hank, he had the man complete elevated over his head, the man lifted his knee and launched it straight into Hanks cheek, you could hear a loud crack and a splash of thick red blood fell from Hanks lips onto the ground, the man fell down to his feet in stance, and turned to face Hank, he was still holding his cheek agony. Nogla was now being repetitively slammed against the wall behind him, his back cracking as the man he was chocking refused to let go of his precious oxygen, but Nogla was not letting he go, he wrapped his legs tight round the man's waist, the more he resisted the more he wrapped, like a venomous snake draining its pray of all its energy before killing it. Hank was now in a fist fight with the blue suit, he threw a punch that was deflected to the side, the man countered with a hard haymaker, it struck Hanks chin with unbelievable force, knocking him straight to the ground, the man then stood over Hank and raised both his hands in the air, as if preparing to bring them down into Hanks skull, crushing it into a pulp. Hank looked up at the man with fear in his eyes, he had blood dripping from his lips and nose, his eye was servilely bruised and his chin was swallow from the brutal punch he had just received. The man brought down his hands with such force that you could hear them break the wind as they thundered down towards Hank, helpless on the ground. Katherine, who had been guarding me, had now darted forward to try and reach Hank before the strike could connect, but the fight had carried him down the corridor to far, she would never reach him in time.

As the mans cupped hands approach the skull of Hank his arms were suddenly pulled back, his back legs struck with a mighty kick sending him straight to his knees, Nogla had finished his fight quick enough to reach Hank, the other man was now dead on the floor just outside the elevator, I could see blood dripping from his eye sockets, they were dark red in colour, I couldn't even see his pupils anymore through the thick oozing blood that had replaced his natural eye colour. His neck was bruised and had cuts dotted all around it from ear to ear, the man's body was lifeless and empty, just lying there peacefully on the floor. I gazed back over to the fight continuing where Hank was lying, it wasn't much of a fight after Nogla got there, the man was now on the floor, his arms popped as Nogla pulled them behind his back, the man's scream filled the corridor, piercing my eardrums. Nogla then wrapped both his hands around the side of the man's face and snapped his neck to the side, there was a sudden snap, and then nothing more. The snap itself sent shivers down my spine, the last blue suit fell to the floor next to Hank, his head cracked against the surface and a pool of blood formed around the man's cold, dead body.

Nogla stood there; staring at the ground, not move, the only movement that came from his body was the dripping blood from his clenched fists.

"Nogla" Katherine whispered, he turned his head down to Hank reaching out towards him with his blood covered hand, the blood from it creating small puddles dashed across the floor. Hank reached up and grasped his hand tightly; Nogla pulled Hank straight up off the floor like he was nothing more than a bag of paper.

"You alright brother?" Nogla asked Hank as he reached his feet, he wiped his bloody hands on the surface of his trousers and then stood up straight to look at Nogla.

"Thank you man, I thought I was a goner then! I owe you my lii . . . ." The air stood still, there was one loud noise then complete silence, everyone froze, Hank was standing there only his eyes were now empty, his facial expression still. His lips stuck, trying to finish his word, but it was now a word he would never get to finish, it had become forever his last word. Nogla raised his hand to wipe the blood from his face; the whole front of his body was no covered in a thick sheet of dark red. The sound slowly came back in the form of a loud ringing sensation. Hank dropped to the floor, his hands clenching his blood covered stomach, the blood seeped through the cracks in his fingers.

My eyes wandered from Hanks lifeless corpse lying face down on the ground beneath Noglas feet to the large group of blue shirted men that were now standing at the far end of the corridor, the weapon still smoking from the barrel where the round had left it and punctured

Hanks back, cracking through his spine and ribcage, ripping his insides into pieces as the button struck the inside of his stomach, tearing his arteries and veins from all parts of his torso. The man was holding a hand held weapon, it was longer than a normal hand gun and had unusual blue lights across one side of it, the clip in the handle seemed to be bigger than the handle itself because it was hanging out of the bottom of the weapon slightly.

"HhhhhhaaaaNNNNKKK!!" Katherine's voice screamed, getting louder and louder as the ringing in my ears quietened.

Nogla grabbed the dead blue suited man from the floor and raised him up in front of him, his body shot out little pockets of blood all over the floor, the wall and ceiling was painted a dark red with the blood of the man as the rounds from their weapons emptied into his flesh. Nogla was using the man as a human shield, every single blue suited man had now raised his weapon and was trying to strike Nogla with a shot, they appeared to be hitting their dead comrade instead. A few bullets seemed to wiz pass my head, I could hear them striking the walls around us and behind us, the sound of shoots filled the air, the ringing from my ears was almost as loud as the shots themselves. I grabbed Katherine and threw her to the floor to avoid her from getting struck by a fired bullet. The walls becoming dashed with small holes from the gunfire, I held my arm over Katherine to keep her under the line of fire. She was still in shock from watching Hank die before her very eyes. I darted my eyes up to see what Nogla was doing, he was slowly walking back towards us, still holding the body out in front of him, the blue suits were still constantly firing their weapons trying to hit Nogla, as he got closer he looked back at us, only for a split second before he lifted his leg and swung it towards a door next to him, the door cracked and flew open. The white walls surrounding us had now been painted red with the blood of Hank and the other two men, the fact that Nogla was holding one while the other Federation soldiers fired bullets into didn't help the constant flow of blood, the walls themselves now appeared to be bleeding.

Nogla held the body with one hand and signalled back to me to move inside the doorway with the other, the men had now began pacing forward, still firing their weapons trying hit us. I don't think they could really see us behind Nogla and the body he was holding up to block their view. I grabbed Katherine by her collar and lifted her over my shoulder, she was curled up in a ball on the floor, her hands over her head, I couldn't pick her because she'd be too high, and in the view of the soldiers firing at us. So I stayed on my hands and knees, and pulled her towards me, throwing her arms over my shoulders and chucking her whole body onto my back, I raised my head up slightly to lift my legs to a crouching stance, and scurried across the floor towards the open door. Jumping throw the doorway, Katherine fell and slid across the floor slightly, I turned whilst laying on the floor to look back into the corridor, Nogla threw the body to the ground and dived through the doorframe, two rounds struck his legs as he dove throw the air, the blood shot out of his open wounds. He let out a small moan as he crashed onto the floor, kicking his leg at the door to shut it.

We were all laying on the floor now, panting and breathing heavily, we could hear the Federation soldiers trying to break through the door behind us that Nogla had just slammed shut, due to the way he shut it, it was now jammed, he knocked it off its hinges and the door had dug into the wall itself, there was no way they would be able to break through that anytime soon.

"I can't believe he's gone" Katherine cried from the floor, she had curled herself into a ball again, her legs rolled up in front of her face, her arms locked around her knees.

"There's nothing we can do now" Nogla muttered through his panting breaths.

"Leo help me up" he barked at me. I didn't know Hank like the rest of them, he seemed like such a nice man, saved my life more than once and if it wasn't for him we would have never made it this far, so I wasn't as upset as I thought the other two would be, but it was still a sad loss to have, we all knew the risks, I just didn't think the biggest, strongest one of us would be the first to go.

I scrambled to my feet and walked over toward Nogla, he was leaning on one knee and had his other leg stretched across the floor, you could see the two holes where the bullets went in, one was continuously bleeding, spitting out blood over the white floor. The other wound seemed to not be bleeding at all; perhaps the bullet was still inside, stopping the blood from flowing out. Nogla raised his arms for me to help him up, I grasped his hands and pulled him to his feet, he screamed out in pain as he blood covered leg struck the floor.

"Are you alright?" I asked him with concern in my voice.

"Yeah, take me to the wall over there" he moaned, pointing at the wall to the left side to the doorway.

"If I'm right, beyond this wall should be the server room, we can upload the device from their and download what we need." He continued as I carried him over to the side of the room. As we approached it he pulled what looked like one of the blue suits side arms from inside his white and now red jacket.

"Stand back" he said pushing me away from him, barely holding himself up.

Pointing his weapon at the wall he fired a dozen shoots into the same spot, he raised the side arm slightly and repeated the same amount of shots above the hole he had just made. The dust from the walls filled the air, I could taste it on the back of my throat, it stung my eyes making them hard to open, I had to squint them to see what Nogla was doing. He stopped following a pattern and began mindlessly shooting into the wall, it started to open up and you could make out a room on the other side, the sides of the hole he created began to smoke from the intense heat caused by the weapon. The sound of the weapon firing deafened me; the ringing was so loud it started to give me a headache. Before I knew it the sound stopped, the ringing continued, Nogla was still pressing the trigger of the side arm but nothing was happening, he turned it around and began whacking the wall with brute force, chipping away at the last parts of the hole that were blocking the way, the hole was still too small for any of us to fit through. He was swinging his arms with such force that it only took a few seconds for him to double the size of the hole in the wall. I could see raw emotion in his facial expression amongst the mist of dust that now filled the room, his eyes were tear filled and red, his teeth were gripped tight, he looked like he was about to break down and burst into tears.

"Take this" Nogla said pulling a small device from the pocket of his trousers. The dust settled and I could see him sitting on the floor by the busted hole in the wall, the smoke still coming out from certain parts of it due to the heat. He was holding the device in his raised hand, reaching out for me to take it.

"Go through into the other room, you will see a large screen, underneath the screen there will be a long line of sockets, place this device in the third one from the left. It is programmed to download all the software we need within a few seconds." He explained as I leant towards him to grab the device from his hand. As I grasped the device he held it tight for a moment so I couldn't remove it. I looked up at him to see that he was staring at me, his eyes red raw, his face worn and tired.

"When the light turns from red to green remove it quickly and come back here, I'll get Kath ready; we are going to have to leave immediately so make sure that you are back through that hole as soon as that light turns green." There was a slight pause and we were just awkwardly staring at each other for a moment.

"This is the part where you saw you understand" he moaned.

"Nogla I won't let you down, just make sure you and Kate are ready when I come back." I said grabbing his hand. He looked at me with approval, giving me a slight nod as I stood up and made my way through the small hole Nogla made in the wall. I glanced back at Kath to see if she had moved in anyway, she was still frozen, lying on the floor in the same position as before, her arms wrapped around her legs, poor girl, she grew up with Hank, seeing him die like that in front of her, there are no words to describe what she must be feeling, what she must be going through, I hope Nogla can persuade her to move otherwise we are not going anywhere when I return.

I placed my hand on the side of the wall to bring my body forward; I could feel the heat burning through my gloves. My clothes scrapped against the busted rubble, I felt a few parts of my jacket tear as I pulled my body through and up to a standing position, I turned my head back to see my legs clearly so I could thread it through the wall behind me. As I placed my leg safely on the ground below I turned my head back to the front of me and that's when I first got a good look at the room. The smoke and dust had seeped through into here and filled the room with a haze that was hard to see through, amongst the dust was thousands of different colour lights coming off computer equipment darted around the room, there was a large silver desk in this surprisingly small room, it was across the centre of the room, there was nothing on it at all, just built in monitors and screens, some other equipment that I had never seen before, small grey boxes with flashing lights and then around the side of the room were much larger grey boxes with lights and sockets dashed among them.

Right on the other side of the silver desk was the large screen that Nogla had told me about, it ten times the size of any of the other monitors in the room and only had one little white light located on the bottom of it, directly in the centre. Below where the light was were the sockets, they started from one side of the monitor and finished at the other, there was at least thirty.

"Third from the left" I quietly whispered under my voice, navigating my way around the large desk towards the screen that was attached to the wall behind it. Looking down I counted three along from the left and then cautiously raised my hand and placed the device into the socket. Almost immediately the light came on, it was a pink, red colour and was rather dimly lit. I averted my eyes upward to the screen above, it was now on, there was thousands of small boxes opening up and green and white text typing across the screen faster than any man or woman could ever type, a few images opened as well, but they flashed by so fast that it was impossible to clearly make out what they were, one look like a picture of this building from the outside, the light on the device began getting brighter and brighter, the red becoming a dark blood red.

The brighter the light got the quicker the text moved across the screen and the quicker the images flashed by, more boxes opened and closed with different things inside them, some had more moving text, others had images of charts and graphs. To be honest I didn't know what I was looking at, everything shot by across the screen too fast for me to take in and acknowledge what it was that was happening. I turned my head back to the hole and anxiously starred at it for a moment, hoping that they were both safe in there and that the blue suits hadn't yet got in. There was banging against the door when I left, they may have been waiting outside for us, just waiting for us to eventually leave. Perhaps they knew another way to get inside the room and were in progress of doing just that. Then I had a sinister thought, my heart rose slightly, I could feel it in the back of my throat. I dragged my eyes from the hole to across the room; there was a closed white door in the centre of the wall. The amount of noise that Nogla made to get into this room was incredibly, I could still hear ringing as if someone was holding a bell beside my ear. There is no way that they didn't hear that, and if they did then there is nothing stopping them from crashing through that door and killing me, then capturing the device as well as finding Nogla and Kath in the next room and killing them too.

My eyes wandered back to the device, the light was now shining a steady green, without wasting any time I plucked the device straight from the socket, I clicked as I pulled it from the screen and watched it as the glowing green light shit off, turning back to nothing. As I darted around the desk to leave the room, placing one hand above the hole and ducking slightly, something caught me out of the corner of my eye. The screen was still on, displaying the last subjects of the downloaded data, amongst the text boxes and images was one that I could clearly make out, my eyes locked onto it, sending shivers down my spine, my heart sunk, I felt sweat start to trickle down my face. I turned suddenly to slide back through the hole into the other room; I cut my neck on the rubble that was pointing out from parts of the hole.

"We have to go, we have to go now!" I screamed as I re-entered the room, standing to my feet, I could feel warm blood form on my neck where the jagged rocks had cut into my skin. Nogla looked up at me, he was leaning over Katherine, he had torn both his sleeves off his white jacket and wrapped them around the wounds on his leg.

"There was something on the screen" I tried to mutter out through my panting breaths.

"What?" Nogla asked in anticipation, standing up and pacing slowly towards me.

"A picture of the base, the inside of OUR BASE! The bed sits and even people sleeping in them!" I yelled my heart racing.

Noglas expression suddenly changed.

"Pick her up now" he barked at me, walking over to the door that was burrowed into the wall around it. I rushed over to Katherine, picking her clean off the ground and throwing her over shoulders, her legs dropped down the right side of my face, her arms and head over my left. I walked quickly over to Nogla, standing directly behind him. He was now right in front of the door we had come through.

"You ready?" He asked me, his eyes fixed on the broken door. What was he thinking of doing? If a hand full of blue suits couldn't get through that door I doubt we'd be able to leave through it.

"Yes" I murmured in reply.

"My shadow Leo, be my shadow" he whispered, lowering his body down and tensing his arms, his left arm was fully extended to cover his face, his right slightly behind his back, without any time to spare he charged forwards towards the closed door.

Nogla impacted the door with such strength that the door swung open, striking a man on the other side, sending him straight to the floor. Nogla continued thundering forwards, lifting a second man, that was standing right in front of the doorway, clear off his feet, he held the man by his sides, still racing forwards, there was a second door in front of them both, with building momentum they reached the door on the opposite side of the corridor and broke it down with easy, the door made a loud clank as it struck the hard ground below. Nogla struck the man into a metal railing on the other side, sending the man straight over it; he disappeared from my vision completely as he fell beyond the metal railing.

"Shadow" I muttered, rushing forward through the broken door, all the while Katherine's body was flailing around on my back and shoulders. I darted through the corridor to the opening at the other side, my eyes didn't move once from the vision of what was directly in front of me, there could have been hundreds of men either side of those doors, but this was no time to stare at them if there was.

Reaching the other side I could see what the railing was that Nogla had thrown the man over, it was a staircase, I peered over the edge to see the man's lifeless corpse hundreds of feet below, the staircase went down to our left and up to our right, the walls were grey, the railings a shining silver, other than a small red patch of blood where the man had crashed into the hard steel railing.

"Down" Nogla snapped, rushing to turn left to proceed down the stairs.

"Not down" I quickly said, I peered down the centre of the staircase to see a long line of blue blurs moving quickly up the stairs, occasionally there would be a splash of white in between gaps of blue, I assumed this was the other people inside the building, like the man at the desk, coming to assist in our capture or to help kill us.

Nogla looked over the railing as well to see these men climbing the stairs towards us.

"Up then" he again snapped, darting past me and rushing up the stairs.

The sound of feet striking the stairs filled the air, the smell of blood and sweat was now too familiar for me to even notice that it was the only stench in the air. Nogla had thundered ahead, I could just see his feet hoping over the stairs, climbing them as quickly as he could, despite his leg wounds he made the climb quicker than I did, but then again I had Katherine's body dancing around on my back, my arms grew tired and weary the more we climbed the stairs, she wasn't heavy but as well as running up more stairs then I could stop to count and holding her, my energy was being quickly drained from my body. I would have turned my head to see if any of our pursuers were gaining, but Katherine would have completely blocked my view from seeing if they were close, and I was intensely focusing on each step at the moment, one slip with her on my back and we'd both tumble down the flights of stairs to greet the men behind us.

I turned left, over and over and over again, getting higher up the building, until finally I turned to see Nogla whacking a door. The door was at the top of the staircase, it was a large white door with a small handle on it, Nogla had gripped this hand with one hand and had begun repetitively slamming his body in the door using his other hand as a buffer between his body and the door. As I climbed the last of the stairs to approach him the door shot open as Noglas body connected with great force one last time, he stumbled through the door to the other side, trying to regain his balance. As the door swung open I was struck by a wonderful breeze, the wind glided through the opening down the stairs, my hair fluttered as it passed through it, I felt it hit the sweat falling down my face and gently cool each drop. As I rushed towards the door I also felt something else, it was still night, and now raining, the clouds from earlier had finally let go off all the water they were holding and thrown it down on us. The rain struck my face, trickling down, replacing what used to be sweat. It cooled my temperature instantly, so soothing and relaxing after climbing all those stairs.

The rain wasn't the only thing that struck me as I left the staircase and stepped out onto what seemed to be the roof of the building we had just been inside. There was bright lights from every direction, gazing into the sky above I could see Mechanics darted around us, each one circling the roof with patience, like a lion circling its prey, looking for a weakness before striking. The vehicles themselves were as black as the night sky itself, located at the front of the vehicle was a large light that appeared to be shining directly at us on this roof, each one was identical in design, they also appeared to be large than the previous Mechanics I had seen.

"Place your hands in the air and wait to be detained" a deep voice echoed from one of the vehicles.

"Leo quick" Nogla said, rushing over towards what seemed to be a large ventilation duct, there were several placed all over the roof top. I quickly ran over towards him, Katherine still resting on my shoulders. Nogla had made it to the duct before the firing began, each Mechanic unleashed an endless wave over bullet fire, they scattered around the ground of the roof, and around my feet, splashing the already formed puddles up into my face, the raining poured from the sky as well as the bullets, each hitting the roof with force.

I threw Katherine from my shoulders as I approached the duct, Nogla opened his arms to catch her, she flew straight into his open arms and he brought her close to his chest, slowly placing her on the floor, I dived through the air to quickly get my body behind cover.

"Any ideas" I yelled at Nogla as we both sat there, the sound of gunfire filled the air, each round struck the duct and made a loud ringing noise, there were hundreds each second which just caused the duct to begin singing this loud ring constantly. My only guess was the men chasing us has now also made it to the roof and would soon join in on the firing, or even just walk around the corner and kill us, we had no weapons to defend ourselves, and were vastly outnumbered, it would be like shooting fish in a barrel for them.

"Sorry mate, I think this is the end of the road for us" Nogla answered. He reached over and gripped my hand, shaking it.

"It's been a pleasure" he said as he shook my hand.

Before I could answer to reply to him I suddenly felt a tingle, had I been shot? Map the tingle began where Nogla was gripping me and began shooting down my arm and around my body, my eyes grew heavy and my head filled with this intense pain! I screamed, letting go of Noglas hand in the process, my head felt like something was pushing into the inside of my skull, cracking the bone, trying to split my head open. I screamed louder as the pain grew more intense.

"LEO!" Nogla yelled reaching out for me; I grabbed his hand out of instinct as it approached me. Then suddenly the pain was gone, I felt different, I felt full of energy, awake, I wanted to fight, I could feel my heart beat, it was not fast but instead slow and steady in my chest, I could hear it out loud, thundering in the sir around me, I could hear every drop of rain strike the ground below my feet, each bullet not only hitting the duct we were hiding behind but also leaving the weapon it was being fired from. My eyes wandered up from the ground to gaze at Nogla.

"My shadow" I said to him with complete calm in my voice, the Awakening drug had finally kicked in, and to my surprise, it felt good!

CHAPTER 21

FIRE FIGHT

WHITEOUT HESITATION I darted my head around the corner of the ventilation duct, I could see six mechanics in total, around a dozen men of the ground, but that number was slowly increasing as more men emerge from the entrance to the stairs, and also men were now repelling down from the vehicles above. Two of the mechanics had opened their side doors, there was two long ropes coming from each door, and men were now sliding down from the vehicles to join the ones already firing on the roof. I brought my head back around the corner of the vent. Right before my very eyes I could see thousands of different versions of me, all doing different things, some jumped clean off the roof, others stood up and were gunned down, so sat here and waited it out, only one seemed to come close to being the correct choice, I felt my mind process all these outcomes in the blink of an eye before it locked with one that seemed the most logical, I gazed back towards Nogla.

"Stay here" I harshly snapped before I turned and dashed around the corner, kicking my legs into the ground to throw myself at high speed into the line of fire, I forgot what it felt like to know you're doing something but have no way to stop your own body from doing it, to becoming a prisoner behind your own eyes, watching someone else control your every action, and seeing it happen before it has, the feeling is indescribable.

There was a man standing a few feet in front of me, he fired a gunshot towards me, I ducked before he could pull the trigger and threw my clenched fist upward, hitting the bottom of the weapon sending it flying into the air. Before the weapon could land I kicked the man in his knee, the bone snapped and sent him dropping to the floor in front of me, both my hands shot out in different directions. My right grabbed the man in front of me to stop him falling to the floor, my left shot out behind me, grasping the weapon as it fell from the sky, I snapped my hand to point the weapon at a blue suit who was now targeting me, I pulled the trigger twice sending two shots into his flesh, one pierced his skull, killing him instantly, the other struck his chest and I considered it to be nothing more than a double tap shot, to make sure there was no way that man would be getting up. The man I had sent to his knees was now riddled with bullet wounds, his body was being used as covering from the men in front of me, I pointed the weapon near two more men that were behind the view of my human shield, squeezing the trigger gently I sent two bullets soaring through the air, they struck each man directly between the eyes, their heads snapped back as the round sunk into their skulls. One managed to get a shot of before I could, he sent a bullet into the back of the man I was holding, the bullet burnt the flesh off my arm as it grazed my skin before sinking into its final destination.

I kicked the ground to stand up quickly, all the while grasping the dead body of the blue suit in my bloody hands. I darted my body forward towards the entrance to the stairs, the men around me were firing their weapons furiously into their fallen comrade, the bullets punctured his flesh, splashing blood across my face and the ground below, the rain quickly rinsed the blood down my cheeks, wiping my face clean once more. Approaching the door I released the corpse, sending flying down the stairs, knocking two men who were climbing it to the ground, they bounced of the stairs and fell down them, tumbling over their own legs, they soon disappeared down the flights. One man at the top of the stairs managed to jump to the side, dodging the falling body, I ran in between the two men outside of the door, ducking underneath the punches that they both threw, and jumped into the air, my legs raised. My hands grasped the doorframe and I flung my legs forward, striking the man at the top of the stairs directly in the chin, he let out a groan in pain before falling backwards to join the others down the stairs.

After my legs connected I swung them back, throwing my body to the floor, the two men turned around to look at me, I was now sitting upon the wet ground in between them, the rain drops danced around my body. I raised my hands to their belts, pulling their secondary side arms from it; I brought the weapons up, tightly gripped in both my hands, the weapons now resting underneath of each man's skull. Both men looked down at me, doing their best to move their other side arms quickly to point then down at me, but it was too late. My fingers pulled both triggers back, sending rounds out of the chamber into both men's skulls, there was a loud crack as the bullet passed deep inside them, their head simultaneously snapped back, their bodies flopped as they fell from their feet to greet the water covered ground below. I stayed in the same position, one knee placed firmly on the ground, the other leg raised, both weapons pointing up in the air towards where the two men's head used to be. The light from the Mechanics shone brightly on the ground, reflecting in the small puddles that had now formed, I looked up towards one of the ones that had two long climbing ropes hanging out of the open side doors. The search light bounced of the raindrops in mid-air, causing them to release a handful of different colours; they danced from raindrop to raindrop as the light moved throughout the air.

There was still many soldiers around me, I counted for under one of the vehicles, however they were hidden behind another air duct, I could see two moving around each side from the directions of their feet underneath. Beside the second air duct were three more men, they had now hidden themselves behind cover and were out of my line of sight, other than that the rest were in the open, but they had turned to try and retreat behind the scattered ventilation systems. I stood up slowly, the rain bouncing of my head, dripping down my nose; all the while the two weapons were still raised beside my head. I glanced over to the vehicle in the sky that had no men underneath it, the two ropes still dangling from it; I could see four sets of feet preparing to scale down the rope to join the others on the roof.

Out of the corner of my eye I saw a man raise his weapon to point it at me, I snapped my right hand down firing three shoots into his flesh, sending him jolting backwards, my left hand lowered and fire six more shots towards the three men hiding behind the air duct, the bullets bounced of the surface of the metal grate, they were not meant to hit anyone, only to keep them behind the cover while I moved. I jumped forward and began sprinting towards the hanging rope, my hands moved through the air around me, splitting the falling rain before it hit the ground, firing shots at everyone I could see, one struck a man in the leg, his screams pierced my ears, they were easily heard over the sound of the weapons firing. Two more men received headshots, sending the contents of the brain propelling from the back of their skulls.

The four men had now reached each side of the ventilation duct; they were reading their weapons aiming at me. Both of my weapons were now cessing to fire, I was a few feet from the container they were using as cover, there was two dead bodies lying face down in front of the container, as I approached the bullet riddle duct I jumped onto one of the lifeless bodies to improve my height by a few inches, the extra height was needed for the leap, I kicked the body and threw myself soaring into the air above. The search light from the Mechanic was shining bright in my face making it hard to see exactly where it was I was going to land, the blue suits below had all began firing their weapons now, dragging them to face up whilst counting to press repetitively down on the trigger. The relentless drone of gunfire had now become less frequent, the men appeared to be falling back more than running towards me now, other than the four that were directly below, they had a good opportunity to take a shot, having me so close to them and directly within their vision. The smell of smoke and some kind of gunpowder filled the air, mixing with the sweat and blood to cause a thick, strong smelling aroma.

I could feel the air shift as the bullets hissed passed me, it sounded like a small winged insect buzzing around my ears but only for a fraction of a second. My feet struck the top of the vent; I brought my whole body down towards it and rolled forward, trying to build momentum for the next leap. As I un-tucked from my roll I pushed off the ground, my legs fully extended, the second Mechanic had now began to dispense the four soldiers inside of it, they were sliding down the ropes, each at the same time, gripping it tightly, their eyes focused on the ground below to prepare them for their landing, each were carrying a weapon, the blue suits all seemed to have the same weapon and would keep a spare one attached to their belt. I averted my eyes back to the Mechanic I was jumping towards, my jump was too low to make it directly into the open door at the side, however I would easily be able to reach the rope that was hanging off the inside of it.

There was loud hiss followed by agonising pain as a bullet struck my side, I could feeling it digging into my flesh, piercing it and enter my body, it ripped open my skin and nestled just deep enough to stay hidden, the pain shoot itself all over my body, an uncomfortable tingling feeling over wheeled me. I reached out with my hands to grasp the rope, lifting my arms caused further pain to my side; I dropped my handguns in mid-air so I'd be able to grab the rope with both hands. More bullets continued to dash past me, missing me by nothing more than the length of a hair. My hands wrapped around the rope tight, my legs flew forward as they carried on flying through the air, I reached up and gripped the rope higher up, if I didn't move quick then I would surely be riddled with bullet holes.

My hands scrambled to climb the black rope as quickly as I could, all the while the men below continued to fire their weapons at me, due to the sudden change in position however they all had to move around the containers into the open to be able to see me well enough to take a sufficient shot, this gave me just enough time to reach the Mechanic. Despite being shot, and all the running and fighting I had been doing I felt completely fine, the pain in my leg had already faded to almost nothing and I felt like a could run a marathon, my heart rate still staying at a steadied low pace, I was completely focused, determined and calm. I felt I'm control, even though it seemed very clear that I was not, I felt like I was making all these decisions, that I knew exactly what I was doing, but deep down I knew that there is no way that I could ever fight like this on my own, not without the help of the Awakening drug.

My right hand flung itself inside the vehicle, my left hand shortly followed, the material on the floor was cold and had ripples in it, they must have been for grip do the soldiers could move around whilst the vehicle was flying without worrying about losing grip and falling over, or worse. The inside was rather empty, there were three short lines of seats, and three seats in a line, which meant the back of the Mechanic could fit roughly nine people. In between each section of seating was a small rack, there were dozens of the blue suits hand guns darted about inside the rack, giving me the strong opinion that is was in fact a weapons rack. However located at the bottom of each one were three large rucksacks, strange considering none of the men who exited these vehicles had rucksacks on. On the walls were small screens, each one seemed to show images of the perimeter surrounding the Mechanic.

Suddenly the rate of fire increased, rounds struck the ceiling of the vehicle I was climbing into, some bounced off the surface and struck the floor in front of me, the hissing increased, it was joined with the loud ringing sound of metal being struck from these bullets. I could only assume that the men had now relocated on the ground below to get a better shot of me, I managed to pull my legs inside the back of the vehicle quickly without receiving further injuries to my body. As I entered the vehicle safely I glanced up, there was a blue suited soldiers foot charging towards my undefended face, I managed to roll myself out of the way before his mighty boot cracked me in my skull, his leg shot into the air, sending him sliding across the floor, he fell straight from the Mechanic to the hard ground below, I couldn't hear whether or not he hit the ground or the vent because the sound of constant gunfire was too overwhelming to hear anything else or make out any other sound for that matter.

"Guess those grips on the floor don't work" I muttered under my breath, feeling them beneath my hand

My eyes shot forward, staring into the opening leading to where the pilot was flying this vehicle, I stood up slowly and began walking forward, there was no door, just an opening that led from the area I was in, into the cockpit. I could see one man sitting at the controls, there was no steering wheel, just hundreds of buttons darted around the dashboard and onto of the ceiling, the side of the cockpit was covered in computer equipment, there was also a handful of monitors that projected images of outside. I gazed into one of the monitors and saw four blue suits moving in towards Nogla and Katherine, without hesitation I pulled a weapon of the side rack and pointed it at the back of the man's skull, I pulled the trigger and painted the windscreen with his blood, his head fell forward, the vehicle began to shake as the man's body lent on some controls, I pulled him from the chair and threw his body to the ground, placing myself in his chair and wiping the blood from the control panned and buttons.

Once again I could see a thousand different versions of me pressing buttons and controls, a few versions left the vehicle altogether or went in the back and found an explosive device and using it to destroy the Mechanic itself, or throwing it outside the open door in the back. The scenarios played themselves over and over again in my head all within the fraction of a second, before one clicked, my eyes closed for a moment, thinking it through, they then shot open, staring forward. I raised both hands and began pressing buttons at random, the vehicle began shaking even more and then darted itself forward, I could only see through a small part of the front of the windscreen due to the man's blood being splashed all over it. The rain was thundering down, scattering across the window, I wasn't sure if these vehicles had wipers for this kind of weather. The Mechanic dropped down slightly, the sound of gunfire increased as the other Mechanics opened fire at me, their built in weapons far superior then the small hand gun the blue suits had. Each shell that struck jolted the vehicle with intense force.

I continued pressing buttons and pulling switches, it felt random to me, but they all seemed to work, the vehicle was flying around the building at great speed, it moved forward and then quickly rotated left, the g-force of the turn sent me back into my seat, I struggled to keep my hands on the controls. Outside of the window I could see a large building in front of me, it was not the one I has just been inside, it looked more like the one that had been opposite us, I pressed a few more buttons and the vehicle once again shot left, I looked into a screen located on the wall just to the side of me, the screen was showing the roof of the Federation building, I could see two blue suits walking towards an air duct, in the background behind them was four more Mechanic vehicles, they were all firing at me, a few missed, the ones that hit didn't seem to do as much damage as I would suspect them to do, especially with a weapon of such force as the one that they had equipped, the vehicle itself must be made from a stronger material then the normal Mechanic, they look roughly the same, just larger, most vehicles themselves looked almost identical to Earth based cars, only, of course, the Mechanics could fly.

As I flew the vehicle forward I could suddenly see Katherine and Nogla sitting behind the air duct that the two soldiers were walking towards, on the other side of the vent was yet another two soldiers walking towards them, all four had their weapons drawn and were firing the occasional shot at either myself or the duct. I pressed a button and the vehicle moved closer towards Kath and Nogla, I could see Nogla picked up Kath, placing her over his shoulders, he struggled to get to his, probably because of his leg injuries. When he finally pulled himself to his feet he took one quick look behind him before sprinting forward towards the Mechanic, the hatch in the back was still open, and I was now close to them, it was only a short run to safety, only there was no cover, just an open roof and small gap between the roof and vehicle itself, I tried to close the gap as much as I could, the vehicle moaned and I pulled it closer and closer towards the building, if I got any closer I risked crashing all together.

The four men had now spotted Nogla making his escape; even a few of the other Federation vehicles had turned their view to him. You could see the flashes of light as their weapons fired, the rounds soaring throw the air, splitting the rain in half as they sunk into the side of the vehicle and the ground between myself and Nogla, suddenly there was a red splatter from his back, and then another one from his leg, the same one that had previously swallowed to bullets, he continued running, un fazed by the growing number of bullets his body now carried beneath his skin. Each step he took sent the water on the ground gliding into the air, forming a perfect circle around each foot as it dropped into the growing puddles. All the Federation lights were now shining this way, they had lit up the path so much that when I looked at the roof through the screen at Nogla running it looked less like night time and more like day.

One of the other vehicles sent a large shell into the ground just behind Nogla, it sent large chunks of concrete and water into the air, they crashed around the roof, so hit Nogla, some even travelled far enough to hit their own men. My eyes darted back to the control panel in front of me

"Too far" I whispered to myself, furiously pressing buttons on the dashboard, the vehicle suddenly swung round, the front of it now facing towards the roof and the other Federation soldiers and Mechanics, each vehicle had a large cannon shaped weapon located underneath of it, at the front in the bottom right hand corner, these were the ones that they were using to fire at me and the one they had just used to fire at Nogla and Kath, I too also had one.

My hand lent forward and pulled a level, I looked up through the glass in front of me, gazing through the trickles of blood that had now dripped onto the dashboard and my legs beneath that, turning the material of my trouser into slowly growing red colour, they were already wet from the rain so I could not feel it when the blood began to fall onto my legs, soaking into my clothes. There was a large flash of light as my cannon heated up and fired a round, the round flew just inches past Nogla and struck the ventilation duct behind them. Vents on buildings, especially ones as large as these, usually have a large amount of electric energy inside, and some can even be powered by certain types of fuel, which is why it is an extremely bad idea to fire explosive weaponry directly into one, unless you are purposely trying to create a large explosion.

There was a pause, the air stood still as the round entered the large air duct, it only took a few seconds for it to react, the night sky lit up with a large flash of light as a ball of fire penetrated the top of the air duct, thundering upward, the fans flew out of the metal and shot off in all different directions, disappearing into the surrounding darkness. The ball of fire continued to grow, I could feel the heat from inside here, the vehicles were now hidden behind the large wall of fire I had created, the men that were previously firing at us had been engulfed by the flames, they vanished, swallowed by the explosion. My eyes dropped from the rising fireball towards Nogla who had now reached the side of the roof, only his was not stopping, Katherine was bouncing all over his shoulders, his arms wrapped around her as he ran, trying to keep her secure.

As he quickly approached the edge of the roof he continued at high speed, it became clear that stopping was not part of his plan, he wasn't going to wait for me to turn the vehicle back around and stop so he and Kath could safely enter, the edge of the roof passed below his feet as he leapt from it, his left foot rose from the ground beneath it as he pushed off with his right one, jumping high into the dark night sky, only a few feet directly in front of me, he was now so close I could make out the raindrops on his face, glistening in the light from my search light. They both began to fall slowly, if I didn't do anything soon they would most defiantly fall to their deaths. Without a moment to waste I began hitting the buttons again, my head dropped down to the dashboard as my hands danced around, pressing everything in sight, pulling switches and twisting nobs. Honestly despite my body taking control of my movements I did previously feel like I had some say over my actions but now it felt like I didn't at all, my body had taken over, acting from core instinct. Whatever I seemed to be pressing it appeared to work, the vehicle seemed to know exactly what I wanted it to do, as it shot itself around, rotating much faster in mid-air than it did before, my head and hands simultaneously jolted back, the force threw me into the back of my chair, my eyes moved up to staring out the window again.

The buildings around the vehicle became nothing more than a mindless blur of lights and dark colours. There was a loud thud from inside the back of the vehicle, the blur formed back into the normal scenery it was before, I could see the building directly in front clearly once again.
"Nogla" I shouted, trying to see if he had made it into the back on the Mechanic, which had now begun shaking from the continued gunfire, now that we had stopped rotating it was easy for them to target us and proceed to attempt to shoot us out of the sky.
"Leo Go!" Kath voice yelled, not Noglas, I didn't even know Kath was awake, what happened to Nogla. Unfortunately there was no time to think about it, there was now a loud beeping sound coming from a flashing red light above one of the monitors, the vehicle had taken on a great deal of damage, it wasn't clear how much more it would be able to take before we fell to the cold, wet ground below.

CHAPTER 22

RUN

RATTLING ECHOED THROUGH the air, the smell of burning metal and blood filled my lungs, my head and arms were shaking as each round struck the vehicle, the loud beeping only grew louder with each direct hit.

"Hold on" I shouted as I pressed two large green buttons on the dashboard sending the vehicle plummeting down towards to the ground below. I could see the building in front disappear beyond my view; the only thing through the windshield that I could now see was the side of the building and the ground below it, the lights in the building dashed past the window as we thundered down.

The ground grew larger as we shot down to meet it, the lights from the pursuing vehicles were beginning to scatter around us, as well as the constant firing from their weapons, piercing the air surrounding us, lighting up the wet surface below. The Mechanic started shaking furiously as we continued to get struck by their cannons. The cockpit filled with the occasional red flash, the light in the corner turning on and off faster. The ground approached quickly, my hands placed on the dashboard, I pressed two more buttons and the vehicle began to pull up from its plummet towards the floor.

The ground became the ground once more and not the destination of our current heading. The night sky now had red lines dancing throughout it, no longer completely black in colour, I couldn't see the sun rising over any of the buildings in the area, but I could tell night was almost no longer upon us from the changing contrast of the sky. The vehicle pulled up to face down a small walkway, just big enough to fit squeeze through without causing further damage to this Federation Mechanic. As daylight approached, the pouring rain continued. The Valarian people had now started to wake up, the doors of the buildings down this walkway had been opened, people oozed into the street, the walkway quickly began to fill up with curious eyes, each one stopping to gaze up at the chase above this heads. The night was still here, although the sun was rising it was still very dark and yet everyone seemed to be waking up, people in this city really didn't waste any time sleeping. I glanced up from the window, just above us was the invisible roads, packed with other Mechanics darting around the sky. I did not want to bring the chase to those people; the collateral damage would be too high. The Federation didn't seem to care, as we weaved from street to street, dancing in and out of buildings they continued their constant firing, most shots missed and struck surrounding buildings, sending a mixture of glass and concrete to the ground below, knocking passers-by off their feet, I couldn't see if anyone was injured, we were moving too fast to make out clearly what was going on below.

I pressed a large blue button and the vehicle jumped down lower, now only a few feet from the ground below, the cannon fire raised the pathway beneath us, shadowing us inside a wall on concrete. The noise rung deep into my skull, echoing through one and out the other. The windscreen became pelleted with dashes of rubble, the blood from the blue suit had almost completely gone, making my vision of the area better, however the rubble was now obscuring my vision once again.

"Leo" Katherine's voice cried from inside the back of the vehicle, her voice sang through my body, I felt my limbs turn to jelly, my arms and legs became heavy. I pressed one final button launching the Mechanic down a dark alleyway; we clipped the side as we darted through the opening. The weapons firing struck the surrounding buildings as we quickly turned, catching the Federation soldiers off guard.

My head began to become light and dizzy; the world seemed to move around me as I struggled to keep my eyes open. There was a small turning to the left coming up, I could hear a loud explosion erupt from behind the Mechanic, I looked to my left into one of the screens located on the side, there was a puddle of fire on the ground below, the rain slowly began putting it out, in the midst of the fire was a Federation vehicle, it must have missed the entrance to the alley we entered, crashing into the building opposite the pathway as it failed to turn the corner. We quickly approached the next alleyway to the left, my head dropped down as my hand slapped the final button on the dashboard, my eyes slammed shut, my body felt drained to the core, I felt weak and lifeless all of a sudden, the effects of the pill had begun to wear off. Having your brain so active for such a long period of time, and your body as well means that when the Awakening drug begins to fade and leave your system, your body finds it hard to cope with the sudden change, sending you into a dramatic crash, your bones feel weak, your head begins to ache, I feel like I haven't slept in years.

It was too late, my hand had slapped the button a moment too late, the corner into the alley had already passed my vision, however we had just began our turn left, only there was no path waiting to greet us, just a tall, skinny grey building, the vehicle thundered towards it at high speed, my eyes just opened in time, peeking through the thin squint of my eyelids, they could make out the fuzzy blur of the windows and walls growing larger as we prepared to crash. I removed my arms and hands from the controls and placed them over my eyes, shielding myself from the imminent impact.
"Katherine" I muttered under my breath, my voice cracked, weak and broken from the lack of energy.

The vehicle plummeted into the side of the tall skyscrapers, smashing the glass of the windows and tearing the concrete from the structures that supported it, the Mechanic shock furiously, the windscreen cracked and exploded, the glass flew into my arms, ripping my cloths and tearing deep into my flesh. I fell from my chair and struck the floor below, my body bounced and slammed back down, my bones cracked as my legs whacked into the hard metal material. The force of us falling flew me around the cockpit, sending me crashing into the walls around me, cutting myself further on the broken glass scattered all around the vehicle. My body darted up toward the ceiling, my head bashed against the surface, we must have flipped over and the ceiling had now become the ground. The force of the rotating continued to shot me from wall to wall, ceiling to floor, my head danced around my shoulders as I tried to hold it in place but failed miserably. Buttons popped from the console and joined me in being propelled around the cockpit. The walls dented and cracked as we fell to the ground below.

Suddenly I found myself stuck to the ceiling of the vehicle. The thuds had stopped, the banging and constant rotating stopped as well, only I felt like we had not stopped moving, my eyes gazed through the shattered windscreen, the building in front was falling, the speed growing. Then it hit me, we were falling, we must have rolled out of the rubble we caused within the building and were now falling through the air to the ground below, the rain seemed to of stopped, the morning light shorn from the cracked window, reflecting different colours through the shattered glass. I closed my eyes and waited for the impact of the crash, the wind shot in through the holes in the walls and broken glass, my hair danced as the wind soared throughout it.

There was a brief moment of emptiness, the air stood still so did time itself, the vehicle seemed to almost hover in mid-air, before the final crash hit, I heard a loud thundering sound and then nothing, the my head banged against the floor knocking me completely unconscious sending me into a deed sleep. Would I wake again? If only I managed to keep the effects of the drug a while longer, I could have got us the entire way home with ease, now none of us might make it back, and if none of us did then the device wouldn't either and this whole journey becomes irrelevant, Hank would have died for nothing. As my mind wandered from Hank I began to think about Nogla and why he didn't reply to me when he and Kath entered the vehicle, and did they survive the crash? Did I even survive? Perhaps this was death, eternity with nothing to do but talk to myself inside the emptiness of my mind.

"Pick him up and go!" A voice echoed through the darkness around me.
"Come with us, please! If we all go now we might just make it" a softer voice replied. My eyes began to flicker, trying to open; at least I now knew I was not dead, not yet anyway.
"Here take these" the deep voice ordered. My head spinning inside my own thoughts.
"Please! Come with us, please, please!" The softer voice now begged, I could hear raw emotion in the voice, the voice quivered as

the person sputtered out their words, they were crying, I could hear the heavy berthing from their nose, and the occasional sniff to send the snot leaving their nostril back inside the nose it was oozing out of.

"Go Now! That's an order!" The deep voice echoed, the voice repeated itself in the depths of my mind, I could feel intense heat pressing up against my face, the smell of burning flesh filled the air, and burning metal. It mucked the strong previous scent of the soldier's thick, dark red blood. My mind fell once again into the darkness, my own thoughts faded into nothing more than quiet words occasionally echoing inside my skull, I could feel my eyes grow heavy, despite the fact that I couldn't even open them, I was drifting off again, fading into nothing, who was talking? The voices repeated themselves over and over again as I wandered mindlessly into a dark, cold sleep, one I prayed I would wake from.

"KATHERINE!" I woke screaming, the heat was gone, I was no longer inside a Federation Mechanic, in fact I was inside a room, it was a small dirty room, on the floor around me were a dozen rucksacks, the only other thing in this dull, dark room was the old bed I was lying on. There was one light on the centre of the ceiling, it was flickering on and off, surrounding the light was patches of dirt and damp, they were all over the wall and floor as well. The smell of rotting wood masked the smell of the damp. I could feel my body begin to wake once more, my legs felt achy and bruised but moveable, my arms felt the same only ten times worse, when I looked down at them I could see that the glass that had been stuck in them had been removed and replace with white bandages, the bandages had splatters of blood around the seams of it however.

"Leo, you're awake" a soft voice whispered from the door in front of the bed I was lying on.

"Katherine?" I asked, turning my body to look towards the door, I hissed in pain as my arms scrapped against the surface of my clothes.

"Yeah" she said, walking into the room, she was wearing a small pair of shorts and a t-shirt, the shirt was a dark grey colour whereas the shorts were a tree like green, her hair was tied back and she looked like she had cleaned up as there was no blood on her nor were there any open wounds.

"What happened? Where are we?" I asked her as she approached the bed, she sat down and then without saying a word flung her arms around me, bursting into tears, I could feel them drip warmly down my neck onto my back. I brought my arms up behind her and wrapped them around her waist, embracing her.

"Hey, hey, what's wrong?" I softly asked her, rubbing my hands up and down on her back. She quivered slightly, before answering.

"Noglas gone" she cried out through her panting breaths and sniffs, continuing to cry over my shoulder. Nogla was dead? Without him how would we make it home, I couldn't protect Kath, and the condition she's in I doubt she could protect me.

"How do you know? What happened to him? I thought you were both safe in the back of the Mechanic?" I nervously asked, I knew I had to find out what happened, but part of me didn't want to know the truth, to many people seemed to be dying over this stupid data that we had to collect, and both of those men should have gone after me, not before.

"We were, but his injuries were to severe, he would have never made it back to the safe house, he had been shot four times Leo, he barely made it off the roof, he passed out from the pain as soon as we fell inside the vehicle" she continued. Of course, that's why he didn't reply to me when he first got into the Mechanic, he was unconscious.

"Why didn't he try? We could have carried him!" I asked.

"I tried, but he wouldn't let me, he took some of the weapons of the side and said he'd cover our escape, there were so many Federation units around us, if he didn't do what he did . . . . She paused, I could, feel the tears now reaching the bottom of my back, growing colder as the made their way down my body, I then noticed that I was only wearing trousers, my top had been removed, probably to get to the glass in my arms easily, without having to constantly move my shirt out of the way.

"I can't believe he's gone" I said to break the silence, Kath had stopped speaking and I couldn't hear her crying anymore either. I pulled her back off me to get a better look at her. Her eyes were now closed and her body was limp, she had cried herself to sleep.

"Kath" I whispered.

"Let her sleep" a woman's voice ordered from behind the door, I turned my eyes from Kath to the person at the door. They poked their head through to reveal who they were, it was Laura, I suddenly realised where we were, Katherine must have carried me back to the safe house herself, she was such a small woman, where she managed to muster the strength to carry me so far I will never know.

"Come on Leo, get some food, you don't have long before you will have to leave again." Laura said, waving her hand towards her, insinuating that I get up and walk over to the door.

As I began walking to the door I turned my head to check on Kath, she was lying face down on the bed, her legs hanging of the edge of the side of it, before I got up I had pulled the sheet over her to keep her warm, the building wasn't cold but it wasn't warm either.

"Can I have a shirt Laura?" I asked, turning my head back round to now face her instead.

"Urm check inside there" she answered, pointing at a bag next to the door, it was the exact same one that we had all worn to the Federation tower, I bent down and unzipped the main pocket, removing a small white top from inside. Returning to my standing position I began to raise my bandaged arms to try and place the white shirt on myself, the pain struck me fast as my arms stretched, letting out vicious screams, I tried to bite my lip so I would not wake Katherine.

"Here let me help" Laura said, she grabbed the sleeves of the shirt and pulled them over my arms, the blood had begun to drip from around the bandage onto the floor and my chest. My arms raised, she pulled the head opening around me and down to sit upon my shoulders, the pain was phenomenal.

Finally the T-shirt was over my head and arms, Laura then pulled it down and over my chest, I had cuts and bruises darted all over me, I looked like I fell into a tunnel of brambles and had to climb my way out.

"Thank you" I said, pulling the top down to my waist.

"No problem" she replied, her hands were still on me, she had them both placed on my chest, I looked at her as she gazed back towards me, I think she had a soft spot for me, she looked much younger than Kath, and younger than me, she must have only been a teenager.

"This way" she said through an embarrassed cough, jolting her head towards the door as she walked through the broken wooden frame into the following room.

I recognised the room immediately, it was the one we had been sitting in before, the same sofas were under the window opposite the door we walked through, there were grey curtains, they looked to have previously been white but due to not being cleaned in a long time the dirt and dust in the air had turned them a sluggish grey colour.

"There, eat" Laura said pointing at a table, the same table that had the pot of Raptor meat among other disgusting things. It looked like the exact same pot was still there, steaming away, the same contents inside it. Even though it tasted good, really good, especially compare to the revolting mush they fed me back at the rebel base, I didn't feel like filling my stomach with the waste from another creature.

The two men from earlier were still in the corner using the computer equipment, one was wearing shaded glasses that covered up most of his face, the other had saggy features and was also wearing glasses only they weren't shaded. Both of them had their hair parted to one side; however the room was dark which made it hard to make out their exact facial features.

"I think I'll pass" I said, straining my voice, my body killing me, just standing was hurting.

"Leo, you . . . ." My ears began to ring; I could hear them singing loud, the high pitch reaching new heights. I blinked my eyes over and over again, trying to look through the squinting slit between my eyelids. The only thing I could make out was my hand on the ground in front of me, gripping the floor beneath me, small pieces of glasses dashed around my finger tips and palm.

CHAPTER 23

SAFE AT LAST?

THERE WAS A bright light shining onto the ground in front of me, it reflected off the broken glass, turning each little piece into a small rainbow filled with hundreds of different combinations of colours. What happened? One minute I was talking to Laura, debating with her over whether or not to eat from the pot of steaming filth. I raised my head slowly to gaze around the room, I could see a pair of dark eyes staring into mine, only a few feet from my head, they were cold and empty, there was a small stream of blood bleeding from them, dripping down their cheek. As I tried to focus my vision the face became clearer, and then I recognised who it was, who the cold eyes belonged to that we gazing into mine through my hazy vision, it was Laura, she was lying on the glass covered ground in front of me, her body drained of all emotion, all feeling, completely lifeless.

Pressing my hand on the ground I tried to raise myself up to discover what exactly had happened, where it all went wrong. The two men were still alive, I could see one of them in front of me, he was holding a hand gun, firing towards the window, into the light that was moving rapidly around the room. It looked as if a giant was holding a flashlight, trying to find something he'd lost of the ground of this building.

"Get up!" The man screamed, sliding a spare handgun across the floor towards me, as it left his grasp he was suddenly struck by a blue light, it wrapped itself round his left hand, and circled itself up towards his shoulder blade, the light seemed to be some kind of electronic rope, it wrapped itself around his entire body, engulfing him completely with an electronic pulse, sending him to the floor, his limbs were jolting up and down, spazzing widely out of control. I reached out for the weapon, trying to get my head together, the ringing only got louder as I began to move, my hand gripped the weapon tight, I could feel the cold material on my skin.

I shook my head slightly to try and regain focus, lifting my body to its feet, the weapon dropped down beside my leg, I held it there, the lower it was to the ground, the easier it was to hold. My eyes rose with my body, staring into the light that was pointing straight at me, I was standing in the middle of the room, the window was opposite me, I could smell the blood in the air, it had become a very familiar smell now, only this time the smell had combined with the overwhelming stench of the stew that was inside the pot, the pot had been shot off the table and was now spread across the floor below, little chunks of meat bubbled through the brown stream it had created.

Turning my head to my left I could see the second man, he, as well as the first, was also surrounded by this blue light, circling his body, causing him to flop around the ground like a fish fresh out of water. I pulled my hand from my hip and out of pure instinct pointed the weapon I was holding towards the blinding light; I readied myself, preparing to squeeze the trigger. There was a buzzing sound in the air, it had begun to get louder, the noise was coming from the light in front of me. It sounded like something charging up, perhaps their weapon, the same one that they had fired at the two men now on the floor. My heart sank with fear, my head grew dizzy and faint, my hands became sweaty, barely holding onto the weapon within my grasp. I knew that without the effects of the Awakening drug there was no way I could help these people, or myself for that matter. I didn't know what to do; I couldn't see a hundred of me running around performing different scenarios at once, helping me to figure out exactly what needed to be done to stop the killing of these rebels. I was nothing more than a man, no fighting skills, no high intelligence and no crack shot skills, which is why I'd be surprised if when I fired this weapon it even hit whatever was behind that search light.

As I pulled my finger back, slowly squeezing the trigger the charging sound got more intense, it was now louder than the ringing throughout my eardrums. Suddenly I was sent straight to the ground, I quickly looked at my hands and legs, expecting to see that same blue light that is wrapping itself around the other men, instead all I saw was a hand, a small bandaged hand gabbing my arm, I followed the hand up to the body to see Katherine staring at me.

"Move!" She screamed at me, pulling my hand towards her, attempting to lift me to my knees so we could crawl to safety, staying low underneath the view of the searchlight.

The room filled with hundreds of tiny shards of wood, the pot exploded into nothing more than metal shavings that punctured deep into the wall. The vehicle had started rapidly firing outside the window, destroying the walls around us and everything inside the room itself. The sofas and tables became piles of rubble that filled the air around us and fell to the floor beneath us. Katherine dragged me into the next room, pulling me across the broken pieces of glass and wood, they cut into my hand, sending themselves deep into my skin. As we entered the adjacent room I flicked my legs, kicking the door shut behind me, the door slammed shut, but was instantly reopened with a thunderous bang, destroying it completely, sending the wooden door across the room in three large pieces, they flew over our heads smashing into the surrounding walls exploding into even smaller pieces.

Katherine let out a quiet scream as the continued shots destroyed the building around us, the walls shattered and crumbled; the furniture vanished, turning into nothing more than dust. How did the Federation find us? I was unconscious for the journey back but I assumed that Nogla staying behind meant that this sort of thing wouldn't happen, I couldn't help but feel that the man gave his life for us in vain.

"Leo take this!" Katherine shouted, her voice barely making it over the sound of small explosions and bullet fire. She slid a small bag over towards me, it was much smaller than the rucksacks we had previously been using, being no bigger than my forearm, but it was still able to fit a great deal of items, considering we didn't need to carry much anyway.

"Inside is the device, you must give it to Henry!" She screamed, I didn't reply, I just stared blankly at her, my head dropping down out of instinct as each shot they fired soared above our heads. Was she not coming with me? I couldn't let another person stay behind to insure my safety, especially not Katherine, not after all we'd been through, not after all the people we lost along the way.

"Laura told me he was waiting for us on the other side of the wall! Bring the device to him there! It's all that matters now!" She continued to scream at the top of her lungs.

"I'm not leaving you here Katherine!" I shouted back, sending my splinter filled hand across the floor towards hers, placing it gently upon hers.

"They won't kill me; I'm too valuable to them! But if they find you they will! Please Leo, you have to go, I will be fine, I promise!" She replied, I could see her eyes turn red as a tear fell from her cheek onto our hands, gripping each other's on the ground.

There was a moment of pause as the building started to heat up, the next room had caught fire and began burning, the remains of the sofas were the first to light up, swallowing the curtains into the growing inferno, growing larger by the second as each item became fuel for it. We didn't move, despite all that was happening around us, the building collapsing, the Federation at our doorstep, the burning fire approaching us, we just knelt there, our hands locked with one another, our knees dug into the ground, scratching against glass and wood yet to join the fire. Our eyes fixed, staring into the dark pupils of the other person. We both knew I would have to go, I would have to leave her, even though I didn't want to admit it, I knew she was right, I knew she would be safer than me and if both of us tried to escape, they'd hunt us all the way back to the wall, at least this way I would be able to have a better chance at reaching it and getting to the other side before they caught up with me.

The smell of burning wood and ash filled my lungs, my eyes began frantically blinking, trying to avoid the ash reaching them and adjust to the growing heat. My hand became sweaty, I could feel Katherine's underneath doing the same, the fire had reached the door into out room, setting fire to the doorframe, engulfing the entire other room. The sound of wood cracking became more rapid, the fire was destroying the building, not only turning the items of furniture to ash but the building itself and with us inside it. The heat was so intense; the fire felt like it was inside my skin, burning me from the inside out.

"You have to go now! If you stay any longer we will both surely be killed" she yelled towards me, tears now streaming down her face. I gripped her hand tighter, not wanting to go. She looked down at the ground, breaking eye contact; she pulled her hand from underneath mine and stood up. The fire rose behind her, she was now standing in front of me, kneeling on the floor.

"I can't let you stay here a die with me; I'm sorry, when I go, turn around and look under the rucksacks behind you." She said, her voice nothing more than a whisper, I could no longer hear it, only see her lips moving, they were easy to read however.

What was she talking about? Where could she go? Where could I go? Surely at this point it was too late; we were both going to burn inside the building as it crumbled to the ground. Our bodies disappearing with the rumble, becoming hidden forever, our skin and bones melted and turned to dust, the device along with us, everything we tried to do, everything we set out to accomplish would die with us. I couldn't help but think about my life, I didn't want to die here, I didn't sent to give it up, I felt as if I left Earth and fell straight into the slaughter that is Vala, the real world, maybe if I never questioned my life, never woke up, none of this would be happening. But then again, the Federation would continue to kill and kidnap millions of people like me, forcing them to live fake lives, never breathing a true breath of air, never eating real food, or kissing a real girl, never experiencing anything real for as long as they live.

"Goodbye Leo" Katherine whispered as she turned to face the door.
"Wait, Katherine!" I screamed! She didn't look back, she walked started to walk forward towards the flames, the door itself looked like a gateway to hell, the fire erupting from it, touching the ceiling above, turning the walls to black around it. I scratched the ground below as I tried to quickly scramble myself to my feet, rushing over to Katherine to reach her before she reached it. I lifted my legs, placing each foot firmly on the hot ground below.

By the time I was on my feet it was already too late, I raised my head just in time to see her reach the doorway. The fire was already flickering out, touching her skin, the smell of burning hair and flesh filled the air as she disappeared, her body being surrounded by dark orange flames, swallowing her, her body becoming nothing more than fuel for the flames to continue growing, and just like that, she was gone. Katherine had been eaten by the fire, I couldn't believe it, my heart sank into my stomach, my throat felt like it had an apple stuck in it, blocking each breath from leaving or entering my body, sweat and tears joined to trickle down my burning face. I just stood there, staring the approaching fire, I didn't want to move, I just wanted to stand here and join Kath, being swallowed by the blistering heat and flames. I felt drained, empty and alone, I was alone, Nogla, Hank and now Kath, they had all gone, I was the last one that should have stayed alive, and yet here I was, and they were now gone.

I turned from the flames and quickly rushed toward the bags Kath had mentioned, the fire approached quickly on my back, I could feel it burning through my clothes, torching my skin. I wanted to die but then Kath would have died for nothing, her last wish would die along with me, and I couldn't let that happen, so I had to press on, survive, despite my protest, my feelings. I ran to the pile of bags and dove my hands deep into the pile, throwing them across the room, launching each one from the pile to scatter around the floor. There would be a time to think about Kath, morn for me, but right now I had to escape from this building before it crumbled to the ground, tuning into burning rubble.

The bags were boiling hot and burned my hands, the black material had heated up from the flames, roasting them, raising their temperature painfully high. I continued to through bags around the room, the like grew smaller as each one left it, until there was only two left, in between them was a black sheet. Pulling the two final ones out of the way I could now see a black metal sheeted hatch, it was built into the floor. The whole hatch was pitch black other than a small metal hoop that seemed to be the handle to opening it.

I leant down and tightly grasped the metal handle, it instantly burnt deep into my skin, I could smell my flesh burning as I let go, staring at my hand, there was now a bright red line of burnt skin stretched across the palm of my hand, I screamed out in pain, grabbing my wrist. I turned my head to see how close the flames were, they were now a few feet from my face, and seemed to be gaining much quicker than before. With shear fear in my heart I throw my hand towards the handle, grabbing the heated metal, it seared into my flesh burning, I wrapped my fingers around it, pulling it up, the hatch launched open, crashing to the ground on its side, I darted my eyes to my left and grabbed the bag Katherine had given me, then without hesitating I jumped straight through the hatch, disappearing into the dark hole below, the fire rushed forward, burning my back as I fell into the void, I was out of the building, safe for now.

CHAPTER 24

BACK WHERE WE STARTED

THE HATCH LEAD to a short dark tunnel, it was a short drop to the soft ground below, I struck it hard, twisting my ankle as I fell hard, dropping to the floor. I couldn't tell whether my eyes were open or not, the area around me seemed to be in complete darkness, there were no lights, not even the fire above provided any lights, the hatch must have closed behind me, blocking the flames from pursuing me. I placed my hands on the cold ground around me; it felt like some kind of concrete, cold, rough and hard. Rubbing the ground below I struggled to find the small bag, perhaps there was something inside it that could be used as light, if Katherine knew what this tunnel was and where it went, then she would have known that it would have no light, no way of seeing where it was I was supposed to go.

My hands continued to slide across the surface of the ground below, until they hit a softer material, I knew it was the bag as I picked it up with ease, feeling around it, double checking it was in fact what I had been looking for. I felt for any zips, so I could gain access to the contents inside, as I found one I pulled it open quickly and sent my hand diving down into the small bag. The insides felt peculiar, I could feel a soft item, maybe some clothing, then a smaller harder item, I guessed that perhaps that was the device; I assumed it was in the bag, I don't remember it being placed on me personally and Katherine had defiantly given it to me. Then there was yet another soft item, this one was much smaller, I assumed it was some kind of food.

There were only two more items inside the bag, one was freezing cold, I went to bring it out of the bag but when I did I heard the sound of liquid moving around inside it, so I figured that it must have been a water bottle. The last was a small slender shape, thin and it felt like a metal material, I grasped it and pulled it from the bag, feeling around it in my hands. There was a small indent on the item, pushing my finger into it the item activated, shining a small stream of light into the wall in front of me, lighting up the area around myself and the bag. I placed everything back inside the small carry bag and stood up, shining the flashlight around the tunnel, trying to figure where I was or which way to go.

The tunnel itself smelled of damp and smoke, the smoke from the burning building above must have been seeping into the hatch, mixing with the damp it created a musky stench that filled my lungs. The wall in front of me was made from thick, black bricks, and had water dripping down it, splashing on the ground, not a lot, just the occasional leaking drop from the ceiling. I moved my hand and turned the light to face into the tunnel, one way was completely blocked, there was only one direction in which I could go, the tunnel seemed endless, I the torch shined into the darkness but didn't seem to change the lighting much, just lit up the ground enough to see my feet and where they were walking. I had nothing else to do now, I grabbed the bag and began walking into the dark abyss, the flashlight aimed at the floor below, watching each step that my feet took, deeper into the darkness that engulfed me.

I felt like I had been walking for hours, maybe I had, I had no way of telling the exact time, I only could by guess alone. My legs continued to grow achy and tired with each foot of progress that I made, my body was drained and I had ran out of water and food. The tunnel didn't seem to change at all, the walls stayed the same size, there were no drops down, stairs, ladders or even turnings, not any that I could feel anyway. To me it all seemed to be a long straight line through a dark wet tunnel and nothing more. My head became dizzy, the air inside the tunnel was thick and dense, it seemed to be heating up in temperature as well, my clothes were clinging to my sweating body, the drops of sweet rolling down my forehead and off the tip of my nose.

More hours past as I pressed on, still no exit, still no change to the tunnel. I started to lose hope, questioning whether I would ever make it out of here, maybe Kath had sent me to the wrong exit, maybe she just knew this was the only way I'd survive and therefore the device would remain safe. I kept seeing her face in the walls of the tunnel, hearing her calling my name for the abyss, I thought I saw her and Nogla up ahead at one point, but it was nothing more than my imagination, my mind was breaking, playing tricks on me. I was seeing things, going insane. If I carried on like this I'd never make it out of here, I need water, I need food, I needed real light. Even hearing someone's voice would make a nice change.

"I could of just stayed in bed, stayed with my girlfriend, in my apartment" I said to myself, my voice broken and weary.

"If only Kath hadn't given that pill, I wouldn't have had to come on this journey. I could have stayed at the rebel base." I continued talking to myself, I was losing it, using my own voice to keep myself company.

"Oh Kath" I cried out.

"I can't believe you're gone" I screamed, stopping in my tracks, my sluggish feet that dragging along the floor, barely rising to continue take steps, had now stopped. I fell to the floor, hitting the ground hard with my knees, sending my closed fist crashing into as well. I couldn't stop thinking about Kath and with each thought of her I grew weaker, less determined to keep walking.

"I'm done" I whispered under my voice. I can't do it anymore, all this, all this drama, people dying and killing, it's not me, I am a nobody, a normal quiet man, not a fighter.

As I lied there, staring into the darkness of the tunnel I could see the small flashlight beginning to flicker, it was running out of batteries, the energy had been drained from it as well as me. It fizzled and then cut out completely, sending me into complete darkness once again, I was now lying on the floor not knowing whether I was staring at the inside of my eyelids or the walls around me. To be honest I didn't care anymore, I wasn't going anywhere, I was too tired to move, my lips cracked from lack of water, I was dehydrated and starving and with the images of Kath appearing everywhere inside my mind even if I did have energy I wouldn't want to press on, there was no point.

I closed my eyes, at least I felt like I did, it was impossible to tell I tried to fall asleep on the ground, perhaps die in my sleep, a painless death, that would be a nice way to go, not fighting and losing, not being shot or watching others around me get shot and die, just closing my eyes and never opening the again, no more worries or cares, I found myself wishing for death, just so this nightmare would finally end.

"Leo" a deep voice said from the darkness, I opened my eyes, still lying on my back, staring into nothingness. Had I just imagined that? There is no way someone else could have made it in this tunnel, especially someone who knows my name, I must have imagined it, my mind was playing tricks of me, toying with me, this was just the newest way of it doing it.

"Leo is that you?" The voice asked, I sat up and stared forward, if I couldn't feel my body move I wouldn't even know that I had starting sitting up, nothing changed at all. I was now sitting, staring in the direction where the voice seemed to be coming from. Then there was a single light, it shined out of the darkness, pointing right at me, I looked down at my chest and could see the light shaking slightly on my dirt and sweat covered top, I couldn't be imagining this, someone was in here with me, staring at me, who was it? How did they even get in here? The only logical explanation was that the Federation had somehow found the hatch leading into the long passageway and had entered it, but then that would mean that they would have to approach me from behind, instead they were approaching me from the front, unless I had been walking around in circles, everything looked the same in here, it was very possible that I could have got turned around and had been walking in the wrong direction. If that was the case then how long had I been walking the other way? Minutes? Hours? I could have even sat up facing the wrong direction, in which case I would not have walked the wrong way once, just was now facing it.

None of that would matter now, not if the light shining on my body was indeed the Federation.

"Leo that is you!" The voice yelled in a sigh of release, I could hear rapid footsteps and then five, maybe six more lights turned on, emerging from the darkness to face me. A shadowed figured was moving towards me from the wall of flashlights, the only sound in the air was the persons footsteps, slapping the wet ground as they approached me. I didn't move, I was too tired to move, I just sat there waiting for the shadow to reach me, not knowing whether they were friend or foe, either way I would finally be free of this place, in death or just free in general.

"Thank the stars" the man said as he knelt down in front of me, his shadow only just out of reach, I still could not make out his face or clothing, but I did notice a familiar feeling when he spoke, I had heard his deep voice before.

The man turned the light he was holding from facing the ground below to now facing upward, shining underneath his chin, lighting up the features on his face, his tired sagging face.

"Bet you're happy to see me" the man said with happiness in his voice. I could feel my heart rate rise as I flung myself forward, wrapping my weak arms around his shoulders, embracing the man.

"Jonathon" I muttered, breathing deeply into his shoulder. There were more voices coming from behind the wall of light. I could not see anything other than the lights themselves, which created a barrier between my sight and the people behind them.

"Turn it on" A husky, old voice ordered. The tunnel ahead suddenly lit up, there were hundreds of built in sources of light scattered throughout the tunnel ahead, I turned my eyes towards behind me to see that the darkness still lingered there, barely gripping my foot, it looked so sinister, there was a complete change in the tunnel, one minute it was pitch black, not being able to see your own hand in front of your face, the next it was lit up brighter than the sun itself.

I could easily make out the faces of the people now, each turning of their flashlights, placing them into their rucksacks. There were two people standing at the front of the tunnel, as it was only small in size not all of them would be able to stand in a line, you could only fit around three people before it would get difficult to move and breathe. The one on the left was Trax, her fierce face staring at me, I know she didn't like me, it was written in every expression she ever had when she stared at me, but at this moment in time I didn't care, I was just happy to see her. There was a tall man standing next to her, he had a familiar face but I do not believe that I had previously spoken to him. Both him and Trax were holding large weapons, I had not seen this kind of weapon before, they were black and brown in colour, made from a metal material, they looked a lot like a normal assault rifle, one the soldiers of earth would have, only difference was that they were much large and wide, the weapon was thin in width but stretched far down, nearly reaching their waists. Then there were three more people behind those two, the two closest to the walls were people I did not recognise at all, they both had the handguns that the Federation soldiers used, not the rifles that Trax and the other man had. Then there was the last man, standing in the middle of the group, wearing a brown jacket, black trousers and a long smile stretching from ear to ear.

"Leo" The man said, still smiling, opening his arms for a sign of welcoming. He started walking forward towards me, slowly, quietly.

"Is it in the bag?" He asked as he passed Trax and the other man, pushing them out of the way to get closer to me, I released my arms from Jonathon, he helped me to feet so I could stand once more.

"Have some water" Jonathon said, handing out a small metal flask, the lid was already off of it, I snatched it from his hands sending it straight to my lips, swallowing each drop with delight, my stomach welcomed the water with open arms. My Adams apple raising and falling as I nourished each sip.

"Is it in the bag?" Henry repeated, still pointing at the bag on the ground below. Stumbling to my feet as Jonathon helped me up.

"Don't you want to know where Katherine is? Nogla or Hank!?" I confusingly asked him, he didn't seem bothered at all by the fact that I was on my own, his own people were not with me.

"Leo do you not understand what the mission was? It wasn't to see what the inside of the Federation tower looked like, or for you all to have a good look at the city, they knew the risks, they made their piece, I only expected to see you again." He said, smiling at me. He leant down and pick up the bag, unzipping it straight away and emptying the contents onto the ground, his eyes gazed at the items that had fallen out of it.

"It's not here" he whispered under his breath. His smile faded, his eyes rolled up, staring into mine, a look of anger burned deep into his expression.

"Leo where is the device?" He calming asked, but I could tell he was not calm, it was like when someone has gone past the point of showing that they are angry, their collecting thoughts, overthinking the situation, waiting to strike.

My hand dropped into my trouser leg pocket and emerged with a small silver device, I glared at Henry, holding the device in front of his face, my eyes fixed on him, his fixed on the device.

"Katherine, Hank and Nogla" I said through my grinding teeth. My hand dropped and then rose, flicking the device over towards Henry, it flew through the air and landed in his open palm.

"They all died for that, that piece of metal, don't you ever forget that!" I finished, turning my raised fist into a pointing finger which was directly pointing at Henry. I don't even think he noticed, he was mindlessly staring at the device in his hands, the smile returned, bigger than before.

"How many years has it been, twenty, thirty, I can't even remember when all this first started." He said, his voice calm and quiet, his smile sinister and scary.

"The day I found out about the kidnappings I swore I would out an end to the Federation once and for all, and now, in my hands, I hold the key to destroying them forever." He continued his head turned with his body to face Trax standing behind him.

"Let's burn them down, burn them to the ground for what they've done!" Henry finished, his hand gripped around the device, turning into a fist, his smile turned to determination, it was time to use the device that so many had died for, time to put a stop to them, it was time to win this war.

CHAPTER 25

NOTHING MORE TO LOSE

"**So what now?**" I asked Henry, I didn't know what he would say in reply, whether we would need to return to our base, or we would strike right now, I didn't even know where we were never mind where we were going to go from here.

"Wait before you answer that, where am I? I asked, lifting the bottle to my lips once more, draining it completely dry of all liquid.

"This is an old tunnel that the Federation built to avoid the creatures above, they could go from the city straight to their military outposts without putting themselves in danger. This one links our base and the safe house, we had it blocked off for years, but Laura sent us a message telling us that to get you and Kath back quickly she was going to send you through this old tunnel to us." Jonathon explained, he gazed at the surrounding walls and the structure of this small dark passage.

"So we had to unblock and come down here to look for you, we are actually not that far from the base, only about an hour's walk, you've actually already passed the wall Leo, you're not in the city anymore" Jonathon explained, I found myself feeling relieved to know that I was so close to safety, after all this time, finally.

"To answer your previous question Leo . . . ." Henry had started to talk, however Trax had interrupted him, she quickly walked over her hand gripping a small grey item, she whispered inside Henry's ear, before handing the device. Without hesitating he raised it to his ear and the passage fell silent.

"What's going on" I asked Jonathon, he still had his arm under my shoulder to offer me support.

"I don't know" he replied to me, we all just stood there, completely silent, waiting to find out what Henry was doing. His smile had disappeared, replaced by a shear look of fear; he dropped back towards the wall, placing his back firmly against it.

Henry dropped the device from his ear, I could see his eyes turn red, filled with hate and anger; he then raised the device once more, holding it out towards me.

"It's for you" he muttered under his breath, his hand tightly gripping the grey item, shaking, from fear, anticipation or even exhaustion, I did not know. Reaching out for the device I kept my eyes focused on him, he did not look back at me, instead his head dropped to join a staring contest with the ground below. I grabbed the thing he was holding and brought it towards my ear, just as Henry had done, I could feel fear slowly grow inside of me, was this some kind of trick? Was this all a ploy to get rid of me, I gathered that maybe I was not welcome anymore, the only one who seemed to like me was Jonathon and I got the impression he didn't really have much of a say in the affairs of the rebellion.

The item was now touching my ear, I could feel it warmly pressing against my skin, Henry must have warmed the cold metal up by holding it against his own ear. I didn't say anything, just held it there for a moment; my eyes darted around the ground, trying to make eye contact with anyone of them for some reinsurance. The only one that wasn't looking at the ground was Trax, but she wasn't looking at me, she was standing over Henry, one hand on his hunched over back, the other on her weapon. The rest had a slouched body, there arms dropped as if they were suddenly heavier than before, their heads joined their arms in dropping down to face the wet ground below. I turned my head to look at Jonathon and to my surprise he also had now joined them in dropping his head, I believe he had figured out what exactly was going on, but he just didn't wanted to say anything. It didn't matter whether he did or not the device was pressed against my ear now, shortly I would know what they knew, at least I assumed I would, perhaps this device was going to kill me, but in that case I would find out what it was that they all seemed to know, only by then it would be too late and completely pointless as I would be dead, gone from this world into the next.

"Hello Leo Cathery" a husky voice spoke from the device. I recognised it, but couldn't remember where from, it was a man, middle aged by the sound of it, but that's all I could make out so far.
"Who is this?" I asked in reply.
"Don't you remember me?" The voice continued.
"That's alright; I did not expect you too straight away. I have someone here who would love to talk to you" the voice finished. The sound of shuffling and moving around now came through the device; it lasted a few seconds until a voice finally spoke once more.
"Leo, is that you?" A crying voice asked, I knew who it was instantly.
"Jane?" I replied.
"What's wrong?" I continued.
"Leo whatever you do don . . . ." The voice finished, only it didn't end with silence, Jane's voice was cut off by a loud bang! Then there was silence.
"JANE!" I screamed into the speaker.
"I'm sorry Leo, Jane is no longer with us, she is with Katherine, Nogla, Hank . . . Oh and did I forget to mention that simpleton you all like to call Magic Man!" The voice continued.
"Director" I said through my tightened mouth, my eyes began to become hazy as tears formed, blocking my view of the other staring at me, turning them into nothing but blurry shapes.

"Ah so you do remember me, glad to hear it" the voice said with sarcasm.
"When I find you I'm going to" I tried stating, before being interrupted by him.
"You'll what Leo? The only thing that you will do is die like your pathetic friends, you're all worthless, nobodies, I took your base with ease, my army could take the whole city if I ordered it too, all those disgusting people need order, perhaps I should take the city." The Director continued. I remained quiet, listening to him speak, my hand grew tighter around the device, sweat formed in my palms, my breathing became heavy and fierce, I was so angry I could literally see red before my very eyes.

"Besides, there is still that little angel Teara to think about, and the dozens of other children, a life on Earth is a lot better than an eternity in darkness, wouldn't you agree?" He paused, waiting for an answer, I wasn't going to reply, I didn't want to give the bastard the satisfaction of hearing my broken voice this angry.

"If you want them to live then the best thing to do would be to stay away, maybe go back to the city, you and the rest of the rebels can live as true Valarians, doing honest work for a good night's rest, you'll even get a meal or two out of it" he patronisingly said.

"No? You could always go back to what's left of your base, you may even have one of your episodes and be able to defeat my soldiers that are waiting for you there, I'd love to see you in action against a black suit, woooah wouldn't that be a sight for sore eyes, did I say that right? I believe it was one of the expressions we programmed into your mind" the man didn't shut up, he'd murdered and butchered innocent people and instead of leaving us alone he wanted to rub it in, antagonise us.

"However if the Awakening drug didn't kick in then you'd all be killed before you even made it inside your burning, filthy smoulder of a base. The odds aren't really in your favour, but hey I'm not gonna stop you, pick whichever option you want, we all know the outcome, we don't need a pill to tell us the future in this scenario." There was a pause for a moment, the air grew tense, I could feel the material of the device crushing in my hand, cracking slowly and breaking, if I did not calm down soon it would probably explode into tiny pieces. At least then the Director wouldn't be able to constantly remind us of how screwed we were, how there was nothing we could, everyone we knew was dead, all the children captured, forced to live a fake life like I did, becoming nothing more than part of an experiment for the rest of their planned life.

"Anyway Leo, I'd just like to say one last thing before I leave you to live your amazing new life . . . Welcome to Vala! Goodbye" he finished, that was that, the device cut out and all that was coming through it now was the sound of static.

"What do we do now?" Jonathon asked.

"We go home" one of the guys said.

"You heard him, there is no more home" Trax interrupted. All of them began talking over each other, arguing about what would be the correct step to take, shouting erupted from the tunnel, echoing around us, I just stood there, the device now crushed in my hand, still pressed up against my ear, I was frozen with anger, the voices around me were impossible to make out, they were just murmurs within my eardrums. I couldn't help but think about what I had just been told, the very fact that all these amazing people I had been introduced to are now gone, and this guy was rubbing it in, telling us to turn back and live inside the city, hidden, broken, nothing more than people who just gave up, letting the Federation continue to rule with an iron fist.

"We strike right now" Henry called out, the passageway fell silent, everyone stopped talking and gazed over towards him, leaning on the wall, his head dropped, he looked like a broken man, not the same confident cocky person who was smiling constantly beforehand.

"Right now they are returning to the facility outside the walls, they have our people with them, they will be tired and have their numbers cut in half by having to keep some of their soldiers at our base, waiting for us to return. We heard him say there were black suits there as well, which means there will be less at the facility itself. The way I see it we have a handful of choices, we can fight them now and maybe have a chance to save our people and even upload the virus into their systems, achieving exactly what we set out to achieve. Or we go back to our destroyed base, fight the suits there and see if we can defeat them. But then what? They'll just send more to kill us if we somehow manage to win." He had got off the wall and begun walking around the tunnel, pacing between us all, his face red, his eyes swollen perhaps from crying.

"Or we can give up, turn around and go back to Vala, live in the city and work in one of the factories." Then he stopped, standing still, he raised his head and darted his eyes around from one of us to the other.

"So what's it gonna be?" He asked us all.

"Honestly Henry there is nothing I want more than to crush them, but even with their numbers depleted, how can we get there? And how will we get inside without being caught?" Trax asked.

"Above us right now is a Federation truck, we were originally going to use it when we were ready to break into the facility, uploading the data to their main operating systems, but now seems as good as time as any, it should pass automatically right through the entrance and dock us in the loading bay, we will be inside, undetected.

We all starred at him, one question on our minds.
"How did you know to have the vehicle ready, right above us now, right we are standing? That seems a bit suspicious don't you think?" Jonathon said, stepping forward towards Henry.
"You see that, over there?" He asked, pointing at a ladder built into the surrounding wall.
"There are at least ten of them between here and our base, each one has a vehicle at the top of it, programmed into the main road from the city to the facility, we live inside an old Federation outpost, it was abandoned but not empty, there were a dozen vehicles programmed to travel to the city, all we had to do was switch the programming in the vehicle to take us to them instead, then we placed them outside our base, in case something like this happened, that way we'd have plenty of backups to breach their facility, so no, not a coincidence, not suspicious, it's called good planning." Henry explained.

"We don't have time for this, what's it gonna be?" He asked again.
"Are you coming with me, or staying here" he finished, looking around at us all. Each person dropped their eyes to the ground, trying not to make eye contact with him, they were all scared, going up against the most powerful organisation with nothing more than a handful of weapons and people to wield them, the obvious outcome is what the director said, that we'd get slaughtered. But when it comes down to it there really is no other choice, when you consider the other options I'd rather die fighting then live hiding, I'd rather die on my feet then live a life on my knees.

"Boss of course we're all with you, let's make them pay, for our brothers and sisters!" Trax loudly said, raising her hand and placing it on Henrys shoulders. I stared at the others; they had all raised their heads in agreement, even Jonathon. They gripped their weapons and nodded towards Henry as his eyes crossed over each of them. Until finally they turned their gaze to me, not only the boss but also the other men, including Trax and Jon.
"Leo, we can't do this without you" Henry said, staring at me, he held his hand out towards me, wanting me to reach out and shake it

with approval. I was nervous, afraid, the chances of me having another episode were slim to none, which meant I would have to fight the suits in the building with just my own mind, my own skills, not that I had any.

My eyes looked at his hand, suspended in mid-air; they then followed his arm up before locking in sync with his.

"After everything we've been through, all the people who have died, everything the Federation has put us through and is continuing to put thousands, millions of innocent children in those machines against their will, it's not right, we can't just let it happen, give up and go back to the city, and if we fight them at our base we will be killed before we even make it close, there is no decision that is the right one, they all end in bloodshed, but there is only one, one decision that has even a slight chance of succeeding. So Henry, I am with you, let's do this." I quietly said, reaching out a grabbing his hand to shake it, he let out a small smile before shaking my hand back, it was time to fight.

CHAPTER 26

RIGHT IN THE CORNER OF YOUR EYE

"COME ON! THE wind is picking up!" Trax screamed as I climbed out of the tunnel, I was the last one to leave it; I had to make sure everyone had got out safely and nothing was left behind. The conditions above had dramatically deteriorated, the wind was strong enough to lift us from our feet now, if the truck hadn't been connected to the ground by a built in magnet then it too would not last on the road long before it would swerve off and crash, stopping our mission before it had even begun.

Henry went first; he managed to connect a rope to the back of the truck so we could climb inside from the tunnel without the wind taking us off into the night. The sky above was dark, however the fog around us, like before, made it impossible to even really see the night sky. The wind struck us with brute force, hitting me like a punch, sending the air flying out of my lungs, gliding off with the wind as it flew past. The vehicle itself was more like an army truck then the truck I had in mind, it was a large metal truck with a door at the back that opened into a large room, there were four seats either side of the room at the back, the insides didn't have much technology, at least not the back of it, only two small monitors and a periscope in the middle so people could see out of the top of the truck. The colour of it was a light, shiny silver, but the night made it look like a darker colour, nearly completely black.

Trax grabbed my hands and placed them on the rope in front of me, sending me across it towards the open back of the truck, I couldn't turn my head to see if she was following me, only I assumed that she would be, if I could survive the intense weather then surely she could, she was much stronger than I was, and much more used to this sort of stuff then I was. I could see the other people ready in the back of the vehicle in front, they all had seat belts wrapped around their waists to stop them from being pulled out of the open back, dragged off into the cold night, at least while the door was open so all of us could get inside. The only one that I could not see in the back was Henry; he must be controlling the vehicle from the front, driving it. There was a small door that looked like it lead into the front of the vehicle, only it appeared to be tightly shut I wasn't even sure if it could be opened from this side.

"Hurry up Leo" Jonathon shouted as I approached the rear of the vehicle, as I made it inside the wind died down, still strong but no longer strong enough to remove the breaths from my lungs before I'd even breathed them myself. I reached out and grabbed the seat closest to the door, the outside was dark, the only light came from the ceiling of the inside of the vehicle, there was a large red light, just one in the centre of the room, this was the only supply of light for us to see where we were going as there were no moons or stars in the sky to help us see the way any better than we could. I let go off the rope with my other hand and sat down on the chair, my airs popped from the sudden changed in the amount of wind being sent into them.

"Quick, wrap that around you" one of the men shouted over the sound of the wind, pointing at the seatbelt that was attached to the side of the chair. I grabbed it with both hands and quickly pulled it from one side to the other, clicking it into the receiver, locking it firmly in place. The man looked at me and gave me a thumbs up, Trax wasn't far behind, she walked in without even holding the rope and slapped a button on the inside of the door, her hand was raised over her face to shield her from the strong winds, how she could even see where she was going seemed like a mystery. The button she pressed made the door rise and close, locking us in the vehicle and cutting of the wind from reaching us. I could still hear it howling from outside, but no longer feel it rushing through my hair and down my clothes, freezing me to the bone.

"Let's go!" Trax shouted, walking to the opposite seat, also near the door. She hit the roof of the vehicle, as some kind of signal to Henry to let him know that we were all in here, and we were all ready. Then she sat down and strapped herself in as we all previously did, I could feel the tension in the air, the fear had engulfed us all, I knew even Trax must have been afraid, despite what she would have us believe. We were all thinking the worst, all ready to face our certain deaths, all ready, to go into the den of the dragon itself.

Vibrations came from the chair I was sitting on; they went through my body and started shaking. Henry must have turned the truck on, causing the vehicle to shake.

"Hang on guys, gonna be a bumpy ride" Trax yelled at us all, the vehicle had started moving. I think the shaking wasn't coming from the truck moving, but more from the wind outside, crashing into the side of it over and over again.

"So what's the plan?" Jonathon shouted, the wind outside caused a loud humming sound, making it very difficult to hear him speak.

"We dock up in the loading area; we exit the vehicle, split into teams. Leo, you will go with Jonathon and Calum. Robert and Henry will come with me." Trax ordered.

"How will we know where to go?" I asked in reply. Trax smiled at me, her head bouncing as the vehicle did before finally replying.

"You won't, the only one who knew their way round the facility was Kath, and she's gone now, hence why we are splitting up, cover more ground, meaning we have a better chance of finding our friends, otherwise we could be in there for days looking around." She finished, still cockily smiling at me.

"How are you Leo? Feel one of your episodes coming on?" Jonathon asked me. There was a small glimmer of hope in his eyes.

"I'm afraid not Jon, I don't think we're going to get that lucky." I replied to him, dropping my head in shame, I'm useless without having an episode, I can't fight at all, there is no point in me going with them, all I am is a liability.

"We can do this without you spazzing out!" Trax interrupted.

"Maybe, but we would have a much better chance if he did, plus I would also love to see him in action, I've never witnessed the effects of the Awaking drug first hand, well I have seen what the pill does to normal people, not that you're not normal, I'm just going to shut up now." Jonathon waffled. Trax just spoke her head with annoyance.

I couldn't help but think about Katherine and the journey we had just done, everything from waking up and complaining about cereal, to waking up again and being told my life was never real and I'm going to die within a few hours of actually breathing in real breaths. Then there was the rebel base, a disgusting building which I doubt I will ever get to see from the outside, and that adorable girl Teara. My fist clenched as I begun to think about her, thinking about what the Director was doing to her, what kind of life she would be forced to live if we failed. Then there was the city, the amazingly beautiful city, I will never forget that view from the top of the wall, the lights shining through the fog, the flying cars darting around buildings, the buildings that were so tall they disappeared into the clouds, it's something you had to see to believe, something that my imagination could never grasp of think of, not in a million years.

Maybe I would get lucky, maybe the drug would kick in, turning me into a super solider once again, I'd be able to infiltrate the base single handily and rescue all those who were captured, killing everything that got in my way, including that Director, finally the world would be rid of him. The things the Federation do to the people in the city as well as the people in the facility, even the rebels, it's unforgivable, they must be punished. It can't go on anymore, although I had a strong feeling that one day it would be stopped, that day was just not today.

Looking around the back of the vehicle I could see two men, both tall and skinny with short hair. They were also both holding weapons, against some people they would pose a threat, but against the soldiers we faced in the tower, they would be slaughtered. And considering those were one of the lowest strength soldiers, the ones that Awakening didn't really bound well with, imagine what a handful of black suits would do to us, the ones that the drug fell in love with, the best of the best. Even me with an episode in place, would be killed before I even got close enough to begin fighting back.

Then my wandering mind fixed on Katherine, despite losing so many, Laura, Nogla, Hank . . . . The only one that made me want to die just so

I could see them once more was her. I've never felt like anyone the way I did her, even the kiss, it wasn't done under the best of circumstances, but it felt right, it felt so good, and that would now forever be the first and last time that I get to feel her lips against mine. I wanted to make them pay, for this hole I now feel inside of me, for this pain they've caused me, I won't them all to experience a pain like this, and die feeling it, so it's the last thing they ever remember.

"Leo get so rest, in fact we all should, the journey will be a few hours, we have to travel quite far around the outside of the wall before we reach our final destination." Trax ordered. No one argued with her, who'd want to, she could probably crush anyone of us with ease. The two other men nodded and shut their eyes, trying to fall asleep and rest, even if it was just for a moment, so when they woke they felt rested and ready for a fight. I turned my head left and looked at Jonathon; he was already out cold, snoring even louder than Hank did. I guess it wasn't just me who had a long day, we all had, they had been waiting for the one key for victory to return, and then when it finally did it was followed by the worst news imaginable. That wasn't even the end of the day, the night was still young and we still had a job to do.

Closing my eyes as ordered I tried to block the thought of Kath out of my head, I would never fall asleep unless I managed to stop thinking about her, her gorgeous face, amazing smile, ruined hair, petite body, everything. The more I tried not to think about her the more I did, that's always the case though, when you tell yourself not to think about something it's always the first thing in your mind, the thing right at the front of your queue of thoughts. Part of me still didn't sent to wake from my sleep, if I did ever manage to fall asleep, because then I would finally be left alone, the only person barking orders at me, telling me to help them, the only person would could cause me pain, the only person who I would ever see, would be me. Lonely perhaps, but free nether the less.

The last thought that crossed my mind before I drifted of, the vehicle still shaking, the thumbing of wind echoing, was the thought of my bed. I think that's why I finally fell asleep, all I could think about was my bed on Earth, that warm duvet stretched over my body, the sound of construction work on the roads outside, my pet rolled up at my feet, my girlfriend curled up, slotted perfectly in sync with my own body. The mornings were amazing; I'd always wake up first and just lie there for a moment. Everything felt great, it felt real, the only part of my pathetic life that did for some reason, maybe it was because it was the only part I actually enjoyed, everything else was just predictable.

Then I was asleep, my eyes tightly shut, the one thing that was different about my bed this time, was the image of having Katherine in it with, not my blood sucking harpy of a girlfriend, just the window open, the smell of fresh air striking me gently, moving the sheets underneath me, and sending the fantastic smell of Kath in my direction. Falling asleep with her in my arms and the smell of her in my lungs, I wish I could have experienced that once before she died, just once.

"Leo get up now!" A man's voice said, I felt a sharp quick pain at the bottom of my leg, just above my foot. I opened my eyes quickly to see Calum, one of the guys, standing in front of me, staring at me. He had slick back hair, making it look shorter than it actually was. He had two scars on his cheeks and a rather large chin. He was dressed in the same black clothing I was in when I left for the city; I think he had always been wearing it, just never paid attention to what it was that he was wearing beforehand.

"Here" he said, handing me a Federation handgun, I struggled to open my eyes fully and seemed to have a blinding headache, naps never did agree with me, when people used to tell me that they would have a nap when they got home and feel completely refreshed I always thought they were full of shit, whenever I had one I felt a hundred times worse than before, insanely hot and stuffy, like I was on the come down from a cold.

I reached out and grabbed the weapon from his hands, gripping it tight and placing it in one of my larger trousers pockets.

"Do you know how to use it?" He asked me as he stood up, walking back slightly.

"Urm I have used one before, but I don't think that counts. I'm guessing you point and shoot?" I asked, trying to sit my body back up straight as I seemed to of fallen down slightly, my body hanging off the chair, the seatbelt raised almost under my chin. He looked at me and laughed as he moved over towards Trax.

"That's the gist of it, yeah!" He explained. I realised that I could no longer hers the thuds of the wind hitting the side of the truck, or feel the shakes each time it did.

"Where are we?" I asked, un-clipping the belt, trying to scramble to my feet to join the others standing up, the only one that wasn't, was Jonathon, he was staring at his lap; it looked like he might even still be asleep.

No one seemed to answer me at first, they were all fiddling around with their equipment, attaching things to their clothing and checking to make sure their weapons were loaded. Between us we each appeared to have one handgun, two of us, Trax and Calum had the strange assault rifles that I saw earlier.

"We are here Leo" Henry said, emerging from the driver's area, the metal door was now wide open.

"Is everyone ready? Within the minute we will dock into the loading area. As soon as that time comes I want everyone mobile and ready to exit the back of the vehicle." He snapped at Trax, walking over to her, holding his hand out to receive a weapon. Trax slapped a handgun into his palm; Henry looked at her with confused eyes, as if he expected to be given something differently.

"Sorry boss but we need one with each group and I'm a better shot then you, so you will have to make do with that" she replied, nodding her head at the weapon in his hand.

"Jonathon, get up!" Henry barked at him, Jonathon stumbled and fell to the ground; he hit it hard, sending a clanging sound around the truck.

"Sorry" he muttered, staggering to his feet.

"Weapon" he asked, holding out his hand as Henry had done. Trax and Henry exchanged a short look, there was a moment of pause before he nodded, allowing Trax to give him a weapon. She pulled another one from her right leg pocket and threw it over towards him; it dropped down through his open hands and struck the metal floor, sending yet another clang through our ears. Trax sighed with anger as Jon dropped to the floor to pick the handgun back up, he held it tight in his hands, a look of fear splattered across his face, the poor man had probably never seen any combat before this. With everyone kidnapped or dead now, this was the best the rebellion had to offer, two tall men, one butch woman, on man who's knowledge was in everything but fighting, and another who was so blinded by wanting to take down the Federation that he had completely forgotten about all the people who died to get the device that could make this all possible, the device hidden inside his clothing somewhere.

Then there was me a nobody, no fighting skill, no shooting skill, just a very open mind which at any moment could be taken over by pure instinct, driving to solve the situation with the best possible outcome, of course if that happened the others would breathe a sigh of relief. I'm sure that they would rather have the man who instinctively knew how to kill then one who couldn't do if he tried thinking about what was the easiest way to do for hours.

"When that door opens, Calum you take your team left, we will turn right. The loading docks are usually empty so we shouldn't have any problems straight away, the machines that dock here are programmed to stay locked until the soldiers can get here, as ours is the older model it will automatically open as soon as it docks, however we will not have long before they get here to expect it, so move fast!" Henry ordered us.

"No bags Jonathon" Trax barked, staring at Jon who had picked up his rucksack from the floor and placed it on his back.

"You are going to want to move fast, the only things we bring are our weapons and the device, nothing more" she continued. Jon listened instantly, it was hard to argue with that statement, he dropped the bag from his back, which also landed on the floor releasing a third loud clang. Everyone rolled their eyes with disappointment.

"Sorry guys" he whispered, his head dropped in shame, he was shaking from how scared he was, the gun jolting and bouncing around inside his gripped palm.

"You're going to be fine; I'm not going to let anything happen to you, alright?" I said to him, trying to relax him and calm his nerves, I didn't want a man standing behind me, pointing his weapon ahead of him, his finger shaking on the trigger.

He looked back at me with a small, thin, nervous smile, his hand still shaking, but not as much.

There was a loud thud from outside the truck, and then the sound of some sort of hydraulics system moving around replaced the thud. The door began to slowly open, falling out away from us. Everyone stood up straight, their weapons pointing in front of them. Calum and Trax took point, as they had the better guns, in stood behind Calum and Jon behind me. Henry stood behind Trax with Robert behind him. All eyes were locked on the opening door, waiting for it to fully extend so we could begin our mission, we were here, scared and ready. I hoped I would never have to return to this place, hard to believe that I lived my whole life in this very building, in one machine, completely oblivious to the world that surround me.

CHAPTER 27

Dig Deep

"**Go go go**" Trax shouted as the door attached itself to the platform outside, we all ran forward towards the white wall in front of us, the other team turned left as they stated and Calum lead us to the right, running fast, even with no enemies around, we had to move fast before they got here. As we left the truck I could get a better look of the area, again all the inside walls were pure white in colour, there was at least twenty trucks attached to the docking station, which was just a raised platform of the ground, sort of like the ones some supermarkets had back on Earth, it allowed the vehicle to back up and people to empty the contents of it without having to change height levels. The trucks were much larger than the one we had come in, they looked exactly the same other than the fact that they tripled ours in size. The room was very larger; behind the trucks was a line of closed doors, each the exact size of the truck that sat in front of it.

We ran fast across the loading platform, trying to find a door on the side, if a solider spotted us now we would be shot down like dogs before we even made it off the platform. I could hear Jonathon panting behind me, he sounded tired already, we had only ran around one hundred metres, and he was only carrying a handgun, obviously he was very unfit. Calum in front of me was keeping the same pace, moving his head rapidly around as he jogged, trying to spot a way to leave this room, or see if there were any Federation units nearby. The further we ran the more my heart rate increased, not just because I was growing increasingly tired, but also because I knew that at any moment a handful of Federation soldiers would saunter in here and kill all three of us. I wonder if Henry's group had made it out of here yet, or if they were still running like us. I would have turned around and checked to see if I could see them behind us, but I didn't want to lose focus of the task at hand, and so long as I could hear Jonathon behind me I had no real reason to turn and face back.

"There" Calum shouted, pointing at a small steel door located on the left side of the platform, we picked up the pace as we approached it, Calum grabbed the handle and pushed it instantly open, holding it while Jonathon and I ran through out of the docking area. We both stopped and turned around on the other side of the door, to make sure that Calum was following us through; he closed the door quickly and held his weapon with both hands once more.

"No time for a break lads, keep moving" he said, jolting the weapon behind us, insisting that we continue to move, I gazed over at Jon, he was hunched over with his hands on his knees trying to regain his breath.

"Come on Jon, we don't have to run anymore, but we do need to keep moving" I explained, placing my hand on his back. He looked up at me and nodded, before tuning the other way and slowly walking away from the door we had just come through.

The following area wasn't a room, but instead a corridor, and a very familiar one at best. The walls were all the same brand of white, as were the many doors darted around in them. The ceiling and even the floor beneath our feet was also white, there were built in lights, each a few feet from the next, they reflected off the ground due to it being so clean. The corridor looked exactly like the one I was in last time I was here, being dragged along the ground to my death. I couldn't help but feel like this time wasn't very different, only I was walking the other way, not being dragged; it still felt like it was to my death however.

"Where to now?" Calum asked, walking in front of myself and Jonathon once more to take the lead, I was happy he was in front of us, his weapon was much larger than ours and therefore I assumed that he would also have a much better chance of killing any suits that attacked us.

"How should I know?" Jon coughed out through his panting breath as he struggled to keep walking without rest.

"Not you, you!" Calum explained, pointing the barrel of his gun back at me, not in a threatening way, just in a way where he wanted to make sure we knew who the question was directed at.

"How the hell should I know?" I replied with a confused expression. He didn't turn back to face us, just carried on walking, his paced slowed dramatically and our voices became quiet whispers, we were trying to sneak down the corridor, silently, remaining undetected. So far it seemed completely deserted; there were no people to be seen, no soldiers coming down the corridor towards us, just an endless row of doors.

Maybe all the men were at our base, perhaps they expected us to go there and not come here, I wouldn't of predicted that we would strike now, not when we were so weak, but then again it is also when the Federation would be most weakest. Or I could be very wrong and this was all just a big trap, a way to get the last of the rebellion in one place to kill us all, but if they didn't know we had the device then why would they think we'd come here, I don't think Henry would have come here just to rescue the rest of his people, he would only come here if he knew that there was a way to destroy them once and for all. If the Director knew what Henry was like then he would surely have guessed that we would return to our base and fight the soldiers there, which would explain why it was so empty here. Unless he knew we had the device.

"Out of the three of us you're the only one who's actually been here" he stated.

"And no disrespect but you have spent your entire life within these walls" Jonathon explained.

"Well I don't know if you noticed but they didn't exactly let us get up and walk around the building, and the only time I actually saw these walls was when I was running past them, trying to escape." I answered, my voice frustrated with the stupid question, how the hell was I supposed to know where we were supposed to go, everywhere in this building looked the same, every turn, every corridor, even the doors were the same damn colour.

"Alright, plan B then, we walk until we find something, as we don't know what's on the other side of these doors there's no pointing opening them. Plus you'd think that the room they were keeping thousands of people prisoner would have a bigger door leading inside of it, or the server room, which are the only two places that have any significance to us." Calum explained, pressing forward, he quicken his pace as to cover more ground quicker, if we were going to continue forward we wouldn't want to be doing it for long, if this was the main corridor leading to the loading bay then at any moment there would be Federation suits walking through it to investigate our vehicle.

"How are you Leo?" Jonathon asked, he had regained most of his energy by the sound of his voice.
"Honestly I'm alright, just very angry and anxious, I don't like the idea of walking in a constant straight line." I answered.
"If you were in the forest of Vala would you keep changing direction, or would you stay the course of one direction? Tell me, if two people choose different paths, one sticking to the rising sun, one changing direction every couple of hours, who would find their way out first?" Calum asked us. Honestly it was a good point, I hadn't thought of it like that, the chances were much better that we would find something of significance if we just stayed our current course, if we started opening every door then we would never find anything or anyone, this place was like a giant white maze, full of closed doors and no clues or signs to help find your way around. Everyone who worked here must have to learn the whole structure off by heart as to not get lost.

We carried on walking for a while, the corridor seemed endless, there was no end in sight and we were starting to lose hope, speeding up and slowly down occasionally. I kept hoping to see a different coloured door, wall or anything, anything to suggest that we should change out direction.
"This is getting us nowhere!" I said, still trying to keep my voice quiet but getting angry due to the time we were wasting, I had lost track of time and realised that if we spent hours walking around this place, not finding anything then the Federation would eventually return and find us here, lurking around their base. We had come too far to let that happen, getting caught cluelessly walking around, they'd laugh at us as the unloaded their rounds into our flesh, closing our eyes forever.

"Alright we can't keep doing this, I think we should split up" Calum said, stopping and turning around, he lowered his weapon to point at the floor.

"I agree" I replied to him.

"I don't, there's no way I'm walking around this dreadful place on my own, I don't know how to use this bloody thing, I could stumble across a five year old girl with a skipping rope and she'd still have a better chance of killing me then I would killing her with a gun in my hand" Jonathon whimpered. Calum and I glanced at each other, we both knew he was right, I wasn't a good fighter or shot, but at least I had the drug pumping through my veins, Jon had nothing, he had probably never even held a weapon before Trax gave him one.

"Fine, you come with me, Leo will you be alright on your own?" Calum asked.

"I guess we'll find out" I nervously replied. I didn't really want to split up, but I knew it would be better than walking down this endless corridor.

"Good luck mate" Calum said, holding out his hand, I reached out and grabbed it, shaking it. He nodded and turned around, opening the door behind him. He walked through it, his weapon once again raised to point in front of him. Jonathon trailed behind, as he entered the door behind him he turned his head to look at me, I was standing still, watching them walk away from me. Jonathon let out a little smile and nod, before turning around and walking through the open white door, closing it behind him. I was now alone.

As the door closed behind them I also turned around, wrapping my hand around the white door handle, pulling it down and opening the door, I suddenly felt very scared, if I came across anyone I would be killed instantly, firing my weapon wouldn't make a difference as the soldiers I would be firing it at would be much stronger and much better at firing theirs at me then I would be to them. The following room was a small white one; it had a table in the middle of it, exactly the same look as the one I was in with the Director when I first woke into Vala. The table was the only thing in the room this time however, there were no chairs on either side of it, and no man sitting in the chairs condescendingly talking to me, putting me down or simply trying to scare me.

I entered the room and the door closed behind me, it let out a quiet click as the handle slotted back into place. I turned my head to once again look at the door, to make sure it was closed behind me, only when I turned my head I noticed that there was no door, just a white wall, how is that possible, I could of sworn I just walked through a door right behind me, right where this wall now stood. I gazed at the wall for a moment before lifting my hand and rubbing it up and down the wall, trying to make sure that I was not imagining it. The material felt like a wall, not a door, there was no hidden handle, no tricks, it was a solid wall.

My gaze once again turned back to the table in front of me, only when I return my stare to the table I discovered I was no longer alone in the room. There was a person with, standing on the other side of the table, standing there, covered in blood, dripping on the ground below, it created a small puddle surrounding the person, the blood grew on the floor, sliding across the surface of it towards my feet. I squinted my eyes, trying to make out the persons disfigured face, it was hidden underneath their long hair. There was a sudden smell of burning flesh in the air, I could smell burning hair with a mixture of blood, I could even taste it at the back of my throat. I didn't say anything to the person, I didn't want to spook them, or for the person to do anything that would spook me.

Lifting my feet slowly I walked into the puddle of blood, treading lightly, approaching the table that was in between us. The closer I got, the stronger my fear grew, I found myself shaking, my heart thumbed in my chest, the sound of it beating filled my ears. I slowly reached into my pocket and pulled my weapon out from it, holding it with my right hand, stretched down by my leg. My grip tightened around the handle of it, my finger placed gently on the trigger, ready to raise the handgun at the first sign of trouble. I looked closer at the persons face, they appeared to be a girl, a servilely burned girl, all her skin had peeled from her bones, her hair was seared and torn, I could see parts of her scalp where she had lost all of hair completely.

"Hello" I called out to the woman, her head jolted up, her red eyes starred right at me, they looked like the eyes from the fog around the wall, dark red eyes gazing into my soul, as her head raised some hair moved from covering her face and I recognised the person standing before, I could feel my heart stand still as I looked at her burnt face.

"Kath" I whispered, the woman didn't say anything, just stood there staring at me for a moment, how could this be possible? Kath died in the fire, I saw her walk into the flames, she couldn't be standing in front of me now, she didn't even look well enough to be standing, her skin was falling off her, hit the blood covered floor below, sending ripples throughout it, I could feel the ripples hit my feet, one by one, they bounced off of my shoes and sent smaller ripples around the soles of my feet.

Not knowing what to do I just stood there, staring at her. She suddenly smiled, I could feel the room heating up, the blood began to boil and bubble around her, steam rose from it. The heat kept rising, sweat started to drip off my head and splash into the blood below. Katherine opened her mouth and let out a horrendous scream, it made me jump, I felt terrified, the scream pierced my eardrums, I raised my hands to cover them. The blood around her feet turned to fire, raising up, swallowing her body once more, the heat burning my face as the fire rose to the ceiling, Katherine continuing to scream.

"KATHERINE!" I shouted at the top of my lungs, reaching out for her with hand. The fire erupted, turning into a large fireball; I shielded my eyes from the bright light. As my hands rose to cover my face the heat from the room disappeared, turning back to normal, what had happened?

My eyes blinked slowly, opening to see the back of my arm, I lowered my arm to stare back into the room, everything was gone, the blood on the floor, the heat, even Katherine. The only thing that was now left was the table that was there before, could I have imagined that? It felt so real; I could feel the heat from the fire on my skin, burning into my flesh. I also now noticed a door had appeared on the other side of the table, it was the same as the one behind me, only the one behind me was still gone; the only way that I could now leave the room was through the newly made door.

I started walking forward towards the newly formed door, passing the table, my eyes were fixed on the ground where Katherine had been standing, I kept expecting to see her rise from the ground once more, or even notice a small drop of blood, something left over from what I had just witnessed, that way I would know I am not crazy, and I would know that what I had seen actually happened and wasn't a figment of my imagination. As I approached the closed door I lifted my hand and gripped the handle, there was a moment of hesitation, I knew this door was not here before; I wasn't going insane, something wasn't right. I turned my head once more to see if anything had changed, maybe she would be standing there once more, but everything was still the same, the same table in the middle of the same boring white room. I felt more at ease then before, perhaps it was just all in my head; I lowered my weapon into my pocket once again, hiding it from sight.

My hand pulled down, opening the door, it pulled towards me to reveal the room on the other side, this room was completely different to the previous ones, and the corridors, there was almost no white in the next room and the size of it was vast and massive. At first there was a walkway, a rather large one; it was like a giant metal balcony, made from steel grates. There were two doors either side of the walkway and a spiral staircase leading down, I couldn't see to what it led down too, but I knew it was insanely big whatever it was as the balcony only took up a small part of the overall room, a fraction of a section. It appeared to look over something, but from the entrance of the door that I just walked in, even gazing through the gaps in the metal grated walkway, I couldn't make out what it was exactly.

The ceiling of the room wasn't white and tidy like the previous ones, it was black and had dangling lights, hundreds of them, lighting up the surrounding area. The walls were a dull green colour, it looked more like the inside of a warehouse them the inside of a high tech facility. There was something else in the room, I dropped my eyes from the ceiling to see two men standing in front of me, they were standing on the walkway, I couldn't make out their faces at first, but I could see that one was holding the other by the throat. There was a sudden snapping sound, the man being held by the throat jolted slightly, and then became limp. My eyes adjusted and I could make out the one standing up straight, holding the other still by the neck.

"You!" I said with fierce anger in my voice. The man looked over at me and smiled, his smile was sinister and devilish. He then released his grip, dropping the second person to the floor; their body hit the ground hard, creating a slight thud. The persons arm flopped out, extended along the floor, their eyes empty and dead. I could see their face clearly now, their tired, droopy face, the red hand mark still fresh on their neck.

"Henry!" I quietly whispered under my breath.

"God no!" My heart sank, we had lost.

Chapter 28

It's All Over Now

THE DIRECTOR STOOD in front of me; blood dripping from his hands, the lifeless body of Henry was stretched out across the metal grates below. The Director was still staring at me, he didn't even look down at the man he had just killed, his eyes were fixed on my, his evil smile still slapped across his face. I can't believe Henry was now dead, he was our leader, the leader of the entire rebellion, we had lost so many people and now we had lost the one in-charge, out of all the people to lose at this moment in time he was the one last on list. What do we do now? And where was Trax or Robert? What happened to them? Maybe their group split up as well as ours, I hope their all safe, that still gives us some chance of succeeding, or if we failed we would still have enough survivors to try and start from scratch. Wait, what about the device? Henry had it; if we lose that we lose everything.

"Right now I assume you're thinking about what you can do next, how you can defeat me, and also what about your precious device. Am I right?" The Director asked through his smile. I could feel my blood boil inside my body, my rage building up. The Director removed an item from his pocket and dangled it in front of him.

"Do you want to hear a funny story Leo? When I tell you you're going to laugh and laugh." He continued all the while staring at me, grinning. I didn't move, I knew I could take him in a fight, especially if Henry failed, he seemed much stronger than me and much smarter, how would I stand a chance. I bit my lip and tried to contain the growing anger within me.

The Director began pacing around the corpse, moving his eyes from the floor back up to me, rubbing the blood off of his hands, it dripped through the grates and fell further down. Then he tossed the device into the air, flicking it over the metal railing behind him, it fell far to the ground below. All hope was truly lost.

"You see Leo what you and the Rebels didn't seem to think about was the very fact that the Federation, the very organisation you were trying to bring down, invented a drug that could help people predict the future, see the best outcomes from our millions of experiments. Did you not stop to think that maybe this meant that we knew what you were going to do? What the Rebels were going to do?" He asked, pausing to gaze up at me, his face had now turned serious. He was standing over Henry's body, his hands moving around as he spoke.

"From the moment you left this facility we knew exactly what you would do, what they would ask you to do, theirs plans, EVERYTHING!" He shouted.

"Do you really believe that you could escape a place like this as easily as you did? We let you go! You led us right or the base of the Rebels! Then we just had to pick you off one by one, the mistakes that you all made just kept coming and coming. The first being sending their two best fighters into the city with you on a suicide mission, so of course they died. The second was leaving the base with the last of the fighters to insure that the device you collected would be brought back safely, leaving the base wide open, we walked straight in, butchered all the adults and gained a great supply of young ones to join our on-going experiment, I have you to thank for that." He again paused looking over at me, smiling.

"Thank you!" He said.

That was it, the last straw, I felt my heart rise, I kicked the ground and sprinted forward, running directly at him, my fist raised ready to strike him, I let out a mighty scream as I got close. But the only thing my fist struck was the cold air around him, he kicked the front of my leg, dropping straight to the metal ground below, he then dropped his raised leg on my chest, pinning me down, he continued to push down harder and harder, the air left my lungs, the pressure made it difficult to breathe. I raised my hand and began hitting his leg, as hard as I could, but my punches seemed to have no effect on him at all. I then tried to lift his foot from my chest, but once again all the strength I could muster didn't seem to be enough, the foot didn't even flinch, it was as if it was super glued to my chest, he was too strong for me, I couldn't do anything to hurt him, I was stuck.

"Anyway, where was I?" He asked before continuing.

"Oh yeah, now I remember. Do you not yet understand Leo Cathery? The device isn't even real, it's worthless. We let you enter our tower, how else would we be able to kill you all so easily, didn't you wonder how it was that all those soldiers could arrive out of nowhere so quickly, you hadn't even triggered the alarms, it was a trap from the moment you left the base. You led us to the safe house, which we later destroyed, you walked right into our tower, surrounded by my units, come on! How stupid can you all be?" He laughed, his foot still pushed down hard on my chest.

"The only thing we didn't count on was the Awakening drug taking effect while you were there, that made things much more difficult, we always planned to let you escape so you could lure the rest of the soldiers out on your return. But we were originally going to kill the other two men there!"

"Nogla and Hank!" I angrily interrupted.

"Yes, them" he continued.

"And of course capture Katherine, she was too valuable to kill, oh wait I almost forgot, you don't know yet, do you?" His smile grew once more as he pulled a device out from his pocket, pointing it at the wall where the door was that I had come from.

He pushed his finger down on it, pressing a button, I tilted my head back so I could see the wall he was pointing the device at more clearly. It was no longer a wall; it was now a large glass window, with another white room on the other side. There were two doors at the back of the room, at first I thought that they were black doors, but then I realised something, the doors weren't black at all. There was two large figures standing in front of each one, both taller than the average man, and much more bulky than a normal person, their suits were pitch black, the shirts were also pitch black in colour, ties as well. The men were so large in size that the blocked the view of the white doors behind them completely, they were the fearless black suited Federation soldiers.

But that wasn't the reason the Director was showing me the room, the reason was the seven metal chairs in the centre of the room, and the people tied to each one. In order from left to right I could see, Jonathon, he his head dropped down, along with the others in the chairs, facing the floor below them, bloody faced and bruised. Their clothes ripped and torn. The next person was Trax, how they managed to capture her I will never know, that woman scared even me. Then there was Calum and Robert, after that my eyes widened with surprise, the next two people tied to the chairs were Magic Man and Jane.

Why would the Director let them live? What significance could they have over the other people at the base? Maybe Magic Man, but why Jane? And also why would the Director lie to me about them being dead. The last person was harder to make out; they had their hair dropped over their face, hiding it completely. The body looked familiar, but until I saw the face I wouldn't be able to figure out who the last person was.

"I had to get Henry to bring you all here to me, I guessed that maybe if I told him that I had killed his two highest priority people, which would fill him with enough anger to attack this facility. Don't worry, they will be killed shortly, but until we extract the information from their minds it would probably be most wise to keep them alive, we need to know how many more of you are out there, how many more we need to hunt down and kill before you are all wiped from the face of this planet." The Director explained, his voice filled with happiness.

"The same goes for all the others, between then all we have a database of our own, a Valarian device like the one you had, only mine is in the form of people, and not a trap set up by you, I doubt you're even smart enough to know what the word trap means, if you did you would t keep making so many mistakes and falling directly into them, constantly." He chuckled.

"As for the last person, that was just for this moment right now, that is all for you Leo" he stated, pressing another button on the device. The persons head flung back, the button must have shocked them somehow. I could now clearly make out their face, their worn out, filthy and damaged face.

"That's not possible, I saw her die!" I muttered out through my hazy breaths.

"No, the Katherine that you woke up with in the safe house after the crash, was nothing more than an illusion created by us, we managed to grab her back at the crash, as we already knew where the safe house was we dropped you off there, our new Katherine with you, waiting for a while before striking the base. Honestly the only reason I made you believe that she had died in the fire of that burning building was so that I could destroy your heart! Remove the one thing in this world that you loved, that you cared about, you had nothing here, nothing except her, and I took her from you, now I can do the same with her. I'm going to let Katherine watch me as I kill you, taking you away from her forever, that way you can both experience the worst pain imaginable." He explained through his growing grin.

"Anyway, this is beginning to bore me" he stated, pressing one last button on the device.
"There, now they can all see us, they will have a lovely view of me crushing your chest plate, puncturing your lungs and then they can watch you cough up your own blood, chocking on it as each bit of life leaves your cold body!" He said, I could suddenly feel his foot pushing down harder, pressing against my body! I took one last deep breath, holding it in as best I could, trying to survive, but I knew my death approached, there was nothing I could do, I could gain the strength to move his leg, and I couldn't fight him even if I did, this truly was the end, and Katherine was here to see it, the pain I felt when I believed she died was unimaginable and now she had to go through the same thing, I can't believe I had just found out that she had survived, and now I was going to die, not even getting to say goodbye.

"Sorry it had to be like this Leo, you're quite the amazing specimen, the way the drug bounded with your DNA, that's never happened before, we spend years trying to get the drug to bound with our soldiers and most don't take, but you, if only you could have it active all the time, you'd be unstoppable, even my body didn't take to it as well as you! But I did learn how to use my muscles more efficiently, which is why I can crush your lungs and there's nothing you can do about it! Such a waste of a life!" He said, pressing his heal in deeper, the air I had previously breathed in shot out of my mouth, I couldn't take in anymore, this was it, the ceiling started shaking, the lights grew brighter, darkening the rest of the room somehow.

"Goodbye Leo!" The Director laughed, that cocky grin still across his smug face. His foot literally draining all life from me, how could he be so strong? There must be something I could do, anything, I don't want to die like this, not with everyone staring at me. Come on Awakening! Kick in! Please, I'm begging you, PLEASE!

But nothing happened, no drug to save my life, the room grew darker, the only thing shining through my blurred vision was the light above. Wait a second; I slid my hand slowly across the floor, all energy drained from my weak arms, dragging it up onto my leg and into my pocket. The cold metal material touch my fingertips, I tried pulling it out, my fingers scrambling around it, sliding it into the palm of my hand. There was a sudden clunk! As the weapon fell from my pocket onto the grates below, I cannot believe I had forgotten about it, seeing the Director kill Henry like that just made me focus on him, I forgot about everything else, including the firearm I had previously placed in my trouser leg pocket. I had to act fast, the pressure on my chest continued to grow, it wouldn't be long before I ran out of all energy and wouldn't be able to even grasp the weapon, never mind use it. The Directors eyes widened slowly, he turned his head to look at where the noise had come from, he could see the weapon on the metal grates, my hand wrapped around the handle of it, raising it slowly behind his back, his foot still pressed hard against me.

"Goodbye you son of a bitch!" I muttered through my last breath, squeezing the trigger. The weapon fire one shot, it flew straight into the back of the Director, he let out a piercing scream and stumbled back, removing his foot from my chest, his hands frantically flying around the air, trying to place them on his back all the while filling the room with his whaling cries. I coughed repeatedly as I tried to re-catch my breath, I rolled over onto my front, my eyes gazing through the gaps of the floor below, I could now clearly see what was below us, what this room was for. The whole ground below was covered in beds, thousands of beds, only they were not like normal beds, they were raised off the ground and made completely out of some kind of metal. There was a blue line down the middle of each bed and dozens of random computer equipment connected to the chairs and what lay upon them.
"Oh my god" I whispered.

CHAPTER 29

IT WAS ALL AN ILLUSION

THE CHAIRS OR beds, whatever they were, they were full of people! Thousands of people, strapped up to machines with wires and tubes pumping certain fluids into their bodies. None were moving; each seemed to be lying in the exact same position. They were all different ages, some were elderly, others were my age, a few were no older than ten years old. There was males and females, all hooked up to these machines, to this equipment. They were just like me, this must have been where I was, my whole life, lived in one of these machines, on one of those metal beds, what a wasted life and for what? Some experiment, a way for the Federation to make tonnes of money, selling this drug! Learning the future! They sacrificed all these innocent people for their own personal benefit.

I could feel my body tensing, my strength coming back, I was furious.

"You heartless bastard!" I shouted, standing to my feet, my legs ached and were still tired. I had been drained almost completely, despite regaining my oxygen I had not yet gained full strength; it was growing, coming back, but only slowly. I stumbled as I stood up straight, glaring at the Director, he was still groaning, falling to the floor occasionally. Blood was dripping from the hole in his back, the hole I had made firing a bullet into his spine, I couldn't help but let out a little smile watching him in this much pain, after all the pain he caused us this is no less than he deserves.

"You alright Director? Need a hand? Does it hurt?" I sarcastically asked him, a little smile stretched from cheek to cheek. I raised my hand; the weapon gripped tightly within my grasp, the barrel pointing towards the Director. He was still fumbling around; he hadn't even noticed the fact that I was now standing and about to unload the entire contents of the weapon into his flesh.

"You know something, I should thank you, if it wasn't for you Katherine and the others would not be here to watch you die" I muttered, still trying to catch my breath once more.

"Thank you" I said, squeezing the trigger, the weapon jolted back as a loud bang vibrated through my eardrums. The bullet went soaring through the air, it struck the Director somewhere on his forehead, the contents of his head flew out of the back of his skull as the round exited his body.

Becoming lifeless, his body stumbled around on its feet for a moment, like a chicken which had just had its head cut off. He continued to stumble around before he reached the metal railing behind, his body struck it with force sending him lifting into the air, his legs kept kicking as they raised from the ground, his arms had already fallen over the other side of the metal railings, becoming a counter weight for the rest of his body, pulling it all completely over the railing, sending his corpse plummeting to the ground below. I dropped to my knees as the body disappeared from sight; I had used all of my energy to previously stagger to my feet. There was a loud clank, which let me know that the body had reached the ground. I wanted to see him, see him lying there dead, and take solemn in the fact that I was the one that put him.

My feet were still worn and tired, I couldn't stand, so instead I crawled to the side of the walkway, my knees scrapping across the hard, cold metal grates. As I approached the side of the walkway I grabbed it with my right hand, pulling my head forward and over the side of it, staring down at the body of the Director. His arms were fully extend outwards, as were his legs, he was face up staring at the roof, his body not moving at all but his were wide open, only there was no life in them, he was gone, finally dead. I let out a large sigh of relief in the fact that I had won, then I remember that there was two black suits staring at me through the electronic window that the Director had created. I lifted and turned my head back towards the screen, only it was now gone, the wall that was there before had once again returned to take its place. When the Director died the device he was holding must have broken along with every bone in that man's body. I knew they would be coming for me, but I didn't care, I feel like I had finally done something worthwhile myself, without the help of that drug, just my own mind.

Dropping my head back over the railing to stare at the dead body of the Director once more, I wanted it to be the last thing I ever saw, when the black suits arrived they would kill me without hesitation, at least I could die staring at the work I had achieved. The body looked different, almost like it was flickering, like when a television begins to lose signal. The body continued to flicker before it fizzled, let out a loud buzzing sound and disappeared completely, fading into nothing. My eyes widen, my mouth dropped open. That wasn't the Director; it was nothing more than a hologram! A projection created by the Federation. Then my mind wandered back to when I had seen Kath's burning corpse in the previous room, that must have been the Director again, getting inside my mind, if he could do that, create the heat against my skin, then why not create one of himself, he would be able to kill me and Henry with ease and not even put himself in danger. Only if he wasn't here, where was he?

I reached up and grabbed the railing above my head, pulling myself to a stance, my legs wobbled and shook as I tried to keep them straight, my arms did the same, trying to hold my body up all together.

"No" I muttered, I was not going to let it end like this, let those suits come in here and kill me, I can't let him win, not after all he's done, not after everything the Federation stand for. One thing that was true about this room was the contents of it, the people below me were very real. Strapped up to those machines, living their fake lives inside a world the Federation created, Earth! I darted my eyes across the large room, staring at the thousands of people, until my eyes saw something, something just below the staircase connected to the walkway. At first I just assumed that it was a handful of those machines bunched up together. But at a closer glance I realised it was a large computer system, there was a long, half circled desk, with a dozen monitors and keyboards attached to it. I wonder, does that control the machines? If so, it gives me an idea, the only question is, would I have enough time to follow through with my plan before the suits reached me, I didn't know how close they were or how many were coming, but I had to try.

The staircase wasn't far from me, only a few feet. I started walking towards it, my hand wrapped around the metal railing for support. I had no time to waste, any moment now I could have the Federation in this very room with me. As I approached the staircase I brought my foot down onto the first step, slowly lowering it so I could still maintain my balance. I could feel myself getting stronger so I began to pick up the pace, quickly moving down the metal spiral stairs, each step echoed throughout the large room, the sound would bounce off the walls and circle back. My hands stayed gripped tight on the side of the staircase, I felt stronger but not yet strong enough to carry myself one hundred percent. The only thing that I had to worry about was making sure I reached the computers before the soldiers reached me.

The last step came faster than I thought, I stepped onto it and jumped to the hard ground below, the floor was pitch black in colour, the machines looked much taller down here than they did from up above, I couldn't see over them, they were twice my height in size. The people were still lying down on top of the metal beds with the blue lights, I noticed that the blue light going down the centre of them seemed to be dimming and brightening slightly, like it was loading, or perhaps it was just a way for them to know that it was still functioning correctly. Honestly I didn't know, despite having spent most of my life on one of those beds the only thing I remember about this room was the brief window of it that I was shown the last time I was in this facility, and that was from a great distance, the room looked much different up close, as did the beds.

Darting my eyes around at the people I remembered why it was that I had come down here. My eyes locked onto the main controlling station, it was very close, only slightly to the left of the staircase at the bottom, it was half under the platform above and the rest was out in the open. I made my way quickly towards it, only trying to pause for no longer than a few seconds to regain my energy. Reaching the entrance to the half circle desk I walked through the opening, standing in front of the bright screens. For a moment I just stood there, looking at all the different monitors and what they had on them, I could see inside some people's lives, some were living in mansions, others were living my nightmares, I couldn't help but think about what the Director had said, all those horror movies that I loved so much were real, real people just like me had experienced those fears, gone through so much pain, and I watched as entertainment, I felt sick thinking about it.

As there wasn't that many screens I could only see a handful of different scenarios that people were living, the images changed every so often, showing me a new life and a different scenario. It was time to put an end to this; it was time to wake these people up from their endless dreams. I looked down at the other screens, the ones that were built into the desk, they displayed different images, images of people in their beds, part of me had hoped to just see a large red button that clearly stated a turn off symbol or text, but it wasn't anywhere near that simple. My head felt dizzy just thinking about all these different mistakes, all these different buttons, I could kill one of these people by accident if I pressed the wrong control, I had to make sure I knew exactly what button I was pressing and what it did.

"I don't have time for this!" I yelled my voice echoed throughout the room. I was now growing frustrated, all the controls looked the same, all buttons were the same size and the screens did show pictures of the machines but no instructions on what part of the machines did what or how to shut them all down at once, I couldn't run around turning each one off one by one. I had no way of knowing what to press or what to do, I couldn't just hit all the controls randomly in case it made things worse, all these people were completely innocent and the last thing I wanted to do would be to injure them in anyway.

As my headache grew and the room started shaking around me I found myself quickly greeting the ground below me, dropping to floor, my legs spread out in front of me, my right hand placed on my forehead, trying to focus my head on one thing to stop the room from spinning. I had run out of time, the soldiers would be upon me any second, and there was no way I was going to figure out how this console worked before they got here. All these poor people would end up living a life inside Earth because of me, because I failed them, thousands of people, there was nothing more I could do.

My hand was now covering my eyes, shielding me from the lights of the screens so I could try and weaken my growing headache. Peering through the gaps between my fingers I could see a silver glimmer of something underneath the desk with the main controls on. I moved my hand slowly down from my face and stared under the desk at the silver object. The object looked like some kind of pipe or large wire; it went into the bottom of the desk and dropped down into the ground, displeasing bellow the floor. Something inside me was telling me that the wire I was staring at had some importance, I don't know why, or what the actual significance of the cable was, but I could feel it in my bones, I just had a hunch.

My back was against the over circled half of the desk, I was underneath the walkway above, sitting on the cold ground now gazing at this silver wire. The desk that my back was against didn't have anything on it; it seemed to just be the back of the one in front of me. My hand slid across the ground below, pulling the weapon once again from my trouser pocket, I held it up in front of me, my hand shaking from tiredness and the weight of the weapon itself. I aimed the front of the handgun, trying to make sure it was completely in line with the silver cable, my head was still fuzzy, making it very difficult to see where I was aiming so I decide to fire more than one shot, to make sure I hit the target.

The gun flew back, pushing against my palm as I fired three shots directly at the cable, the first missed hitting the bottom of the desk, the second two however struck the wire spot on, cutting it in half. The bottom of the cable fell to the ground, with nothing to support it to keep it elevated, the top was now nothing more than a few inches long and dangled from the desk, still attached to it. The reaction was almost instant, every machine in the room turned off, shut down completely, the blue lights underneath the people stopped brightening and dimming, they just became dark, no light pulsing through them. Every single piece of computer equipment and the monitors connected to the machines and even the desk that I was sitting behind also shut down, if it wasn't for the lights on the ceiling the whole room would have been engulfed by complete darkness.

Managing to grab the top of the desk, I was able to pull myself to my feet. I gazed out over the sea of people, all lying down on the bed of these machines, but nothing seemed to happen, no one moved, no one woke up, nothing changed other than the lights turning off.

"Oh no!" I whispered as a horrible thought hit me, what if the machines were keeping them alive? Did I just kill all of these people? They live inside the simulation that is Earth, if I just turn off that simulation wouldn't they just die, not wake up.

As the sinister thought passed through my mind I tried moving to the one closest to me, if I could check for a pulse, see the person, even get a closer look at the machine maybe I could do something. I used the desk as leverage for as long as I could, but eventually the desk ran out and I had nothing else to hold on to, I dug deep and used whatever bit if strength I had left, letting go of the desk completely and walking towards the closet metal bed. Each step felt like an accomplishment, I could see the person getting closer and closer and I stumbled towards it, I put out my hands in front of me, making sure that as soon as I got within range of it I would be able to grab the side and use it to stay standing up.

My energy slowly came back to me; I never thought something as simple as cutting off my oxygen would cause me to be so weak, so drowsy. My hands grasped the side of the metal bed, my eyes were gazing at the ground underneath where the person was lying, I pulled them up from the ground, my breath hard and heavy. The person on the bed was a young girl, she had long blonde hair, must of been in her early twenties. Her features were absolutely perfect, spending a life in these machines obviously means that you will never get a single scratch, bruise or scar in your skin, you remain constantly lying down and catch no disease, all of these people were perfectly healthy. Her face had a blank expression on it, she didn't look like someone who was sleeping, but then again I had no idea what people were supposed to look like when they were in these machines, maybe it was all still on, just looked like it was off.

For a moment I just stood over the young girl, staring at her still body, until something happened. Her eyes flickered, like when you watch someone who is dreaming and you can see their eyes moving behind their closed eyelids. My mouth widened with disbelief, was she alive? As I stood there staring at her moving eyes, I couldn't help but worry if I may have made the wrong choice, if perhaps trying to wake these people was the decision I shouldn't have chosen. Then I realised that if I didn't do something, if I didn't try to save these people, they would most likely love their whole life lying down on one of these beds, doing nothing but following a routine given to them, doing what they were told without even knowing they were being told to anything. A programmed life on Earth, it's not right, people should be able to choose how they want to live and that's exactly what I had given these people, a chance to choose.

The woman's eyes opened slowly, they were a pale blue colour, she continued to blink, trying to gain focus, it was the first time she had ever peered through her own eyes after all. There was a noise behind me, and to my right, I looked up, turning my head around to see where the noise were coming from. There were other people waking up, some already sitting on the side of the metal bed, their hands on their heads. Some were just moving around, still lying on their backs, but every single one seemed to be slowly waking from their endless sleep, one by one. I had done it; I had freed the people, everyone just like me, finally free to live a normal life, a real life.

CHAPTER 30

WAKE UP

I COULDN'T HELP but worry about whether or not they'd believe, it took me being tortured to finally be convinced that Vala was real and Earth was in fact fake, I didn't have time to put everyone here through the same test I went through, nor did I really want to or know how to, it was the most horrible pain I had ever experienced, funny how it was from the people who we're supposed to be the good guys. Actually I'm lying, the worst pain I had ever felt was watching Katherine walk into the flames, leaving my life forever, or so I thought. Of course Katherine, I hope they were all safe, with any luck they escaped, if the black suits left the room to come and find me it would at least give them all a chance to quickly escape, I guess I would find out soon enough. That was another good point, where were the black suits? They should of gotten here by now, they should of reached me a while ago, or someone, anyone who worked here, but no one had entered the room since I had, something didn't feel right.

Once again I was standing behind the desk, my hands on the top of the silver surface, my head held high, staring out across the thousands of people, each leaving their bedsits, walking over towards me, some were helping others get up and walk, all of them were struggling, some fell to the ground, others mastered it rather quickly, as none had never used their legs before it must have been an odd sensation, of course, me of all people would know, but then again I did have a bit more time to adjust. Every single person was wearing the same uniform, it was completely white, underneath they had a black T-shirt on, and the trousers they were all wearing seemed to have a black strip going down the front and the back of them, so did the sleeves on their white tops. The uniform looked rather tight, not sure why they were wearing one to be honest, maybe just so the Federation would always be able to tell how came from the machines and who didn't.

My legs rose as I pulled myself onto the desk, I was slipped slightly and almost fell off, but I managed to find my feet in the end, standing higher up, my feet strongly placed on the metal material of the silver desk below.

"I know this must be confusing, and I know you will all have a lot of questions, and it want to answer them, but now is not the time for that. I ask only that you follow me to the exits so we can leave this building, do not ask why, just trust me." I yelled, loud enough so they could all hear me. Of course they listened, they had no clue what was going on or why they were here, even where here was. They all knew if they wanted answers the only thing to do would be to come with me, as I made my way back up the stairs I looked back to see if any were actually pursuing me. A few feet behind me walking up the stairs was the blonde girl I had stood over, the one that I had seen as she woke up. Behind her was even more people, all following me up the stairs. Looking of the side of the staircase I could see every single person making their way to the spiral stairs leading to the platform above, they were all queuing patiently, waiting for me to make it to the top, wanting answers.

Amazing to think that all of these people had lived different lives, each had been someone else, rich, poor, in danger or loved, I would love nothing more than to sit down and listen to the endless stories of their lives on Earth, here about what they had to do, who they had become, maybe some of them had seen others before on a television show or in a movie, it was remarkable to think about. As soon as we were all safe I would tell them the truth, whether they'd believe me or not was up to them, so long as they were safe I didn't really care what they chose to believe. Only knowing one way out of this building I would lead them all through the long corridors and passages back to the loading bay, maybe there would be a way to open the doors to the outside world, even use some of those vehicles to get these people out of here quickly before the Federation reached us.

It was only when I reached the top of the staircase that I realised just how large this room was, it stretched so far back that I couldn't actually make out the back of it, all I could see was the blur of the lights on the ceiling and the hundreds of people on the dark ground below. There was so many, much more than I had thought, I forgot that the Federation had been doing this for so long, kidnapping so many people, there must have been way over ten thousand people in this room alone, I hope that this was the only room like this is the base. Somewhere amongst the people I hoped that Teara was safe, walking towards this very platform, and all the other children from the rebellion base, hopefully they were all safe now, being shown the way by the massive number of people.

"Follow me" I said, looking at the blonde woman closest to me, she nodded slightly as I reached out for her, she reached back, grasping my hand, I could tell she was scared, they were all scared, I wanted them to all know that I wasn't a threat in anyway and that I was here to help them. We made our way through the door at the top of the stairs, over the other side of the platform and past the table in the room, through into the long corridor. A long line of people one by one walked through the building, following me as I lead them to their freedom. The corridor was of course a long walk, I was glad that it was only one straight line, it was impossible for anyone to get lost that way, all they needed to do was look at the back of the person in front of them and focus just on that.

Despite the large amount of people it was surprisingly quiet, from what I could hear no one was actually talking, they were all quiet, just walking, one by one, not a word left their lips. It is likely that maybe they didn't know how to yet, they hadn't ever spoken through their own mouth before, however that seemed unlikely as I didn't seem to struggle when I woke, I found my words quickly. The more likely reason was that they generally didn't know what to say, being woken from their life into this random building and told to follow someone, what words would you want to say. Their all probably so confused that they are just trying to think things through, talking comes later.

The corridor seemed much smaller than I remember, but I believe that was more due to the fact that it was packed to the sides with random people, all walking in one direction, that had the effect of making the walls seem to be closer than they actually were. The door appeared ahead of us, slowly growing as we got closer to it, the hall echoed with the sound of footsteps, I couldn't help but smile as we all walked together, thousands just like me, we had beaten the Federation, for now anyway.

"What's going on?" The blonde woman asked, I turned around to look at her, still walking towards the door at the end of the corridor.

"You wouldn't believe me if I told you, I didn't at first" I replied, turning my gaze back to the door.

"If you wait I'll show you" I continued.

As I reached the door I grasped the handle and pulled it open, to my surprise I was greeted by someone on the other side, they came thundering through the open door and wrapped their arms around me. I couldn't make out who they were, they had their head buried in my neck, I could smell a familiar smell, the persons hair smelt wonderful, I knew who it was after I took one deep breath, breathing in the smell of the persons hair.

"Kath" I whispered, raising my arms and bringing her closer to me, gripping her tight.

"Urm Leo, who are all these people?" She asked, releasing me from her grasp and walking past me towards the people behind.

"I couldn't leave them there, they are coming with us" I replied. Katherine didn't seem to mind, she had now walked over to the blonde woman closest to me.

"My name is Katherine, what is your name?" Kath said, holding out her hand as a sign of greeting.

The woman just stood there for a moment, her eyes darted between me and Katherine before she finally packed up the courage to answer the question.

"My name is Elizabeth." She murmured, the poor girl was scared stiff, I wasn't going to ask her a question myself, not until she felt comfortable around us. Katherine turned to me and smiled.

"I know there are a lot of them but . . . ." Before I could finish Kath spoke

"We will find a place for them, don't worry" she interrupted, I smiled back, I should have known she wouldn't object, how could anyone? This was always the goal of the Rebellion, to free those like me, and that is exactly what I have done, freed all of these innocent people.

"Come on, the others are waiting for us, they are trying to get the doors open" Katherine said, leading us all into the other room, where the loading bay was.

"Follow us people, we will explain on the way" Katherine said, turning around and looking over all the people, she kept smiling, she looked so much more happier than I had ever seen her, even though we had been through a lot it all seemed worth it now. As I walked through to the other room I could see the long line of trucks, still exactly where they were before, I can imagine that no one really knew how to use them which made them all completely useless. It also meant that we would most likely end up walking out of here, I didn't know how far the city was from here or the rebel base, we could end up walking for a while, even if we made it to the wall there would be no way we could sneak such a large number of people into the city without being seen. If we were lucky we might find another abandoned old Federation base, like the one the rebellion previously had. If we did them we could all seek refugee within its walls.

There was a large amount of noise coming from the far end of the room; it appeared to be coming from behind the trucks, over near where the doors to the outside were. Katherine had jumped down off the raised part of the walkway and was now walking past one of the trucks; she went round the back of it and disappeared. I followed her, climbing down off the platform and walking past the truck, as I turned past the back of it I could see the others in the corner, by one of the doors at the far end, they were trying to do something, maybe get it open, it was hard to tell from this distance what exactly they were trying to do.

"Leo!" A woman's voice cried. Jane had spotted me and had begun running at full speed towards me. She jumped in the air and wrapped her arms and legs around me, sending me to my knees.

"I'm so happy to see you!" She cried, gripping me tight. Honestly, I was very happy to see her as well, and all of the others, just knowing that we were all safe, everything seemed to be working out. However one question was still stuck in my mind, this was supposed to be one of the main facilities to the Federation, yet there was not a soul in sight, something didn't quite add up.

"You to Jane! Thought we'd lost you for a moment then!" I said with a sigh of relief.

"Magic Man and Jonathon are trying to open the doors to the outside, the weather is stable at the moment, if we hurry we can lead everyone to an old Federation outpost, it's just outside the forest." She explained, releasing me from her grip and turning to walk back over to the others, it was strange having an army of people watching my every move and yet remaining completely silent. As I walked over towards the others so did the large group behind me, they stretched back to the vehicle and then disappeared behind it, the rest were spread out over the raised platform, I could see them through the gaps between the trucks, each wide eyed and awaiting guidance

"How long until the doors are open?" I asked as I approached the guys, they seemed to have a panel on the side of the door open and were fiddling with some wires and cables inside of it.
"3 . . . 2 . . . 1 . . ." Magic Man said, cockiness in his voice.
"By the way it's good to see you Leo!" He continued, as his voice faded, becoming nothing more than echo, the sound of hydraulics replaced it; every single door that the vehicles could use as an entrance began to shake, vibrating and slowly started to rise up. Everyone behind us paced forward, standing a few feet from our reach, watching the doors rise as well. We all held our breath, waiting to see if the extreme weather was actually stable for now, if it wasn't then we wouldn't be able to go anyway, we'd have to wait here until it was safe for everyone to leave.

The sun rays peered through the gap at the bottom of the metal doors as they detached themselves from the ground below, the room was already lit up from the strong lighting that was inside the room already, however the light from the sun outside had now increased the brightness of the room dramatically, practically blinding us all as it carried on getting brighter, the doors opening more and more. Most people now had their hands raised to shield their sensitive eyes from the bright sun, thousands of people watching, waiting to see the outside of Vala for the first time. Amazing to think that I didn't technically see the outside of this planet until I was beyond the wall of the city, preparing to scale the beast of a structure.

I had never seen Vala like this before, the facility itself was surrounded by long green fields, they seemed endless in size. I expected some sort of courtyard to be outside the large doors but instead there was just one large road, it thinned out the further it went on, turning into a road that would not be able to fit any more than two trucks at a time. It was strange seeing flatland like this; there were no hills anywhere, just these lush green fields. The fog had all disappeared, making it easy to see everything outside, the sun was shining bright in the sky, I tired moving my head up to gaze at it properly for the first time but it was too bright to even get my eyes close too. Another thing that had changed was the weather, there was no rain, no wind, not even a cloud in the light blue sky, for the first time since I had woken on this planet I was able to stand beyond the wall and not worry about the intense weather conditions carrying me off into the air above, never to be found. I was surprised not to be able to see the city, or the walls of the city, it just showed us all how far we really were from it, the ground around the city was completely flat and as there was no fog, if it was close, we would be able to see it with ease.

CHAPTER 31

Hunted

"**E**VERYONE, FOLLOW US" I called out, loud enough so everyone behind could hear, we were all standing in the doorways, gazing out across the green land in front of us. Most people had moved forward to stand in the doorways as well, they were evenly spread out, a handful of them under each one. I lifted my right foot and stepped out of the facility, walking slowly forward, as I did so I could feel a cold feeling on my hand, it was the same cold feeling that I had learned to love. Katherine had reached out for me and was gripping my hand tightly, walking forward with me as I did, standing right by my side. The Trax followed us first; she was the most confident out of the group so it made sense for her to want to be close to the front, leading the way. The other five trailed behind, they stuck close together, not saying a word. Behind them was the army of people, each scared and nervous, struck with confusion and frustration, it would take a long time for all these people to adjust to Vala, to believe that this world was the real world and the world that they had grown to understand as life, was nothing more than a simulation.

As we walked forward, leaving the building behind us, hoping never to return again, Katherine had begun to turn the massive group to the right, placing the doors of the Federation base on our right as well. I stared back at the complex for a moment, expecting to see a large building towering from the grass below, but instead there was just more green land, the ground slopped down towards the metal doors where people were streaming out of, a long line now followed us all the way from the building to the backs of Katherine and I. It was then that I realised the whole facility was located underground, hidden completely from sight, even the doors disappeared the further you got away from it, making it impossible to see, it looked like it had been hidden on purpose. Why were they trying to hide it? Maybe from the dangerous creatures of Vala? Or perhaps just the rebels? I thought maybe the people who lived in the city didn't know that the Federation were holding these experiments out of the safety of the walls, however even if that was the case there would still be no reason to build the base underground because the Valarian people would most likely never leave the confines of the city, making it pointless to hide from them.

The longer we walked the bigger the group seemed to get, as the ground around us grew flatter and everyone now leaving the building you could see the sheer number of people that we had rescued. The group was now one large cluster of scattered figures, some had begun socialising with one another, others were still too afraid to speak and were keeping to themselves. A couple of people seemed to be wandering off slightly, straggling away from the main group. I couldn't count the exact number of people, if I tried I would be here for days, all I could assume was that there was a couple thousand. Inside the facility there looked to be a lot more, but now outside the facility, although the number was still great, it wasn't as large as I had first thought. If the Federation had been running these tests for hundreds of years then you'd think by now that they would have millions of people locked up in these machines. I do believe that if they could get away with having that many people in the facility, they would have, but a large amount of people like that missing, children taken away from their homes at such a staggering rate, people would start to notice, and one day they would rise up against the Federation, putting an end to the experiments altogether. So in a way it was smart by keeping the figures much lower, still high when you consider each one is a human, a living person, but not in the millions.

There was a large figure now forming to the right of us, at first I could not make it out, but the more we walked, the clear the figure became. It was the forest that I had heard so much about, the forest that engulfed the rest of the planet around the city, I remember the director telling me about all the vicious creatures that lived on this planet, some that no one had ever layer eyes one, all harbouring within the shelter of the tall trees. The trees were tall, as tall as the buildings within Vala, they were a dark green colour, with vines draping from the tops of them, the shrubbery around the forest was wild and untamed, very different from the green fields we were walking on, the grass beneath our feet was much smaller, it looked fresh cut, which didn't really make sense considering it was an endless field, no one could cut something this large this well.

The more we walked the larger the forest got, becoming clearer to make out, the tree line stood strong, below the tall trees was a darkness, the thick head of the forest shielded the sun rays from reaching the ground, creating an ocean of pitch black.

"Aren't we getting a bit close to the forest Kath?" I asked as we continued walking.

"The base we are going to is closer to the forest than the city, this means further from the Federation and stronger walls in cads they ever find us, the walls and structures of the bunkers built close to the forest were much stronger than the one we were previously in, as the real dangers from the Federation lie within the darkness of those woods, not the city of Vala." She explained, I felt like she didn't need to explain in such detail as instead of calming my mind she had made me feel worse. Knowing now that inside the forest were things even the Federation were scared of, and we were about to become their new neighbours.

Suddenly Katherine stopped, she gripped my hand tight, the large group behind us slowed and turned to a halt as we did. I darted my eyes of over towards Katherine, she wasn't staring at anything in particular, instead she seemed to be focused one something within her thoughts, thinking about something important.

"Katherine" I whispered, moving my head in close to hers, I turned around for a moment to see what the rest of the group were now doing, most people had already begun sitting down, we had walked far, it made sense for them all to be growing tired. The other six of the original people were talking amongst themselves, occasionally batting an eye in our direction; I couldn't hear any words, just random mumbles as they congregated.

"Oh god" she hissed, slowly turning her view away from the direction we were walking, looking back the way we had just came. I too turned my head to look in the same direction as her, I couldn't see anything though, just the heads of thousands of people looking at us both as we stared over them into the distance, the sun was still high in the sky, making it difficult to widen my eyes, I raised my hand or try and get a better view of what it was Katherine was looking at. At first I assumed maybe she had lost it, we had all had a long couple of days, it was only normal that she would start feeling a bit fuzzy, seeing things, or hearing things, she was just tired so I understood, but then, I started to hear something.

The ground shook, sending vibrations up my legs through my body, the thousands of heads staring at us had turned their gaze to behind them, looking into the distance as we were. A loud drone filled the air around us; the dirt of the floor seemed to be bouncing slightly, moving across the surface of the grass, the shaking carried on, getting more and more intense, the droning sound turning into a loud hum. The whole group was now staring at it, even us, every single pair of eyes locked on the cloud of dust on the ground, growing, moving fast, straight towards us. Could it be some of those raptors we had saw earlier? We were outside of the wall, there must be a few of them around here somewhere, however they might not like the sunlight, none of that really mattered, I just tried to think of something else and not what the true answer clearly was.

"Leo, what do we do?!" Katherine asked her hand gripping mine tight, I could feel the growing sweat form between our palms as we became more anxious, fear had replaced every feeling in my body, knowing that even with the help of the Awakening drug, there was no scenario where we would all come out of this alive. The air in the distance filled with flying vehicles, some were familiar looking, they were shaped and moved like the Mechanics within the city, however others were very different, they had wings with propeller engines of the tips of them, like two small helicopter blades within a tiny circle of metal. They had long thin noses and cockpits like a space rocket. It scared me how easy it was to see the detail of the vehicles, the large trucks carrying soldiers, thundering towards us. Some had large cannons strapped to the top of them; they didn't have wheels but instead had tracks, roughly the same as the tanks of Earth.

Regardless of what they looked like it was the amount that sent shivers down my spine, there were so many Federation vehicles heading towards us that they blocked out the light from the sun, I lowered my hand as the flying ones engulfed it completely. The dust cloud grew larger the closer they got, the group had begun to huddle up, thousands of people slowly moved towards Katherine and I, even our friends looked at us for guidance, what could we say? What could we do? Any moment their army would be upon us, we would be slaughtered, the people I had just saved from a life inside the machines they were born in would now be killed hours into their real lives, never truly getting to live. At least now it made sense why it was so easy to escape, why thousands of people could leave one of the most heavily defended places on Vala, they wanted us out in the open, we wouldn't be hiding behind walls or in rooms. Rather than playing a game of hide and seek with thousands of people they would simply run them down in a beautiful green field, there would be nowhere to run, nowhere to hide, and no risk of damage to their own base, we spoon fed them our own demise.

Unless there was somewhere to run, a place to hide, I assumed by Kath's reaction that the base we were heading for was still far away otherwise she would have suggested that we go there. And even if we now did head there, some of us even making it inside the walls we'd never be safe, the Federation would know exactly where we were and would know the complex better than us as it was previously their own. However there was one other place to go, somewhere, where even the Federation wouldn't be able to find us, somewhere, where all of us, every single person in this group, the thousands of eyes looking to me for help, for leadership, Katherine's now among them, would all have a chance of reaching it safely. The Federation approaching, the people shaking with fear, the ground beneath out feet joining the shaking of the people, there was only one place to go. I turned my head quickly to Katherine, she gazed back at me, tears dropping down her soft cheeks, her eyes scared from the horror that face us, I took a deep breath and moved my head towards her ears, so she could hear my voice over the loud droning sound of vehicles moving in our direction, racing through the green fields. My warm breath hit the side of her face as I muttered a faint whisper.

"The forest!"

To Be Continued . . . .

SPECIAL THANKS

THESE ARE ALL the people who I owe a great deal of thanks to, those who stood by me through writing this book and those who helped with its completion. If it wasn't for these people there would not a Vala! Thank you all so much!

Ely Rivera—My Publishing Consultant, I can honestly say that if it wasn't for this man I would never have gotten this published! Or finished.

Alice Elkins—Proof reader and commenter

Jess Davis—Proof reader and commenter

Emily O'Callaghan—Proof reader and commenter

Myles Fitzpatrick—My little brother for his help on some of the ideas within the story

Calum Mcgregg—Helped me with character names on occasion

Katrina Fitzpatrick—My big sister with all her support over the period of time it took me to finish this book

Oliver Townsend—A great friend who listened to the plot line as I created the world of Vala, giving me feedback

Zachary and Leza Fitzpatrick—My parents for reading the story as well, while it was just a few scribbles on scrap paper

And to all my family and friends for their continued support! Thank You so much! If it wasn't for all of you I would have never of finished this book, or even thought about publishing it! I hope you all enjoy it and I hope that you are all looking forward to the next one!

Printed in Great Britain
by Amazon